Never the Twain

Never The Twain
First published in Indonesian in 1928
by Balai Pustaka under the title Salah Asuhan
Balai Pustaka, Jl. Gunung Sahari 4
Jakarta, Indonesia

English language edition copyright © 2010 The Lontar Foundation
English translation copyright © 2010 Robin Susanto
Introduction copyright © 2010 Thomas M. Hunter, Jr.
All rights reserved

Publication of the Modern Library of Indonesia Series, of which this book is one title,
has been made possible by the generous assistance of the Djarum Foundation.
Additional assistance provided by the Ford Foundation.

Design and layout by Irma Isnaedi (DesignLab)
Cover illustration: detail from *Minangkabau Village* by Wakidi;
image courtesy of OHD Museum of Modern & Contemporary Indonesian Art
Printed in Indonesia by PT Subur Printing

ISBN No. 978-979-8083-54-9

MODERN LIBRARY OF INDONESIA

ABDOEL MOEIS

Never the Twain

Translated by Robin Susanto
with an introduction by Thomas M. Hunter, Jr.

LONTAR

Jakarta, Indonesia

Contents

Introduction

The novel *Salah Asuhan*, translated here as *Never the Twain*, is without a doubt among the most popular works of modern Indonesian fiction. In a country where print runs rarely extend beyond a first or second printing, *Salah Asuhan* has far surpassed the norm, both in terms of longevity and volume of distribution. First published in 1928, the years that followed saw numerous editions and printings, as well as the production of a popular dramatization for television.

The 1956 printing of *Salah Asuhan* is especially noteworthy for its cover, which captures in a single image one of the central themes of the work. In the foreground we see a young man wearing neatly tailored trousers, pin-stripe shirt, tie and pocket-handkerchief looking over his shoulder with an expression of disdain and contempt. This is Hanafi, a young man of the Minangkabau region of western Sumatra who has returned to his homeland after a Western-style education in Batavia, then colonial capital of the Dutch East Indies. Behind Hanafi we see a traditional Minangkabau house, easily recognized by the boat-like outline of the gable roof, pitched high "fore and aft" and connected by a graceful, low-slung curve. For Indonesian readers the image of a Minang house calls up immediate resonance. Some of these echoes are literary: in the 1920s a number of Minang writers began to produce novels written in "standard Malay" for Balai Pustaka, the government publishing house originally set up to promote literacy through works of literature that would not threaten the colonial status quo. Even though edited under watchful eyes, these works often played with and manipulated colonial realities. A depiction of a Minang house on the cover of a Balai Pustaka novel thus calls to mind a literary genre that in many Indonesian minds is associated with the first stages of building a national identity.

Another resonance of the Minang traditional house are the socio-cultural patterns that had a defining effect on the so-called "Minang novels" that were published by Balai Pustaka. The Minangkabau people are matri-local, meaning that inheritance of property is by way of the female line, and that men marry into the residences of their wives. Coupled with a strongly orthodox practice of Islam that prohibits close contact between young men and women once they enter puberty, this means that young men are often not welcome in the homes of their mothers and sisters once they have come of age. For young Minang men this has led to the practice of seeking one's fortune abroad—"abroad" meaning somewhere outside the region, often in Java or another island—and then returning to the "homeland" to claim a bride, a place within a "traditional house" and a place within the extended kinship networks of Minang society.

For Marah Rusli, a Minang author famous for his novel *Sitti Nurbaya* published in 1922, the "home-abroad" aspects of Minang social life provided fertile ground for an early exploration of the tension between "custom and tradition" (*adat*) and modernity. This novel focuses on a modern marriage undertaken "abroad" that is contested in the homeland by the maternal uncle of the groom. Here another well-known aspect of Minang social life would likely echo in the minds of many Indonesian readers: among the Minangkabau people the strongest bond of familial responsibility is between the mother's older brother and her children, rather than directly between the mother's husband and their children.

For Abdoel Moeis,*) author of *Salah Asuhan*, the "home-abroad" dynamics of Minang social life also offered a unique opportunity to explore conflict between tradition and modernity. While a marriage—or rather two marriages—and a "debt of conscience" to Hanafi's maternal uncle are focal points of this novel, the main source of tension is within Hanafi himself. Because of his Western education, Hanafi first rejects the affirmations offered by custom and tradition, then begins a process of complete alienation from his native beliefs and behavior required to fulfill the terms of *gelijkstelling*, a colonial-era legal process whose ultimate goal was equal status with Dutch nationals.

The complication to Hanafi's move away from tradition in *Salah Asuhan* is an inter-racial marriage that Moeis exploits brilliantly to reveal the human impact of colonial legislation aimed at preserving apartheid while accepting the mixed nature of colonial society. As Hanafi begins to turn away from his roots he moves ever closer to Corrie, a girl of mixed Indo-European descent whose father is French, her deceased mother native. In following the story of Corrie's original rejection of Hanafi, her eventual change of mind, and the ensuing pressures and difficulties, Moeis explores the schism between colonial and traditional realities with a master hand. Hanafi's shallow use of the vocabulary of Dutch liberalism to defend his rejection of tradition is set against his mother's apparently innate or "native" ability to read his moods through subtle changes in his behavior and expression. His misreading of an arranged marriage with the daughter of his maternal uncle as a crude economic pay-off is contrasted with the patience and reason displayed both by his mother and hapless Minang wife. Even domestic elements are drawn in to support the contrast between Hanafi's mimic Western-ness and what are called the "enduring values" of the homeland.

---

*) Following contemporary orthographic conventions, the author's name is often spelled "Abdul Muis", the way it is pronounced in Indonesian, but his official name is "Abdoel Moeis", which we use here at his heir's specific request.

Hanafi prefers the clutter of Dutch drawing rooms and their implied separation from spaces outside the control of colonial domesticity; his mother prefers the kitchen and sitting mat of the verandah, places that open out to the wider world of the Minang village. The story of Hanafi and Corrie sets this novel firmly within the romantic tradition, inviting comparisons with classics like *Jane Eyre*, whose study of domesticity threatened by colonial shadows is an ingredient that also looms large in *Salah Asuhan*. The progress of the tale is best left to the exploration of the reader, while technical discussions of the particulars of translation may be best left for more academic discussions. However, it may be of use to note that Moeis makes use of two distinct traditions when dealing with the subject of emotion or "feeling." In the Malay world, including the Minangkabau area of West Sumatra, a sharp contrast is often drawn between "reason and will" (*akal*) and "feeling" (*rasa* or *perasaan*) in the sense of "base desire" (*nafsu*). While many studies have shown that reason is usually counted as a male characteristic, in *Salah Asuhan* it is clear that Hanafi is more consistently the victim of desire, while the women in his life—his mother, his Minang wife, and even Corrie—consistently demonstrate more reason. Later in *Salah Asuhan*, during Hanafi's discussions with his Dutch friend Piet, another version of feeling is brought to the foreground to explain the difficulties that threaten Hanafi's marriage. This is feeling in the Javanese sense, an attention to the subtleties of human emotion and communication quite outside the realm of discursive language.

From the biography of Moeis we know that his use of a single multi-valent term to convey differing aspects of human psychology was no accident, but the product of a life rich in experience. Born in 1890, Moeis was actively involved in the early years of institution building that marked the beginnings of the nationalist period. After an apprenticeship as a civil servant he left government service for journalism, quickly becoming involved in nationalist publications like *Kaoem Moeda*, a paper he co-founded in 1912. Shortly after this, Moeis joined the Syarikat Islam (Islamic Union), rising quickly through the ranks to become its representative to the Netherlands in negotiations aimed at trading off a native defense force in the Indies for direct representation in the Dutch parliamentary system. During the same period he was married to a Sundanese woman from West Java and began to establish his household there.

Within several years he became an important member of the central leadership of the Islamic Union. In this position he campaigned against growing Communist influence in the organization, but was also very active in union activities. In 1919 he was arrested when a Dutch Controleur in North Sulawesi was murdered just after he had completed a speaking tour there. However, he remained undeterred in his union activities until 1922 when he was arrested following the breakup of a strike called by his pawnshop union. He was exiled along with Tan Malaka, the fiery Minang Communist, and only allowed to return to Java in 1926.

From correspondence with Balai Pustaka that Moeis initiated in late 1927 we can sense that he experienced a major change of direction during his three years in exile. Not long after his return to his home in Garut, West Java, in 1926 he was loaned five hectares of land by the Dutch forestry service, with the condition that he plant each with 1,500 seedlings, while in early 1927 he submitted a manuscript for *Salah Asuhan* to Balai Pustaka. In a sense, these two events suggest the victory of Dutch paternalism, but they may also reflect a deeper resolve to grapple with complex issues of national, religious, and ethnic identity that had bedeviled the first phase of Indonesian nationalism. In a letter from Moeis dated November 28, 1927 he explains his purpose in writing *Salah Asuhan* in conciliatory terms that belie his background as an Islamic Union activist:

> *...this novel is in no way intended to widen the gap*
> *between West and East, to inflame feelings of enmity,*

*or to belittle a particular race in any way. On the
contrary my purpose is only to bring the truth to light
and to entreat young people of the Indies who receive
a Western education to refrain from mere imitation
of Western ways.*

Internal memoranda of Balai Pustaka editors tell us that Moeis'
novel had been allowed to languish for almost a year because it
dealt with the subject of inter-racial marriage in terms that vilified
Corrie, portrayed in Moeis' original manuscript as a woman of pure
Dutch descent. It is said that the original manuscript submitted by
Moeis was intended for the popular press. This may account for
some of the scenes that the Balai Pustaka found offensive, reported
to include a shoot-out in a brothel in which Corrie is wounded at
the hands of a jealous lover.

Alas the original manuscript of *Salah Asuhan* has never come
to light, at least to date, nor do we know whether the loss was
intentional or simply an accident of history. Yet in a sense this is not
the central issue: some may judge Moeis harshly for capitulating
to the demands of the editors of the Balai Pustaka, but there is no
doubt that in doing so he produced a work that stands to this day
as one of the milestones of modern Indonesian literature.

In his approach to the dilemma of hybridity that marks the
colonial experience Moeis adopted a position that calls to mind
later debates on the relative attention that should be given to
tradition and modernity in formulating an Indonesian identity.
Moeis' stance resembles that of Armijn Pané, who insisted that
Indonesians were experiencing a temporary age of confusion arising
from the conditions of coloniality and should thus seek to achieve
a balance between traditional and modern forms of understanding.
The difference between Moeis and Pané is that Moeis adopted the
logic of the supplement in order to achieve a resolution. Tradition,
in its essential wholeness, is the source of individual and social

well-being, but needs the supplement of a Western education that will eventually put Indonesian subjects on an equal footing with the Dutch and other outsiders to the system. The separations implicit in this argument have lived on in Indonesian society, at times producing a brilliant synthesis of local and universal forms of understanding, at others promoting a narrow nationalism that rejects everything that is not considered indigenous or genuine. It is to the lasting credit of Abdoel Moeis that he outlined the terms of the debate brilliantly, and with a sense of humanism that has inspired successive generations of Indonesian readers.

Thomas M. Hunter, Jr.

1

Two Friends

The tennis court in the shade of the almond trees stood empty. Though the sun's light was muted by the trees' dense foliage, the day was still bright, for it was only half past four in the afternoon. It was here, at the tennis court, that many of Solok's distinguished residents gathered every afternoon. Young and old, married and single, Westerners and Easterners alike, all met at the court to play the sport that had become so fashionable throughout the country.

No one was on the court but beneath a shade tree in the clubhouse garden, directly adjacent to the court, a young man and woman were having tea. Both were wearing tennis outfits; their two racquets were leaning against their chairs, but the couple showed no sign of being in a hurry to play.

The comely woman with Western features was refilling their cups of tea. "Well, of course, Han..." she said, while stirring sugar into the cups, "but what would people think if I stopped by your house every day before coming here to play?"

Hanafi, the young man, asked in turn, "What gives anyone the right to object to what another person does with his life? If he does no harm nor causes offense to his fellow man, why should there be a problem? My word, Corrie, if we had to ask people's opinion before doing anything—especially when it's no one else's concern—life would be unbearable."

"I know that Han, but as everything has its limits, consequently there are things that are out of bounds and therefore should not be done. Even things that you might think harm no one may very well be against propriety."

"Propriety? Can what we're doing—sitting across a tea table from each other in broad daylight, at a time of day when people commonly visit one other—be thought of as against propriety?"

"Surely not, but you're a man and I'm a woman and society has certain laws which, although unwritten, must be followed if we are to live at peace within a society that abides by those laws."

"Oh, it's those laws you're talking about! Where do *those* laws end? You're European, a people known for their liberal outlook on relationships between men and women. For Europeans it's not uncommon for a married woman to go out with a man who's not her husband, to walk arm in arm with him, without any laws to stop them, either written or unwritten. Now let's take another example: in Arab societies a woman must cover her body from head to toe, even her face, whereas in America, in many of the big cities on the coasts, men and women can run about in bathing suits, and even go to clubs scantily dressed. Yet if a Western woman were to go out in her pajamas, which covers more of her body than does her dance frock, she will thought to be 'violating propriety'. So what I'm saying is that such talk of propriety is very confusing, especially since it is not written down."

"But it was you, Hanafi, who started talking about the customs and etiquette of different peoples. And it's you who doesn't want to admit that there are differences among them. Every time we discuss this topic you always end up getting upset. It's as if you're ashamed of being native. You think I look down on natives, but my skin is colored too. Under the law I might be classified as European, but my mother was one hundred percent native. I don't like to remind you that remarks of disdain towards native ways are more often heard from your lips than from mine. But anyway, we were saying..."

Hanafi interrupted her: "I know I'm just a native, Corrie; you don't have to keep reminding me."

"My my, Hanafi, you are in a bad mood today! If I didn't know better, I might get the wrong impression. But as we've been friends since childhood, ever since primary school, I know your disposition well. So calm down, Hanafi, and listen to me. We were talking about the customs and traditions of different peoples. Let's not argue about what kind of clothing people in other countries find acceptable; they can argue about that among themselves. All I know is that if tomorrow or the day after it suddenly became fashionable, here in Solok, to go about in a bathing suit, I would not follow that fashion. What should matter to us, Hanafi, is the etiquette of our own cultures.

"It may be true, just as you contend, that in my culture—European culture —relations between men and women are much more liberal. But just because something is commonplace doesn't mean that people won't talk if, for example, a man is seen with a woman who is not his spouse. In your culture, that of the Minangkabau here in West Sumatra, it's quite different. If a man is seen with his spouse, or even with his sister for that matter, casually jesting or going for a walk together, people will consider it odd, not to mention if the woman is not his wife.

"In your culture, it's considered a sin for a man to touch a woman other than his wife. But don't misunderstand me.... Among Westerners if a young man is seen regularly with the same woman, people are going to assume that they're engaged. But among natives ninety-nine percent will surely talk, and the woman's reputation will be questioned. Do you have any idea just how fragile a woman's reputation is, Hanafi, especially among your people? No matter what, Hanafi, you have to remember that you are a native."

"How many times do you have to keep reminding me that you're a Westerner and I'm just a local with colored skin! If this is getting in the way of our friendship, say so, Corrie! If you dislike natives so much, why bother with me?"

Hanafi grabbed the newspaper lying on the table as though he were about to read it but Corrie reached over and ran her fingers over his hand. She smiled and a dimple appeared on her left cheek.

"Hanafi, I hope this is not your way of telling me that the newspaper is more interesting than me."

With renewed desire, Hanafi raised his eyes to the lovely woman opposite him. Hers was a smile that could melt the hardest of hearts, and the beautiful Corrie du Bussée looked especially stunning that day: her scarlet wool sweater hugged her slender torso, showing its shapeliness; her silk headscarf seemed scarcely able to contain her shock of wavy black hair. A few locks of hair, escaping their tress, hung from her finely sculpted temples to the nape of her neck. Her beauty, combined with her haughty temperament, was irresistible. Hanafi simply could not continue his charade.

Hanafi stared into the eyes of the young woman who gazed back on him with what seemed to be pity. He reached for her hand and drew it close to his lips, then kissed her fingers.

As if stung by a scorpion, Corrie snatched her hand from Hanafi's grasp. But then, smiling sweetly, she looked out of the corner of her eyes in the direction of the tennis court.

Vexed to find his hopes so quickly foiled, Hanafi followed Corrie's eyes. The roil he felt inside immediately calmed when he saw Mr. and Mrs. Brom, the bank administrator and his wife, walking towards the court.

Mrs. Brom smiled and waved her racquet at the young pair as she approached. "Oh, look at the two love birds," she cooed, "just like a pair of turtle doves!"

Corrie's cheeks reddened. It was Hanafi who spoke to Mrs. Brom: "You're certainly right to compare Corrie to a dove, which might look tame but will fly away as soon as you reach out your hand to touch it."

Corrie now smiled at the older woman. "How are you?" she asked in Dutch.

"Easy come, easy go," Mrs. Brom answered, but she wasn't going to be put off by small talk. "Sparrows are only five cents each because they're tame and easy to catch, but a bird of paradise is worth its weight in gold."

Corrie and Hanafi shook hands with Mr. and Mrs. Brom. "So tell me, Corrie," Mrs. Brom continued to jest, "...are you a sparrow or a bird of paradise?"

Again, it was Hanafi who replied. "She's a garuda, Madam!"

Now Mr. Brom spoke up: "The garuda is a legendary bird which may or may not exist. But even if it does, mere mortals like Hanafi and I would have no hope of catching it."

"I'm not so sure about that," Corrie answered coyly. "Whoever is steadfast in his beliefs and does not give up easily will surely reach his goal."

Mr. Brom boomed with laughter. "If that's not straightforward, I don't know what is! Well, Hanafi, if there is still room in your heart, I think Miss Corrie wants in."

Corrie continued the banter: "Oh, there's plenty of room in Hanafi's heart, enough for two or even three women!"

"Corrie!" Hanafi exclaimed, but then found himself unable to say another word for his voice had begun to tremble.

More people began to join the small group. One of them was Aminah, a young native woman, who had come along with Mrs. Bergen, the school teacher.

"You're late, Minah," Corrie said cheerfully, then leapt towards her friend as if to escape from the mirthful but risqué chatter.

Soon afterward, the playing began, a set of mixed doubles. Corrie was paired with Hanafi. She liked playing with Hanafi, and not because she wanted to run back and forth beside Hanafi, she asserted, but because she wanted to learn how to play tennis well. If she played against Hanafi—here, at this point in her declaration she would smile and flutter her eye lashes—she'd never learn how to play because Hanafi always gave her easy shots.

In this oft heard repartee, Hanafi would then reply in a voice so low that it could only have been meant for Corrie's ears: "That's it, Corrie, I simply don't have the heart to beat you."

"Nonsense!" she would answer sternly, with a look that would be enough to make Hanafi want to kneel and kiss the tips of her shoes.

After their tennis matches, Hanafi would walk Corrie home yet he seldom went inside her house, not because he was never invited—on the contrary, Corrie's father was unfailingly polite and always asked him in—but because he knew that the invitations from the dour-faced older man were extended to him half-heartedly, for the sake of politeness only.

As he always did, Hanafi stopped outside the front steps of Mr. du Bussée's house and shook Corrie's hand. But today he felt a restlessness in his blood. He was convinced that Corrie reciprocated his love, yet the way she had snatched back her hand from him earlier at the clubhouse had instilled doubt in his heart.

She has to give me a decision now, he said to himself. It's now or never! And so, before they parted, he said to Corrie: "You only have five more days of vacation and you still haven't seen my new sketches. Would you like to come to my house tomorrow, around five? There's something else I want to tell you too."

Corrie fell silent for a moment, casting her eyes downward, as if to count the flagstones that lined the walkway.

Hanafi took her hand. "Is it beneath you to come to my house?"

"No, Hanafi," she finally replied, "I'll come with Aminah."

"No, please come alone."

"But, Hanafi, we must be careful of what people say. Have you forgotten our conversation this afternoon?"

"But the whole of Solok has seen us together, from the time when we were in diapers. You're only going to be here for five more days! We sit together in the garden every day. What's wrong if this time we sit on the front verandah? It's not like I live alone. I live with my mother, you know. Please, Corrie. How about it? Tomorrow at five?"

"Well all right," Corrie replied dreamily.

"Oh, sweetheart!" Hanafi was so happy he immediately clasped her hand in his.

"Hey, watch it, *Mister*!" Corrie said angrily, but still smiling. "This is a public street. We're not there yet."

"Tomorrow at five!"

2

Father and Daughter

Mr. du Bussée was a retired French architect who, in his old age, had isolated himself, living like a hermit. After the death of his wife, a native woman from Solok whom he had properly married in church, he seemed to have withdrawn from all social life. He visited neither friend nor neighbor, and though he was polite to all who came to his house, as the French usually are, guests always somehow knew their visit would not be well-appreciated if they tarried too long.

In his bereavement, Mr. du Bussée found solace in hunting. He might be sixty years old, but there was no jungle he wouldn't explore, no mountain he wouldn't climb, no valley whose depth he wouldn't plumb. As long as he had his automatic rifle in hand, it didn't matter what crossed his path; neither bears nor tigers could make his heart tremble. Whenever his guides heard the thunder of his rifle, they knew they would be soon carrying another trophy back to the village, a jungle beast likely to have been the scourge of surrounding villages.

More than anything else, Mr. du Bussée loved to hunt tigers, and would devote days to a hunting expedition for one. As long as there were whiskey and biscuits in his provisions box, he wouldn't return home without his prize. He dried and tanned the tigers' hides himself, treating them with his own special formula. After they were cured, he would place them, along with the animals' bones and claws, in a wooden box which he had made himself. Then he would send them to Paris for further treatment and cleaning, after which he would sell them, either in Europe or Java. This sideline supplemented Mr. du Bussée's modest pension. Other than that, he lived solely for his daughter, Corrie, whose mother, his wife, died when their daughter was only six years old, and he was still actively working as an architect.

After Corrie finished her primary-school education in Solok, Mr. du Bussée sent her to the Salemba Boarding School, in Batavia. He was not going to let his beloved daughter receive half an education. His heart was heavy during that time. He couldn't leave Solok: not only was it the home and final resting place of his beloved wife, it was also the place where he had found a new life after fleeing France and the European continent with a broken heart. Batavia's hustle and bustle didn't attract him in the least. But how could he be separated from his daughter, the only person other than his wife to whom he had devoted his life?

He was determined that Corrie would have a good education. The inheritance that he would leave her would be modest, at best, so she had to be able to care for herself. And for that she needed a good education. While he often insisted that Corrie deserved "the very best," the truth was that he himself had been quite negligent in supervising her education. After all, she had not started school until she was eight years old, two years after her mother's death, because he couldn't bear to be parted from her, not even for a moment.

After primary school, Corrie's father wavered between sending her to Meer Uitgebreid Lager Onderwijs, known as MULO, the Dutch-language secondary school in Padang, or the Hoogere Burger School, HBS, the four-year secondary school in Batavia for the children of the elite. Corrie easily passed both matriculation exams, but because of her father's indecisiveness and his unwillingness to be separated from her, two years passed before she attended any school at all. So it was that Corrie was sixteen when she bade her father farewell on the pier in Teluk Bayur harbor in Padang, as she boarded a ship bound for Batavia.

This story began when Corrie returned home after her third year at HBS, on holiday. In truth, she had planned to quit her schooling at that time, but her father insisted that she return to Batavia and complete the school's five-year program. But at the age of nineteen Corrie realized that she was no longer a little girl. She knew that her inherited good looks attracted men—young and old, they swarmed about her wherever she went, giving her endless compliments and praises—and that began to work its influence against her basic good nature, her good heart.

She had a keep chest in which she kept letters from her admirers, bound in colorful silk scarves. It was almost shocking how many there were, several of them proposal letters from young men in Batavia who had been captivated by her beauty. Every time Corrie found an envelope in the post with handwriting she didn't recognize, she said to herself, "Which lunatic is it this time?" But all the same, her heart would race as she opened the envelope.

The writing styles of the letters she received were as varied as the men who wrote them, but their underlying message was the same: a declaration of undying love and towering passion. Some of the men who courted her said they would shoot themselves beneath her window at the boarding school if she did not return their love; others said they would drown themselves in the Ciliwung River; still others said they would seek their fortune in America.

Corrie was not in the least moved by these woes and laments, and the young men's threats of leaving behind "this world of tears" served only to elicit fits of laughter in her when she read them. For each threat addressed to her she had a reply, a bit of advice she spoke only to herself, for her own amusement. To the young man who threatened to shoot himself beneath her window she whispered, "Just don't do it after ten o'clock at night, because I am easily frightened in my sleep." To the young man who threatened to drown himself in Batavia's Ciliwung River, "Don't forget to wear a shower cap. You don't want to mess up your hair. And don't forget your overshoes. The Ciliwung is muddy!" To the one who threatened to go to America she advised, "Make sure to use all your tickets for the Deca Amusement Park before you leave; it would be a pity to waste them."

That was how she made fun of those who declared their love. But she didn't hate their letters; in fact she kept every one of them, in that small box her mother had passed down to her. Her reason for keeping them was unclear, even for herself. She never replied to any of them, and if one of the men tried to follow up his letter with a conversation, she would simply say, "It's not proper to bring up such a topic to a school girl."

Hanafi was right; Corrie du Bussée was like a dove.

She neither rejected nor accepted the love of these enamored young men; they were left hoping. She remained sweet to all of them. But if any of them dared to cross the line, she would, just as sweetly, erect a stone wall around herself that made it impossible for the poor fellows even to come close.

Did she understand the meaning of love? She herself didn't know. She certainly enjoyed her admirers' attentions. Their praises and daring glances filled her with delight, like a refreshing drink to one who is parched with thirst. But as soon as one of them became serious and began to hint at love, her heart would suddenly turn cold, and she would despise him, the one whom she had just fancied.

After Hanafi left, Corrie entered the house.

"*Daag*, Papa," she said hello to her father in Dutch as she hurried to the parlor where he was reclining on an easy chair, reading the newspaper and having tea.

"*Daag*, Cor," he replied, looking at his daughter's slightly blushing face.

The ruddy color of her cheeks did not rouse his curiosity; she always looked that way after tennis. But this time he sensed a difference in her bearing.

She threw herself on the sofa as she tossed her tennis racquet into the corner. Deftly, she took off her tennis shoes, and tossed them aside as well. She then sank deeper into the sofa and closed her eyes.

Though he noticed his daughter was acting strangely, Corrie's father said nothing, content for the moment to watch.

Corrie called out the name of the manservant: "Simin!"

"Yes, Miss," came the reply from behind her.

"Get me a glass of tamarind syrup... No, make that vanilla." Then a few moments later, "No, make that Dutch soda instead."

"With ice, Miss?"

"Of course, you idiot, with lots of ice. A pound or two at least."

As if she had not harassed poor Simin enough, Corrie then got up from the sofa, ran to the cabinet, and yelled at him again: "Hurry up. Are you going to let me die of thirst?"

As she said that, she quickly snatched the opened bottle from Simin's hand and poured the bubbly drink into a glass, letting the soda's rising froth spill onto the satin runner on the cabinet top. "The ice, Simin, the ice!" She took one or two gulps of the drink as she stomped her foot on the floor.

Hurriedly, Simin opened the ice box. Just as he was about to wash it, she snatched the ice from his hand and dropped the large chunks of ice into the glass, spilling even more soda onto the runner.

"Well, looks like you're ruined now," she said with a smirk as she watched the stain spread through the runner. She drank a few more gulps of the soda and then went back to recline on the sofa. There she took a deep breath and put the almost empty glass on the coffee table.

"Corrie," her father said gently, "why are you acting like this?"

"Like what, Papa?"

"Strangely. Can't you be more patient? Something must be bothering you."

"Oh, it's nothing, Papa, I'm just tired and thirsty after the game."

"Well, if that's all it is, I'm happy. Why don't you take a rest. It will cool you down. But don't change your clothes right away, or you'll catch cold. And your face, sweetheart, it's beet red."

Wordlessly Corrie stared at the ceiling as if counting the wooden panels. Her father continued reading his newspaper. There was a long moment before she finally broke the silence, "Tell me, Papa, what do you think is the biggest challenge to a mixed marriage?"

"Oh dear, there are so many, and all of them caused by a universal human disease called 'racial pride.' For some reason people seem to find fault in the mingling of races, even when the two people, a man and woman, marry and are very much in love. But as long as the two guilty parties are determined, it's possible for them to remain above the scorn and contempt that society heaps upon them. Look at your mama and me. Her people did not approve of her being with me at all. It was the same with my people. Somehow, what we were doing was wrong. But it wasn't society that we wanted to marry, nor did we depend on society for our livelihood, so we were happy despite the scorn. The only thing was, Corrie, not too many people came to visit us."

"But it was different for you and Mama. You are a Westerner, and Mama was from here, a native. Somehow I think—and I'm not sure why—that it would be different for a native man and a Western woman."

"That's for certain, Corrie; there's a big difference and, again, it's all caused by the same thing: racial pride. Europeans first came here with the belief that it was their right to rule the native people. And if a white man comes to this country without bringing a wife from his homeland, it's not considered dishonorable for him to take a native woman as a concubine. If his mistress bears him children then, according to the Western point of view, he has done a great service to the native people: he has improved their blood. But it's very different for a white woman to marry, and have children with, a native man. First of all, as a Westerner, she would be seen as degrading herself. People would say that she had thrown herself away to the natives. Legally, she would lose her European status. Imagine that! Did you know that once a native has obtained European status, he cannot relinquish it and become a native again? There is no provision in the law that permits a European man to give up his privileged status. But a white woman who marries a native man must relinquish her European status as long as she remains with her husband. And if they have any children, it is even worse for her. She will be seen as having contaminated European blood. Do you see the difference between the two?"

"I see it, Papa, but if—and this is a very big if—if fate would have it that my soul mate should be a native, I think I would do what you and mama did. I would not care what people said. Well, except for you. The only opinion that counts is yours. What would you say, Papa, if that were to happen?"

Mr. du Bussée became serious. He put the newspaper on his lap, and looked searchingly into his daughter's eyes. "Are you asking just out of curiosity, or is there something you want to tell me?"

Her father's reaction startled her. "Oh, no, it's just out of curiosity," she answered hastily. Yet she continued to press him. "So would you approve of it, supposing that were my fate? This is only supposing, of course."

Mr. du Bussée paused for a long moment. He gazed into the distance as he carefully weighed what he was about to say, and then reclined against the back of his chair. Methodically, he filled his pipe, tamped the tobacco, lit it, and slowly puffed: once, twice, three times. "You are still a child, Corrie, too young to worry about such things. But since we do meet but once a year, and I am getting old, very well. Listen to me carefully. Remember that whatever I say comes from my heart, and you know that I want only what is best for you. I hope you will take to heart what I am about to tell you.

"As you know, Corrie, I was born into the French nobility. But I never felt a genuine kinship with them. In my heart, I felt closest to people who had barely enough to eat. And that's why I came to this place, because I couldn't resolve a difference with my family, a difference that was as vast as that between the earth and the sky. In short, although by birth I belong to the bloodline that is the pride of France, I could never in my heart of hearts ever embrace their ways. My family looked down on all peoples of colored skin. They even spurned other Europeans who were not of royal descent and viewed them as belonging to a lower order. For my family, as long as a person was white and of high birth—not to mention wealthy—it didn't matter if he behaved like an animal or wasted all his money. Such a person was honorable. I could never accept that. To me, what I honor in a person is his moral character, what's in his heart. For me, the color of a person's skin, his bloodline, or the state of his money or wealth, do not influence the value of a person I befriend. That's why I chose to banish myself to this place, which is where I met your mother." He suddenly stopped and looked up toward the ceiling. "It's been years since your mother passed away, but not a moment passes that I don't think of her." Tears welled in his eyes.

"So, you wouldn't object if it were my destiny to marry a native man?" Corrie persisted.

Mr. du Bussée swallowed before answering. "I can't say for certain, Corrie. I mean, first I would have to know who the native man is, because not all of them are honorable either. I only hope that when the time comes, when you are old enough, you will have the wisdom to decide for yourself what is right and what is wrong. Because, in the end, the decision will be yours to make. All I want, as a father, is for you to be happy. That's all. Then I can rest in peace in my grave. But in the meantime I am here to give you guidance. That's my obligation as a father."

"But you still haven't answered my question," Corrie insisted. "Say the time has come, and I am old enough to decide for myself, and in my judgment I have decided to marry a native man, an educated native man: prestigious, and of equal status to me; a man I love, and who loves me very much. Would you then approve of the marriage?"

Mr. du Bussée lifted his teacup slowly. He sipped two, three times, and then gathered the newspaper from his lap, folded it and stacked it neatly on a pile with the other newspapers. He took off his glasses, put them in their case, and once more sank into his chair. His words were soft and slow. "Corrie my child, I've told you how I feel, but with something as serious as this, we also have to use our reason. And that's why, if you must have my answer now, I would have to say no.

"You can't compare yourself with your mama and me. I was a man with adequate means and as long as I did my job and fulfilled my official duties, I would not lose my job for marrying a native woman. But in our daily life, people didn't spare us. We were despised by both the East and the West. The Europeans were the worst: how they hated your mother! Because I was a man of position, they showed respect towards me. But not towards your mother. I was always invited to official receptions, but they always neglected to invite your mother. When we passed people on the street, men tipped their hats to me but most appeared not even to notice your mother, who was right there walking beside me. Yet I suffered her shame all the same. It was because your mother was not given her due recognition that we gradually came to isolate ourselves and cut off all contact with the larger society. It wasn't so terrible at first. We loved each other and had enough money to spend, so we never harbored any doubts. For us, it was like other people, the people on the outside, didn't exist. And when you were born, sweetheart, it was as if we had been given both the sun and the moon. We were so happy we didn't care what people thought. But gradually, because of the disdain with which people treated your mother, I began to resent my fellow man. That's why, even now, I don't socialize much. That's why I live a solitary life.

"At that time, being ostracized wasn't so terrible for us. We were content to be together, the three of us; we didn't much care for the company of others. But with you, Corrie, it's different. I know how much you enjoy socializing. And then there's another trait of yours, which I'll come to later. It's one I don't care for very much but one I have learned to accept. Life has taught me that feelings can't be changed, not by the person who feels them, let alone by others. Beliefs might change but not feelings. So tell me, honestly, Corrie, do you feel that your status as a European is far superior to that of the natives?"

"Yes, I do, Papa because that's the truth. I don't feel that the natives deserve my respect, except for Mama, of course."

"So then, Corrie, if your mama was the only brown-skinned person you ever respected, how is it possible that you would ever want to marry a native?"

"I don't know. Maybe I'll meet a native man who has characteristics similar to Mama's, one who is civilized and polite, one who is... no longer a native."

"Fine, then let us suppose you meet a native man who would willingly rid himself of his 'nativeness.' What about his people? Do you think you'd want to associate with them?"

"Why of course not, Papa. You know I don't like to mix with the natives."

"Fine, but your own people will ostracize not only your husband but yourself as well. They will think of you as one who is 'lost'."

"I think that depends on the native man. Take Hanafi for example. All his friends are Europeans. He doesn't even associate with the natives. And he's a clerk besides."

"This is a small place, Corrie, and as long as Hanafi doesn't break any taboos—namely, marrying a Western woman—of course the Europeans will like him. They now think of him as a civilized, well-educated native, but the day he marries a white woman those same people will say that his Western education has gone to his head. And that's when the shunning will begin. There are so many examples of that, of native men who marry Western women.

"Now let us suppose that you and your husband decide to move to Batavia. Surely you will want to make friends with other Europeans, to visit their houses and to have them visit you. But believe me, in that you will be disappointed. No one will step foot in your house, and your visits to other homes will be received only half-heartedly. If that were to happen, what would you feel? How would you feel if you went to the theater with your husband and the ushers refused to show you to your seats, or worse, looked the other way when you tried to get their attention? How would you feel then?

"You can read these things yourself. In the newspaper I just read there was an article about a native man of high birth, and a graduate of a Dutch university who went to a restaurant with some of his European friends. He was dressed in native fashion, with a headdress. The owner of the restaurant objected to his presence there. When his European companions, who were also of high rank, explained to the owner who their friend was and what native title he held, the owner simply shrugged his shoulders and said that the 'directors' of the restaurant had a policy of not allowing natives into the restaurant. That's how strict the rules are in the big cities.

"Your husband's luck would be even worse. At his workplace, I suppose, at first there would only be two or three persons who looked down on him. But they would talk, and soon all of the staff would be on his back. If he happened to have an understanding boss, he'd be lucky, but even then he could lose his job.

"Only then would you begin to understand your destiny and, when that happened, especially if the time of courtship had passed, you would feel a kind of venom begin to poison your heart and threaten the relationship between you. No matter how much two people love each other, a time will come when they have a fight. It might be over something small. Say, one day you worked all day in the kitchen to cook his favorite dish. Meanwhile, he's had an argument at the office with his boss and when he gets home he's in such a bad mood that he can hardly eat. You'll think he doesn't appreciate you and soon words are flying: words you don't mean, words that would be better left unsaid. In your anger you'll tell him that you regretted marrying him and his kind.

"By saying such a thing, you will have injured him irrevocably. And he, too, will regret ever having married a Western woman, especially when there were many women as good as you among his own people. He'll feel that you aren't the only one who has been banished from his people all for the sake of love. He too has been cut off from his family. Maybe his mother has even disowned him which, for a native man, is a catastrophe. In a moment like that, you will both surely curse the day that you joined together as husband and wife.

"There are so many examples like that, Corrie, far too many. I'm sure there are Westerners who think of native people as their equals, or at least don't look down on them, but they are in the minority. The majority agree with Kipling, who wrote 'East is East, West is West, and never the twain shall meet.' I think I have said enough, Corrie. When you have seen more of the world with your own eyes, I am sure you will agree with what I've just said."

Corrie lay silently on the sofa.

The manservant Simin came to the door. "Dinner is ready, sir," he said.

Corrie stood to give her father a kiss on the forehead. "After hearing your advice, I suddenly don't feel so well," she told him. "I think I'll skip dinner and go upstairs."

"At the very least, I'm glad that you've taken my advice to heart," he said to her. "You are my daughter and I trust that you won't do anything to ruin your life or break your father's heart. You've probably caught a chill, is all. Why don't you take an aspirin?"

3

Oil and Water

When Hanafi was a child and before he had completed primary school in Solok, his mother sent him to Batavia to study. She said that she didn't want to compromise on her only son's education; her only son who had to make do without a father. Her finances were good then, so she could afford to send him to board with a respectable Dutch family. Her intention was that Hanafi would learn modern ways, so he could raise his family's status.

After primary school, Hanafi went to HBS, which he attended for three years. At that time, his mother, feeling the approach of old age, could no longer contain her longing to be with her only son, so his schooling was cut short. With the help of his father's friends, who finally yielded to his mother's repeated appeals, Hanafi obtained a post as a clerk in the Assistant District Commissioner's office in Solok. In due time, he advanced to become a senior clerk.

Hanafi's mother had lived her entire life in the village. She was a country woman but for the love of her son she had left her family's long house in Koto Anau to live with Hanafi in Solok. She did not hesitate to spend what money she had to purchase European furniture for their rented house in Solok, because Hanafi, who reminded everyone that he had lived with the Dutch since he was a child, insisted that he could be comfortable only in a house that was furnished in the European fashion.

Everything about the house was European, from the front veranda to the kitchen and the bathroom. Hanafi's mother could not feel at home in such a house. Like most village women, she preferred sitting on the floor; her betel-nut case, spittoon, and cooking utensils in the kitchen were the only objects in the house she felt comfortable with. They were her world.

But Hanafi hated his mother's world and filled every corner of the house with small tables, flower pots, and vases. The things in which his mother had taken refuge, he despised. "Mother, you're from the village and you have village tastes," Hanafi said every time his mother spread her mat on the back veranda to wait for the visits of her friends: her village friends. "Mother, in the long house in Koto Anau you can spread your mat and plunk yourself down on the floor wherever you like, but this is Solok. All my friends are Dutch."

"But my back hurts when I sit on a chair, my feet too. It only feels right to me sitting on the floor, because I have always sat on the floor, ever since I can remember. You know that, Hanafi."

"That's what's wrong. That's what's wrong with our people; they're backward, out of touch with the modern world, sitting on the ground like water buffalo. And that betel-nut chewing; it's too much!"

As time went by, Hanafi's mother no longer protested. Instead she took refuge in the kitchen, where she had cleared some space for herself. And there she would receive her friends. A sadness grew inside her as she witnessed her only son becoming more and more Dutch. He dressed like a Dutchman, and socialized only with the Dutch.

When he spoke Malay, Hanafi used different dialects. With his mother, it was the Riau dialect. And when he addressed those of lower standing, he used the Betawi dialect. It was as if he wanted to cut up his own mother tongue into separate pieces. For Hanafi, anyone who didn't speak Dutch was a nobody. And anything having to do with the Malay world was despicable. The Malay cultural heritage was outdated, Islam a superstition. It was no wonder he felt himself so alienated from his own people. His mother was the only native woman with a place in his heart.

Hanafi often said to his Dutch friends, "The Minangkabau region is so beautiful. It's just too bad that it's populated by the Minangkabau people. If it weren't for my mother, I would have left it a long time ago."

One day, as Hanafi was reclining in an easy chair in the garden, his mother approached him, and sat on a bench next to him.

"Hanafi," she said, "I have been meaning to talk to you for a long time. There is something I want to tell you, but you are always so busy. Can I tell you now, so that it does not become a thorn in my flesh?"

"What's on your mind, Mother? Tell me, it's not good to keep things inside."

"Yes, but that's not why I want to talk to you. What I am about to say is important: for me, for you, for both of us. You must remember that you are my only son. Your father passed away long ago, and I am getting old. You are the only one I have."

Hanafi took out a cigarette and, without looking at his mother, lit it. "Well, I am listening."

"Your aunts and uncles from the village have come here a few times."

"Oh, yes, that is very important, isn't it? If they want good food they can come here all they want, every day. That's fine by me, as long as they come when I am at the office. You know I can't mix with people like that. It's like oil and water."

"They're not coming here for food, Hanafi, but for something very serious. The family long house is falling down."

"And what am I supposed to do? Prop it up?"

"No, Hanafi, you know that's only a figure of speech. But still, it's odd that you have never seen our long house. What's important is that for some time now they have been thinking of making you the village chief."

"Excuse me, did I hear you correctly? Me, a village chief? What, so that I can learn to bow and be bowed to? Fine, as they wish, and I'll make the houseboy my advisor."

"Hanafi! I knew you would deride your elders' good intentions which is why, so as not to offend them, I already said no to the idea. I also said no to their plans for you to marry."

"Thank you, Mother. That was very good of you, because if they had expressed their intentions directly to me, I'm not sure how politely I would have been able to respond. And they, my respected elders, might well have been offended. I'm just wondering: since I have nothing to do with them, why should they have anything to do with me?"

"The fact is, Hanafi, that according to village ways, you are supposed to obey your elders."

Hanafi sat up and looked straight into his mother's eyes. "And this law that says I have to obey them, when did that begin?"

"At the beginning of time, Hanafi."

"Oh, it's one of those laws, is it? Those laws should apply only to those who revere them. For you, Mother, as long as it's not too unreasonable, I will do whatever you wish. As for the others, I don't give a damn what they wish. I don't owe them a thing."

"But Hanafi, if that's how you feel, that you owe them nothing, I feel obliged to explain to you that, in truth, you owe them much."

That startled Hanafi. He looked up for a moment. "As far as I can remember, I've never borrowed any money from them, not a single cent."

"Calm down, Hanafi. Listen carefully to what I am going to tell you. You went to school in Batavia for five years. Your spending money was one hundred rupiah a month, that's six thousand rupiah. Where do you think the money came from?"

"As far as I know, it was from father's life insurance."

"That was three thousand, Hanafi. Where did the other three thousand come from? And what about your clothes, your ticket home, as well as the thousand rupiah to furnish this house?"

"From you, Mother, who else?"

"That's what you don't know, Hanafi. What do I have?"

"You have large plots of paddy fields, and orchards."

"How wrong you are if you think all that is mine alone. No, Hanafi, they are a family inheritance, something to be shared. You are fortunate because the family who shares our portion does not have a son, so you are the only male heir in our house. Out of the goodness of their hearts they let me use the harvest from the family rice fields and orchards to pay for your schooling, because they had great expectations for you: that someday you would be a great man, an educated man on whom they could depend in their old age. So, truly, Hanafi, our debt is great."

"Well, if that's the case, they can calculate exactly how much I owe, and then I can pay them back. I can pay them back in monthly installments."

"Your elders are not expecting money, Hanafi; nor are you obliged to pay back the money. If your debt could be paid with money, that would be easy. What you owe them is not money: it's kindness. You can't repay that with money, no matter how much, not even hundreds or thousands of rupiah. And what troubles me most is your uncle, Sutan Batuah, my own brother. Even with his small salary, he always helped me send money to you in Batavia whenever I didn't have enough. I know he doesn't expect to be paid back with money. He is hoping to marry you to his daughter, Rapiah."

"Good heavens! That child, who once came here with her father, and ran away like a scared kitten as soon as she saw me: is that the woman who has been chosen for me?"

"Yes, that is our intention. Your aunt and uncle didn't have the time to talk to you directly. They were here for only one night, on their way to the village. And they are not planning to stop by on their way back to Bonjol."

"Oh, and why is that? Are they offended now?"

"More than offended, Hanafi. They stayed here overnight, and you, you hardly said a word to them."

"Oh, Mother, I have told you so many times, I feel awkward around that sort of people. I never know what to say."

"Your uncle is a school principal, Hanafi. By country standards, he is an intelligent man."

"But he graduated from the old school system, before they taught Dutch."

"Very well, Hanafi, but whether he is intelligent or not, he is still your uncle, your elder, and according to our tradition you must obey his wishes. Imagine, he came here to see you, his own nephew, because he had waited for you in Bonjol to visit him, but you never came. And then, when he comes here, he finds out that you have become a 'Mister' who thinks he's too good to sit with his elders from the village. Is it any wonder that he left here with a broken heart? You might have invited him to sit at the table, to eat with a spoon and fork, just to let him try it. But, no, you had to disappoint him. Alas, we can't undo what's been done, but now let me tell you what I have been meaning to say.

"When your uncle left, he hadn't come to a decision as to whether or not to take you as his son-in-law. Now I feel that it is my duty to clear things up. So let me ask you once and for all, do you wish to take Rapiah as your wife? Yes or no?"

Hanafi sat up once again, this time laughing loudly. "That's what I can't stand about living here, in Minangkabau. Everyone has an authority over someone else, and to everyone we owe something, whether it be money or kindness. Men and women are married off, matched up by their elders. I like the Dutch way better. When a man is young, his family consists of only his parents and his brothers and sisters. When he's old enough he chooses his own wife. His uncles and aunts and elders, even his parents, can go to hell if they don't like his choice. And after he's married, his family consists only of his wife and children. But here? No! Here we're always meddling in someone else's life: to honor and be honored, to obey and be obeyed, to explain and be explained to, and so on and so forth, forever. Before we marry, when we marry, and when we divorce, there are always people sticking their noses into our lives, people whose intentions aren't always good, either.

"But all that doesn't bother me any more, Mother. I have considered myself to be outside that tradition, no longer bound by it. If they expect me to repay my debt, especially Uncle Sutan Batuah, they will have to be content with money, for there will be no repayment of kindness. I never asked for a loan of kindness.

"And as for my wife, what's the use of you sending me to school in Batavia if all this time you intended to marry me to a village girl? Who among them could be my equal when it comes to knowledge of the world?"

"But you don't know that, Hanafi. Many of our girls have had a decent education, at MULO, or the King's School, for example."

"That's just a charade, Mother. Those children know their ABCs, and a little Dutch, and they think they're educated. But a broad approach to knowledge, what the Dutch call *algemene ontwikkeling*, you can get that only from Dutch-language high school, and from having lived among the Dutch for a long time. Oh, Mother, I can try to explain to you the concepts of *moraal, principes, gewetan* and so on but it won't be of any use. There are no Malay words for those things. And as I have told you before, I want to marry only for *liefde*: for love! Only *liefde* can make man and woman husband and wife, in a meaningful way. The Dutch call a marriage without *liefde* 'gewetenloos,' which is contrary to the values of educated people. And it's against my principles to see a woman offered, as it were, on a platter, garnished with a sum of money, to a man favored by her parents and her elders because of his position and his lineage. Marriage here is no more than a *handelstransacties*, which is repugnant to anyone who understands the meaning of *westersche beschaving*."

Once Hanafi began talking that way, his mother could only fall silent. There would be no use trying to reason with him; the more he talked the less she understood. If she persisted, he would say something like: "It's useless for someone who is *ontwikkeld* and *beschaafd* to talk to a peasant about matters of *filosofie, sociologie*, and 'deep spirituality.'"

After Hanafi spoke these words, his mother fell silent. She wiped her tears with her long scarf, and resigned herself to her fate, which had bestowed upon her such an intelligent son.

Such an exchange had happened two or three times before, always ending with her in tears, but she was hurt more deeply now than ever before. Even if she was an ignorant country woman, it had never occurred to her that her son could be so cruel to his own mother. She now felt that she could no longer open her heart to her only son. Yet she endured her sorrow patiently: perhaps there was still hope that one day he would change.

4

Love him, Love him Not

Corrie was unable to sleep that night. Her every moment was filled with the question, "Do I love Hanafi?", which was immediately followed by the answer, "Oh, but a Dutch woman and a Malay man, it cannot be." Yet there was another voice within her which said, "But a Malay man can obtain European status."

She summoned Hanafi's image into her mind. He was a handsome man, with striking features, and skin not nearly as dark as that of most natives. His education, his manners, and his values were entirely Western. If it weren't for the presence of his ignorant mother, people might very well mistake him for a European, and it was likely that because he despised his own race he would one day apply for European status. His job was one that was usually held by a Dutchman, and if he obtained European status, it was likely that he would continue to rise in position; there might be no limit! Still, Corrie definitely couldn't accept his love because, because, because she didn't love him!

Hanafi was a good friend whom she had known since her childhood days, but he was nothing more than a friend. They had been playmates and, with Hanafi being three years older, he had acted like an older brother for her at their primary school in Solok, often defending her from the teasing of other boys. When she first moved to Batavia, Hanafi extended his stay there for six more months before he returned to West Sumatra. But in those six months they met only two or three times. And after that, when she lived in the boarding school on Salemba Street, they didn't even write to each other. They saw each other only when she came home to Solok for her year-end vacation. But even then, their relationship had never been more than casual, like that of a brother and sister. Also like a brother and sister they quarreled, often heatedly, until one of them lost their temper. But as soon that happened, the other would gently retreat. That was how they had preserved their friendship.

Corrie had begun to realize—especially after entering HBS—that she was a little girl no longer. As such, she had to be careful of her reputation and do everything to ensure that she was not talked about. That was why she visited Hanafi's house only occasionally, and never alone. The same was true when they went for a walk: she always brought along a friend.

She herself did not feel the need to be prudent with Hanafi; it was the talk of others she was wary of. Hanafi was Malay, and she knew that the Malay had strict rules of etiquette concerning how a man should behave toward a woman. When they were in Batavia, Hanafi would take her to the beach to go swimming, without a chaperon. She didn't mind that, for she trusted him as a brother.

And so far Hanafi had acted like a brother; until this vacation, that is. Now, suddenly, as he had that very afternoon, he was acting differently. It was their habit to hold hands, as brothers and sisters often do, but this afternoon, when he caressed and kissed her hand, it had startled her. She had been taken aback: not just because of Mr. and Mrs. Brom's sudden appearance and not because of him kissing her hand, for that, too, was normal for brothers and sisters. When he kissed her hand something else had come over her; her blood had rushed to her head, and her heartbeat had quickened. For her, this was definitely a sign that their brother-sister relationship was starting to change.

Corrie was aware of her own desires and, for the first time that day, recognized the danger inherent in a relationship between a man and a woman. Previously, she had thought that a man and a woman could be friends, without the possible intrusion of feelings that went beyond friendship. It had never occurred to her before then that any of her male friends might think of her as a "woman." She was simply their friend, no different from one of their male friends. That's why she had always laughed at suitors who confessed to undying love for her after having only seen her two or three times in a crowd. Such statements had never incited her passion. More than anything, they seemed to her ridiculous, or annoying to the point that they made her want to tease the boys.

But what about Hanafi? She admitted that she loved Hanafi, but only as a friend. Unfortunately, Hanafi no longer saw her in that same light. He loved her not as a sister but as the woman he wished to marry. Her feelings for him had also changed. But how? She herself didn't know. Did she love him? The question haunted her, making sleep impossible. No matter how tightly she shut her eyes, his face kept coming back into view. Something about him had taken hold of her. He was Western in every way, but his "nativeness" had not completely disappeared. It was his coyly polite manner, typical of native men, that had captured her heart.

She stared at the ceiling for a moment, and then started counting off the buttons on her nightgown: "Love him, love him not, love him, love him not, love him..." Five buttons, it stopped at "love him."

"But of course it stopped at 'love him'," she said to herself, "because there are five buttons. If I had started with 'love him not' it would have stopped at 'love him not'."

A house lizard gave a shrill cry: "*toh-kay!*"

"Aha!" she exclaimed. "A gecko never lies. Let's see how many cries it makes... Love him not. *Toh-kay!* I love him. *Toh-kay!* I love him not. *Toh-kay!* I love him. *Toh-kay.* I love him not. *Toh-kay!* I love him..." But then the gecko stopped.

Cursed gecko, she thought to herself, they usually call five times, but this one went and called six times! "Well, it doesn't matter; I don't love Hanafi. Good heavens, he's a Malay!"

Corrie tried to banish all thoughts of Hanafi. Her head felt heavy, her ears were ringing.

For a while she lay still, her thoughts empty, and then she fell asleep. But almost immediately, Hanafi's face appeared in a disturbing dream, smiling sweetly. In the dream, Hanafi was about to leave her for a faraway place. As they parted, she cried out his name with all her strength, "Hanafi, my love!"

"Corrie, Corrie!" Her father's voice outside her door woke her up. "Wake up, you are having a bad dream."

How upset she was over her foolish dream. She, Corrie du Bussée, screaming in anguish because Hanafi, a Malay, was leaving her. What would her father think if he heard her call out his name? It was all Hanafi's fault. He had no right to disturb her like this. He, whom she had treated as her own brother since childhood, her closest, most trusted friend, he had no right to take away her peace of mind. She made up her mind to tell him. Tomorrow, when she went to his house, she would tell him that he had taken advantage of her trust, that he should forget the whole thing.

Yet as she turned over her thoughts, she realized that if she truly had no feelings for him, she would not be so perturbed by her little game of love him-love him not. If she truly did not love him, she could put a stop to it all with one word. She thought for a while and decided that that is what she would do tomorrow. She would put an end to it, nip it in the bud, with one word. No, she did not love him, and he must abandon all hope. And yet... Poor Hanafi, how much that would hurt him, her dearest friend. Surely the friendship and the siblings' bond they had nurtured since childhood would come to an abrupt end.

As these thoughts crossed her mind she rose from her bed and opened the door for her father.

"Papa," she said when he entered the room, "this afternoon, after tennis, as Hanafi was walking me home, some children were shooting pellet guns at bats that were hanging in the almond tree. One fell right in front of me. It must have frightened me more than I thought for it to enter my dream."

Mr. du Bussée looked into his daughter's blushing face. He felt uncertain, not knowing what to say. But after a moment he finally said, "You are over-excited, Corrie. Your nerves are probably too tense. Why don't you take a Bromural? Let me get it for you."

He left his daughter and returned with a small bottle in his hand. After taking a small tablet from the bottle, he poured a glass of water from the carafe on the small night table.

"Take this. It will calm you down and help you sleep better. Good night."

Quickly she swallowed the tablet, and then went back to bed. The clock struck four, and Corrie fell asleep soon after.

But Hanafi didn't leave her. She had another dream. This time she dreamed that she was playing "Love him, love him not" with the stripes on the mosquito net. The stripes were about twenty centimeters apart, so there were many of them. She began with "love him not," because that was how she truly felt—"Love him not, love him, love him not, love him, love him not…"—but yet again it had stopped at "love him."

That dream upset her greatly, and when she awoke and saw the sun already high in the sky, the dream came back to her.

"Dreams lie!" she huffed, pulling up her blanket as if trying to return to sleep even though the clock had struck seven some time before.

She glanced at the mosquito net. Yes, there were a lot of stripes, at least thirty or more. Let's start with "love him not," she thought, in accordance to reality.

"Love him not, love him, love him not, love him…."

Thirty times they alternated between "love him not" and "love him," and it just happened that at the stripe closest to the end of the bed frame, she ended with "love him."

"Maybe he's put a spell on me," she said to herself as she jumped out of bed. "I am certain I don't love that man. No, no, no! Divining numbers, counting stripes, that's the childish superstition of the Malay. It doesn't matter what the numbers say. They can say 'love' ten times out of ten, I don't give a hang. This afternoon I will tell him what's in my mind, and that's 'love him not.' And if that means the end of our precious friendship, so be it."

But she was greatly upset by the fact that Hanafi was the first man who had ever distracted her in this way; it was like a great wave rolling over her, robbing her of both sleep and appetite. Corrie felt restless all day as she anxiously waited for five o'clock.

Of course I'm in a hurry to see him, she thought, because I want to put an end to his hopes once and for all. With such excuses, she justified her impatience to herself. That's the only reason I feel anxious: the only reason. It's impossible that I'm impatient because I want to see him. That's impossible, absolutely impossible!

All day, she did things and did not know why she did them. She took out her "treasure box" of love letters from her admirers, and brought it to the kitchen. One by one she took out the letters, and fed them to the fire. "There, I hope all of you will see this in a vision tonight, and not waste any more stamps."

5

On the Waves of Emotion

Since four o'clock Corrie had been readying herself in front of the large mirror in her room. First she put on her ocean-blue dress; she was very fond of that color. But as she looked into the mirror she suddenly remembered that lavender, not blue, was Hanafi's favorite color. Immediately she changed into a lavender dress. How frightened she had been when looking in the mirror and seeing the pallor of her skin, so pale from lack of sleep. Lavender brought out her pallor even more. She pondered the fact that she had chosen his favorite color. She should not do that; because she did not love him.

It took her a long time to choose, but she finally settled on red. Satisfied with her choice, Corrie smiled at the mirror and said to herself, "Don't think red stands for passion. No, sir, I chose this color because it's the only one that suits my complexion this afternoon, that's all."

It was only half past four. My watch must have stopped, she thought to herself as she put it onto her wrist. But the watch was working, so how could it be that it was only half past four? She left her room to check the clock in the living room. It also said half past four. I promised to come at five, she thought; if I arrive early, he will think I am too eager to see him.

Corrie began pacing back and forth through the house, examining, as if for the first time, the objects hanging on the wall:

tiger skins, civet pelts, the large thermometer, her father's antique rifles. She examined the whole house from the kitchen to the front veranda. She went into her father's study, read the titles of the books on the shelves, and then went into her room to scrutinize herself one last time: her hair, her dress, and accessories. She peered at her watch again, and then stepped out of the back door. The flagstones that lined the walk way to the front gate caught her attention. When she stepped on the first stone, almost unconsciously, she started counting. Let's try something different this time: "Love him, love him not, love him, love him not, love him, love him not...."

Very carefully, she walked along the flagstone walkway, counting off each stone she stepped on, so as not to make a mistake. But despite her caution, the last stone said "Love him"!

"Oh! Everything says 'love'. No, no! I won't count anything any more. What childish nonsense anyway. It's a quarter to five; if I walk slowly, it will be five o'clock by the time I get there."

"Papa!" she called to her father and walked up to him at the corner of the yard, where he was taking the air.

"I am leaving now, Papa."

"*Daag*, Corrie. Enjoy yourself."

"Thank you, Papa. *Daag*."

She left the front gate, walking much more quickly than she realized.

Hanafi was on the front veranda, rearranging the flowers in a crystal vase, when he saw Corrie walking hurriedly towards the house. Startled, he bolted and ran halfway across the yard to meet her.

"Corrie, that's what I call dependable. Ten to five!"

"Oh, hello, Hanafi," she said panting, looking a bit bashful. "So, my watch was right after all. I thought it was running slow, and I can't trust the clock at home either. I hurried because I thought I was going to be late."

"Lucky for me: that's ten more precious minutes with you. But you know, even if you had come at half past four, you would have found me sitting here waiting for you. Let's go sit down," said Hanafi, taking her hand.

He guided her into a rattan chair directly opposite the crystal vase. Just before she settled into the chair, he once again held her hand firmly, for a long moment, as he looked into her eyes in a way that didn't need to be explained by words. Corrie dropped her gaze; a shade of red suffused her face, and moved more vibrantly to her ears. She felt herself tremble. If Hanafi had been standing any closer he would have heard the fast, heavy beating of her heart. But as it was, he could only surmise her excitement from the way her breast rose and fell, deeply, as if she were panting from physical exertion.

For an instant Corrie almost lost her composure. Her fingers, interlaced with his, were pressing themselves into his hand almost of their own accord, returning his pressure. Then she recovered herself. I don't love him, she said in her mind.

"Hanafi, sit down!" she said firmly, to reestablish some distance.

Hearing her cold voice, Hanafi felt as if he had just been doused with a bucket of cold water. Clumsily, he retreated and let himself sink into the chair across from her. The crystal vase stood between them.

"My turtle dove..." Hanafi said under his breath.

She pretended not to hear.

"So, Hanafi, what is it that you want to talk about?"

Hanafi said nothing. He looked at her for a moment and then dejectedly cast his eyes towards the dusty street.

Corrie grew restless waiting for his reply, and shifted in her seat once, twice. She finally broke the silence: "You are acting strange, Hanafi!"

He was now full of doubt. If he had read her gestures correctly, his turtle dove was flying away just as he was about to catch it. "I thought you knew what I was going to say," he said.

"I am not a fortune teller," she said flatly, though her face revealed her agitation. "Just tell me what is so important." Corrie felt better now. Everything was again under control. She had nearly lost her head, almost been swept away by passion into that blissful but fatal abyss. Yet she had regained her composure. She would not and must not marry a Malay.

Hanafi was still lost. He stared at the tabletop, as if counting the little squares of woven bamboo. "Would you like some tea?" he said at last.

"Yes, very much."

That was a relief, because it meant he could now leave that space, which had begun to suffocate him, making him feel as if the whole universe was closing in on him. Hanafi went into the house, and soon reappeared with a houseboy carrying a tray with a teapot and two matching cups. Slowly, deliberately, Hanafi poured out two cups of tea, and stirred in some sugar. He then went back into the house, before returning with a small sketch book.

"Here are sketches I made when I went to Padang through Sitinjaulaut," he said, almost sighing.

After bringing the cup to her lips a few times, taking small sips, Corrie took the sketch book and started flipping through the pages. But her hands were trembling, and she could not keep her attention on the sketches.

Hanafi asked her if she wanted more tea.

"Thank you, Hanafi. The road to Padang is truly beautiful, isn't it? But what is it that you have asked me to come here for?"

"Oh, Corrie, there is only one more week left of your vacation, and I want to see more of you than just on the tennis court. That's why I asked you to come."

"But there is a time to meet and a time to part," she replied. "For myself, if it wasn't for my papa, I would have left this little town for good a long time ago. I miss the zoo, Deca Park, the harbor, Stafmuziek, and all my friends in Batavia. I don't know how people can stand to live here."

"You know I don't like it here either. But what can I do? My mother and my job are here. Yet over these last few weeks, Solok has been heaven to me. Alas, it will soon end. Once again it will be no more than a lonely town."

As if oblivious to what Hanafi was saying, Corrie gazed into the study, and lost herself in the books that were stacked neatly on the shelves.

"I have read all the books I brought from Batavia," she said, "and the only books on my father's shelves are things like *The New Architecture, Concrete Construction,* and *Hydro Engineering.* Can you lend me something to read, just to pass the time?"

"I have plenty of books, Corrie. Let's go look."

Corrie picked out two volumes, and Hanafi showed her another one, a collection of Shakespeare's plays.

"Yes, that one too," exclaimed Corrie as she took the book from his hands. A carnation had been pressed between the pages, in a passage from *Romeo and Juliet.* Although it was dried, the carnation still retained its color: a deep, dark red.

"What's this, Hanafi?"

"Do you remember, Corrie? One day when we were walking to the tennis court, this flower fell and somehow stuck to your blouse. I don't know if you were aware of it or not, but I picked it up. I knew then that I intended to keep it for the rest of my life."

Corrie felt the blood rushing to her face, making her blush. Her hand trembled as she picked up the flower and caressed it. Again she felt the rush of blood throughout her body. She held up the flower, and for a moment lost herself in its dried petals. Hanafi, seeing how affected she was, could no longer contain himself. Almost against his will, his hands reached toward her waist. He drew her to him, and pressed her breast to his. He kissed her on her cheeks, on her forehead, on her eyes and lips.

Corrie felt lost, as though an electric current was running through her. Her body felt as if it was floating, swooning in the air. She closed her eyes, no longer resisting Hanafi's kisses. She felt an inexpressible sensation wash over her, one she had never felt before. She returned his kisses as if by reflex. Moments passed— who knows how long?—as the young pair lost themselves in each other, oblivious to the world around them.

And then, suddenly, "Mail!" A loud voice could be heard from the veranda.

It was like a lightning bolt, startling them. Hanafi withdrew his hands from Corrie's waist, and she turned away. "I have to go!" she cried. "The mail from Batavia comes today. There must be many letters from my friends," she said hurriedly.

Between heavy breaths, Hanafi said, "Don't go yet. You've been here for less than fifteen minutes. Just now, for a few moments I felt as if I was in heaven. Please don't go."

"Hello," she said to the postman, as she went down the veranda steps. "Any letters for me?"

"A lot."

"Good day, Hanafi. I have letters waiting at home."

Without even a handshake, she ran down the steps, and quickly walked towards the gate. On the way home she kept repeating to herself what a disaster the meeting had been. Her head giving in to my heart. But it won't happen again, she vowed. From now on I will do only what is sensible. Corrie du Bussée will not abandon herself!

Hanafi's eyes followed her from the veranda. Although she had left him so abruptly, his heart was now settled. There was no longer any doubt in his mind. Corrie loved him! He had finally caught his dove, had it firmly clutched in his hand. He went back to the study. The book of plays was still open to the same page. He picked up the carnation and kissed the dried petals again and again.

The three books that Corrie had wanted to borrow lay on the table. He set them aside. If she had not come to fetch them by tomorrow afternoon, he would go himself to Mr. du Bussée's house to bring them to her.

6

Into the Blue Sky

When Corrie arrived at home, a packet of letters from Batavia were waiting for her. Two of them had the appearance of love letters. They follow me even to this hinterland in Sumatra, she said to herself, smiling. I wonder who is so eager to die for me this time?

First she opened an envelope with a handwriting she did not recognize. The letter began with "Dear Beautiful One." She read three more lines. She was right, it was a love letter, but this one said nothing about being eager to die. It was signed Alfred Holstein. Oh yes, she remembered him now: a young man with curly hair who worked for the postal liner. She had spoken to him once or twice, on a street car. Hmm.... This one is certainly bound for the fireplace, she thought to herself. The second letter was signed George Jansen. It was also going to the fire. What a waste of stamps. And then she suddenly felt the urge to reply to all of her suitors, and explain in clear, plain language, that she had no intention of marrying, that marriage had no place in her life.

It seemed natural to her to live the rest of her life without a man. She couldn't help but feel a little squeamish at the thought of a man's hand on her body. No, she couldn't imagine it at all: unless it were Hanafi. She felt no repulsion that afternoon when Hanafi held her in his arms. This troubled her. Why is Hanafi an exception? she asked herself angrily. It can't be because of love, because she did not love him. It must be because he was such a good friend. Yes, that must be the reason.

Satisfied with that explanation, Corrie went on to open the other letters. They were from her school friends who, like herself, had gone home to their parents for the vacation. Meanwhile, afternoon had changed into evening, and darkness had slowly engulfed the sky. After dinner, Corrie excused herself to her room. She told her father she had a headache. It wasn't a lie: her head felt as if it was being pounded with a hammer.

It was then that she decided to cut off all relations with Hanafi. She didn't know if her decision was prompted by her anger at Hanafi's actions that afternoon, or by a genuine kindness towards him, her dear friend whom she did not wish to hurt any more than could be helped.

She quickly undressed and loosened her hair. Usually she would brush her hair and powder her face before retiring. But tonight she did not. She simply tossed herself onto the bed as she was.

She was at a loss to explain the feeling that overcame her when Hanafi embraced and kissed her. The only thing that was clear was that she was thankful for the postman. If it hadn't been for him, who knows what might have happened. She knew that at that moment she had no will of her own; she would have surrendered to Hanafi's desire.

As she lay in bed, the conflict between her head and her heart possessed her again. She now understood that she could not reject Hanafi's love as long as she was in contact with him. Whenever she saw his face, met his gaze, or sensed the awkwardness in his gestures as he confessed his love, she couldn't help but be swept away. That she no longer denied, but she could not, must not, become his wife.

What Hanafi had done disturbed her equanimity even as it aroused her desire. If she wasn't careful, her heart's passion could overtake her mind. As she reflected on her situation, her father's advice suddenly echoed in her mind. She agreed with him wholeheartedly now. Considering that one has to live and be at peace with society, the misery and difficulty of a mixed marriage would far outweigh any benefits. Oh, how good it felt to be once again capable of clear thinking.

Maybe he used a charm, she thought to herself. But that's nonsense! Corrie didn't believe in such superstitions. What possessed her had to be nothing but a weakness of the heart, which she fell victim to every time she was near him. The only solution was to put as much distance as possible between herself and him, and she must be vigilant: one careless moment meant one dangerous step closer to losing herself to the abyss.

With one swift movement she rose and went to the small desk in her room. There, she took pen to paper and, with more determination than ever before, began a letter to Hanafi. It had to be short, she said to herself; but before she knew it, she had written half a page, digressing into irrelevant tangents as she explained the depth of her sadness, which in the end couldn't help sounding as though she was giving him hope for the future. In short, the letter didn't say a firm goodbye but only asked for more time. The page was now full, and the letter was not yet finished. She drew a deep breath, put down the pen, and started reading the letter from the beginning. "Ach," she said when finishing, "this letter is making me feel closer to that man." Quickly, she tore up the letter and took out a fresh sheet of paper, and wrote:

My friend Hanafi,

I have a girlfriend in Bukittinggi who wants to see me. From there we might go to Padang or Lubuksikaping; we are not sure, because she has relatives in both places, and she wanted to show me the countryside. I am not sure when I will be back in Solok.

By the time you receive this letter I will be on the train.

Sincerely,
C. du Bussée

This letter satisfied her; she hoped it would succeed in preventing Hanafi from writing back.

After she put the stamps on the envelope she took out a small suitcase from the closet and packed enough clothes, make-up, and toiletries for a week. Then she fell asleep. The next morning, after breakfast, she told her father she was going to visit her friend, the daughter of the Assistant District Commissioner in Bukittinggi, for a period of time that she hadn't yet decided on.

"But there's only one week left of your vacation," her father said, pleading.

"If I am there for more than two days, you can join me, Papa. We can stay in a hotel."

Mr. du Bussée felt bound to comply with his daughter's wish.

The next day, Hanafi found Corrie's letter when he arrived home from the office. It disturbed him at first. Could it be that she had changed her mind about yesterday afternoon, that she had regretted her actions and decided to leave Solok so she wouldn't have to see him? He was almost overcome by doubt. Her letter was too short, without a single word that could be construed as a testimony to their budding intimacy. She even signed it "C. du Bussée."

Yet like all young men in love, Hanafi found a way to rationalize away his doubt, even transforming it into something that worked in his favor. Corrie is still a child, only nineteen years old, he thought to himself. What happened yesterday afternoon must have truly shocked her, like a dove that has just begun to peck the food from your hand, when it is suddenly seized by the fear that the hand might move to wring its neck. It's a perfectly natural reaction. Corrie would surely come back to Solok, and then he would ask her father for her hand.

He never once suspected that his turtle dove had flown, up and away into the blue sky.

One week had passed since Hanafi received Corrie's letter. Doubts began to take hold of his heart once again. Not only did he miss his beloved, but her vacation was now over and he had not heard a word from her. To make matters worse, he heard from Simin, Mr. du Bussée's houseboy, that Mr. du Bussée left four days ago for Padang, with several large suitcases.

From that he deduced that Corrie was in Padang; but what about her steamer trunks? Corrie would not sail to Batavia without first coming back to Solok, even if it was just for one day, to say good-bye to her friends, and to him. It was unthinkable for her not to do so. And if Corrie had left without informing him, at least there should have been some word from her father. So he concluded that his worries about her sailing away without first seeing him were without any grounds. That conviction cleared his head of all disturbing thoughts. Still, there were the large steamer trunks: these troubled his mind.

He bolted from his house and hastily headed to Mr. du Bussée's place to verify what he had heard. The houseboy, Simin, told him that the trunks belonging to Miss du Bussée were gone. All her belongings had been put in them and packed away, even her dresses, which had to be rushed from the cleaner. As for Mr. du Bussée, he had packed for only three or four days, bringing his clothes in a small leather suitcase.

Everything was clear to him now. Hanafi rushed home and tossed himself onto the sofa. And then he wept. "How could you, Corrie?" he murmured between his sobs.

For a long time he lay there on the sofa, losing track of time. The day had turned into evening, and Buyung, his houseboy, had begun lighting the lamps. Suddenly Hanafi heard him yell: "Fire!"

The kerosene from one of the lamps had spilled onto the woven jute mat which then caught fire. Buyung panicked; instead of shutting off the tap on the kerosene drum, all he could think of was to try to blow out the fire with gasping breaths as he yelled hysterically for help. The fire quickly spread, and neighbors poured into the back yard. Hanafi's mother was the only one calm enough to think. Quickly, she turned off the kerosene tap and the fire was soon extinguished.

While all this was taking place, Hanafi remained lying on the sofa, completely motionless and oblivious to any danger. He watched the commotion passively, as if it were a dream. Not a word escaped from his mouth. Yet his dazed condition didn't escape his mother's notice. For the last few days, she had observed her son's strange behavior anxiously. She had heard from Buyung that his friend Corrie had gone to Batavia, and she knew enough to suspect that Hanafi now missed her. Although he seldom talked to his mother, much less opened his heart to her, she knew what was in his mind. She could read the most subtle expressions of his face, even his gestures. Nothing escaped her, but she said nothing, and acted as if she knew nothing.

His mother had known about his feelings towards Corrie from the very beginning. If she had wanted to, she could have explained to him long ago the true nature of their relationship. She herself believed that Corrie was only toying with him, that she didn't love Hanafi enough to sacrifice herself for him, yet she said nothing to her son, afraid he might turn against her. His intention to marry a white woman not only went against the wishes of her heart, because she was convinced it would lead him astray, but she also believed that such a marriage would irreversibly separate her from her son. Hanafi had lost faith in his religion, that was clear, and she also knew that he looked down on his own people. At this point, she was Hanafi's only link with the world of Islam and the Minangkabau. If that link were severed by marriage to a white woman, she would lose him forever.

From the time Corrie arrived in Solok, at the beginning of her vacation, Hanafi's mother had felt uneasy. Corrie, as young as she was, was perceptive enough to feel uncomfortable whenever Hanafi's mother looked at her. There was jealousy in the old woman's gaze, which enraged Corrie, especially as she felt that such jealousy was groundless. She had no intention whatsoever of coming between a mother and her son. So, as her revenge, Corrie relished nothing more than to show Hanafi's mother how easily she could control him: he would kiss her feet if she told him to.

Hanafi's mother knew that the time was not yet ripe to talk to him about his relationship with Corrie, but this evening's incident with the fire had upset her deeply. After the lamps were lit, she approached him cautiously. "I thought you were asleep," she said to him before asking, "Hanafi, why didn't you get up and put out the fire?"

"Every day I tell that idiot Buyung that he shouldn't turn on the tap until the lamps are well-heated. Maybe a little scare will teach him a lesson, and prove to him that I'm right. Do you hear that, Buyung?" With that, Hanafi flung his back to his mother, who was standing in the doorway, as if he wished to say by this gesture that he didn't want to be disturbed. The old woman sadly shook her head and walked away.

Hanafi remained like that, lying in bed, for days. In his heart, in his mind, in every part of his body, there was only fire and lightning that struck and burned him everywhere. What did he care if the whole house burned to the ground? He was still certain that Corrie would respond to his love. Just one more meeting, and he was sure to steal her heart. And once she was his, he would never let her go. She must have acted the way she did because of her father's interference, or maybe her white women friends had influenced her.

Hanafi cursed himself for being born a Malay. For a long time he lost control over his life, unaware of any of his surroundings. In his mind there was only Corrie.

"Mail!" he heard a loud voice from the yard. As if stung by a scorpion, Hanafi jumped to his feet and rushed to meet the mailman at the door. He was certain there was a letter from Corrie, and he was not mistaken. The postman handed him a pink envelope with Corrie's handwriting, postmarked in Padang. He opened it hurriedly, and pulled out three sheets of paper the same shade of pink as the envelope. First, let's see the signature, he thought to himself. It was "C. du Bussée".

That was a bad sign. If it was a good letter, it would have been signed Corrie. But instead, she used her last name, just as she did on the previous letter.

At first he covered the letter with his hands, afraid to read it. His blood rushed, his ears rang: for a moment all was dark around him. But the letter had to be read; good or bad, anything was better than not knowing.

Slowly, cautiously, he began reading:

My dear friend Hanafi,

This is perhaps the last time you will hear from me, Hanafi. You know, Hanafi, ever since I was a child I have trusted you wholeheartedly, because I have thought of you as an older brother.

How many times have we discussed the subject of mixed marriage between a Dutch woman and a Malay man? And how many times have you responded to my level-headed argument with an outburst of temper, so that I have had to cut short my argument to avoid hurting you? And at the end of it all, still, we have never arrived at the truth of such a difficult matter.

I think you realize that in principle I am against mixed marriages. I can't understand why you have not thought the matter through. Many people wanted to bring together East and West, but in the times that we live in, for most people, East is East and West is West; the gap between them can never be bridged.

Marrying me would mean divorcing yourself from your people, your family and your mother. I know you have said many times that all that means nothing to you. But please forgive me if I have to say that I find such a position reprehensible, especially considering how much you owe your people and your country, not to mention your family and your mother. You have a duty to them, and I cannot respect a man with such an outlook.

Furthermore, I too would be shunned by my people. We would be ostracized from both sides.

Dear Hanafi, let's let bygones be bygones. Let us not say another word about what has happened. I have forgiven you for taking advantage of me when I was weak, for putting my honor as a woman in danger. I have forgiven you for breaching the trust I have put in you since I was a child.

Even now I am still ashamed of my actions on that cursed afternoon, but I have forgiven your transgression. For now let us bury what is past. And I beg of you that you put a fence along your life's path, so that it may not cross mine.

Whether we will ever see each other again, only God knows. But let me ask of you humbly, that you do not seek to contact me until you are married. Henceforth I should be addressed as "Juffrouw du Bussée" until I am married and "Mevrouw So-and-so" after that.

I hope the briny ocean between us can wash away our memories, and all that is past.

Do not think that I am cutting myself off from you just to spite you. Not at all, Hanafi. It is with sadness that I have done so, but it was your actions that put me in danger of making a fatal mistake.

Should you yourself want to cut off all contact with me in the future, I will completely understand.

Sincerely,
C. du Bussée

Hanafi was not at the table for dinner. After he read Corrie's letter, he folded it carefully and put it into his shirt pocket. Then he went straight to his room to lie down. He said he had a headache.

7

Mother and Son

Hanafi did not sleep that night. The love and longing he felt for Corrie had suddenly turned to hate and revenge. It was clear to him now that Corrie had toyed with him, just to amuse herself and pass the time. How could she forsake their relationship so easily, as if she felt nothing for him? He knew, he was sure, that wasn't really the case. It simply could not be, for she had shown him, through her gestures and in so many other little ways, that her heart was his and that she had accepted his love. How else could he have fallen in love so deeply? His love could not have been entirely one-sided.

Once again he went through her letter in his mind. It was obvious that she blamed him for everything. But what had he done wrong? Had he deceived, ensnared, or coerced her? Certainly not! Their relationship was that of two close friends. Nevertheless, he was a man and she was a woman, and suddenly his desire for her as a woman had emerged. She must have known that, indeed she must have approved of it, because she, too—that he knew—felt the same passion. So why was he the guilty party? She had said in her letter that he had endangered her honor, taking advantage of her when she was weak. How base did she think him to be? Didn't she realize that it was she who had enflamed his desire?

There was something else in her letter that irritated him. Although she had said it politely, with carefully chosen words, the fact remained that she had insulted the Malay race. He realized that he himself had no high regard for his people, but somehow hearing Corrie's disdain made him angry. Suddenly Hanafi felt, perhaps for the first time, the urge to defend his people.

If her father forbade her to marry a Malay, her reaction would be understandable. No one could fault a daughter for wanting to obey her father. Yet even if that was the case, there was still no need for her to give him an insulting gesture as she left. If she truly accepted his love, and it was only because of her father that she could not be with him, then why not say so; at least then they might salvage their friendship.

The more he thought about it, the more intense was his resentment towards her. It was acceptable for him to look down on his own people, to be convinced that he should not have been born a Malay, and that his mother was the only civilized Malay person he knew, but to hear the insult from another's lips was different, especially if it was from Corrie's.

He began to feel that the only reason Corrie had treated him with such contempt was because he was a native. It's true: he was a native. But as a friend, she did not have to be so curt; there were other, more respectful, ways of ending his hope.

Morning had broken, and shafts of light penetrated his room through the gaps in the curtain. Hanafi had not slept for a single moment. His brain had been spinning, composing all sorts of counter-insults and attacks to include in his reply to Corrie's letter, but he decided against writing it. He must not show his defeat. Even though she had insulted him greatly, he must hold his head up. Perhaps one day she would realize what she had done.

His feelings about marriage were confused now. Perhaps Corrie was right, that East is East and West is West. Even if there is a union of the two, one day, when the passion is gone the white woman would surely regret her hasty action, especially when loneliness surrounds her, as her ostracism grows intolerable. No, he no longer wanted to marry a Western woman. What had just happened to him with Corrie convinced him of that. But, at the same time, a Malay woman was also out of the question. Among all the women of his own people that he knew, there was not one sophisticated enough for him, not one with whom he could share his thoughts and ideas.

In that state of mind, full of doubt, Hanafi drifted off to sleep. Twice his mother knocked on his door. He answered on the third knock, and told her he was not going to the office because he wasn't feeling well.

Hanafi was indeed seriously ill. For fourteen days he suffered a fever and during those days of delirium, the words he mumbled brought worry to his mother's heart. She gleaned from them that the root of his illness was a desire for revenge.

Eventually, Hanafi's fever subsided and the doctor declared him out of danger. Nonetheless, his mother still waited by his bed, day and night, as he slowly regained his strength. After having been fed only porridge and milk, he was now well enough to have rice.

Patiently his mother waited until he had fully regained his strength. Only then would she tell him the words that for days had lain so heavily on her mind.

In addition to the doctor, a *dukun* was also summoned to heal him, but Hanafi didn't approve of traditional healing methods. He would not take the *dukun*'s medicine; indeed he wouldn't let the person near him.

His mother, on the other hand, firmly believed that Hanafi needed both a Western doctor *and* a *dukun*. A doctor is able to cure only what ails the flesh, whereas she was convinced that the source of Hanafi's illness wasn't physical. The doctor's medicine had to be complemented with medicine for the soul, because every illness has both its visible and invisible manifestations. The doctor could take care of the visible symptoms, but the unseen aspect of the disease could be cured only with incense and prayers. Since Hanafi would not knowingly take the traditional medicine, the *dukun* was made to burn incense in the room next to Hanafi's bedroom. There, the *dukun* said his prayers and sprinkled holy water on a spot on the wall directly behind Hanafi's head. The *dukun* believed that Hanafi was affected by a curse, a spell that not only made him love the white woman for whom he now pined but also made him dislike all other women. The *dukun* was there to free Hanafi from this spell so that he would be able to love another woman.

If Hanafi didn't want to take the *dukun*'s traditional medicine knowingly, then it could be mixed into his food. Since it was liquid in form, it could easily be mixed into his food or his coffee, or even his bath water. Thus no matter how obstinately Hanafi might refuse his own people's methods of treatment, his mother and the *dukun* believed that, sooner or later, as the traditional medicine permeated his system, he would come to his senses.

Hanafi's mother was very grateful to the *dukun* and promised to do anything he told her. She would pay him any sum he asked as long as he was able to restore the health of her only son.

One morning Hanafi came out of his room and lay down on the sofa in the parlor. The Western doctor was no longer calling on Hanafi every day, because Hanafi's fever had completely subsided. The doctor assured him that as long as he had plenty of rest and was able to relax his mind, his recovery would soon be complete. Meanwhile, the *dukun* was also satisfied with his work: he had succeeded in administering to his patient enough medicine to break the spell from which he suffered. He would be more compliant now and willing to accede to his mother's wishes.

And to look at Hanafi lying on the easy chair, who would doubt the *dukun*'s word? His face looked as if he had been sick for months, or even years. He was pale, his eyes were sunk deeply into his skull; both his empty gaze and his gestures indicated that he was oblivious to his surroundings. His mental powers had weakened. Whenever someone said something to him, he would pause for a long time as if thinking, but then he always gave the same reply: "Yes," "No," or "I don't know."

Before the fever and illness had taken hold of him, Hanafi had acted indifferently when the servant almost set the house on fire, but even then it was apparent that he still had his strength. Now, however, he seemed drained, completely lacking in power. His mother believed the *dukun* who said that his weakness meant the medicine had broken him and that this was the first step in his return to normalcy. This made her very happy but also caused her to forget the doctor's advice who said that Hanafi needed rest. So it was with a clear conviction that her words would not be spurned that she sat down on a chair beside him.

Luckily, Hanafi was feeling clear-headed that day, and was in a mood to talk, although clearly, he was not completely recovered, neither physically nor mentally.

"So, how are you feeling now, Hanafi?" his mother began.

"I just have the headache."

"Thank God that's all. Is there anything I can get for you, one of your favorite dishes, perhaps?

"No thank you, Mother."

A long pause, and then his mother said: "The doctor said he would only come if we call him. That must mean you have recovered?"

"I think so, Mother. I'm just feeling weak, that's all."

His mother saw that Hanafi was now in an agreeable mood. She spoke cautiously: "Hanafi, don't you think that at a time like this—when a man is ill, that is—it would be good to have a wife to take care of him?"

Hanafi threw an awkward glance. "Are you tired of looking after me? You know you can always send me to the hospital in Padang Panjang."

"Hanafi, won't you ever listen to me? Does a mother ever tire of looking after her children? What I just said was not for my happiness; it was for your own good!"

Hanafi did not answer right away. He shut his eyes, and tried to think of what to say. Instead, memories of the vacation just past flooded into his mind. For a moment his lips trembled as if her were holding back words that threatened to burst forth.

His mother saw that he was tormented by doubts, and looked down at him kindly.

Hanafi finally opened his eyes and said, with resignation, "It's not that I don't want to take a wife, Mother, but what can I say? 'Tis the heart's desire to hold the mountain, but alas, the arms are too short."

"You know what the elders say, Hanafi, we should not dream of what is beyond our reach. Your father was a respected man and I too occupy a place of honor. You, too, could have a happy life if you take your proper place among your people. In our tradition you have an honored position. A man like you shouldn't have to chase a woman. In fact, you should be able to choose from many. According to the Minangkabau tradition, it is always better for a man to be asked than to ask himself."

"So, how many girls have been offered to you, Mother? How many have there been laid out on a silver platter? And how much have they been offering?"

"You mock our customs, Hanafi. What I am talking about is serious, something a mother must say to her son. Don't you think that a mother wants only what is good for her children? A mother would starve so that her children could eat; she would go naked so that her children could be clothed. Even among the animals a mother's love for her young is plain to see. Even chickens! No matter how tame they are, a hen will suddenly lose all fear if you come too close to her chicks. Believe me, Hanafi, everything I do is for your happiness. I think all religions agree that a person who turns against his mother commits a grave sin. A mother will forgive her child for that, because she loves him but Allah, the Most Exalted, will surely show his anger towards those who have sinned."

"I'm not mocking you, Mother. I'm serious. How many have asked for me?"

"Very many, Hanafi, but most of them I've already turned down because I know you wouldn't like them. We won't even discuss those."

"Well, do you have a suitable candidate? If you do, I'd like to know."

"My own favorite, as I've told you before, is Rapiah, the daughter of Sutan Batuah. I think she would make a good choice. First of all, it would be in keeping with Minangkabau custom for you to marry your uncle's daughter. Secondly, she's not lacking in appearance. Third, she has an adequate education: she graduated from HIS. Fourth, she was well brought up and, after school, continued her practical lessons at home, learning how to cook, sew, and embroider. Fifth, she has a good temperament; she's both kind and patient. Sixth... Oh, Hanafi, she has many more good traits. Must I list them all? I've known that child from the day she was born.

"But most important of all is that—and this has been hard for me to talk to you about—is that we long ago engaged you to Rapiah. Our families exchanged tokens! That's why Sutan Batuah paid all the money he did towards your schooling. But now, with your attitude towards this arrangement being as it is, what can I do now?"

For a long time Hanafi closed his eyes, lost in thought about what his mother just said. For him, her first five favorable points were nonsense. If that's what makes a wife, then he would rather not marry. But the last point she made, the point about them being engaged, troubled him. Rapiah's father had already paid the dowry!

Hanafi reflected upon his fate. His mother was right: he mustn't dream of plumbing the depth of the ocean if all he had was a foot-long line. A rush of anger rose in him once more as he thought of Corrie's refusal. No, marrying a woman he didn't love would not be an act of revenge against her, though she had, in truth, loved him. That he knew, but could the love he had felt ever be resurrected? It had been the first time for him, to love so purely, with all his heart and his will; and look what happened. Hanafi was sure he could not love that way again; that kind of love happened but once in a lifetime, and for only one person. It could never be grafted onto another. He loved the Corrie of his memory. Though she had cut off all physical contact with him, spiritually she had become his purpose in life. If he could not show his love for her physically, then he would love her as he once did, on a spiritual level instead. He could never love another, and thus had no hope of finding a wife though love.

He then thought of the debt he owed his uncle, not just the monetary debt but the debt of kindness his mother had just explained.

"Now the truth comes out," he finally said to his mother. "I have been sold to my uncle and my debt to him, in terms of both money and kindness, can only be wiped clean if I marry Rapiah. That's the way it is, isn't it? What high-stake transactions you conduct, Mother!"

"Oh, Hanafi, you always have to look at the bad side. If that's the way you're going to be, then fine, go ahead. But as you weigh the good and the bad of what I told you, remember that we country folk, in all our dealings, have never thought of harming either you or Rapiah. In our 'transaction,' as you put it, we have thought, in our own simple way, only of your happiness, that's all. And as to your debt to your uncle, he is not waiting for payment, neither for the money nor his kindness. What he gave he gave as a man of honor."

"And how does he feel about the arrangement now?"

"When you were at school he had high hopes. That was when we exchanged the tokens. But now, I couldn't say."

"Why do you say that, Mother?"

"He is afraid of you, Hanafi. He's from the old generation. When he saw you with all your foreign ways, so different from what he had expected, he began to feel uncertain. That's why he left our house in such a hurry, almost as if he were running away."

"Then why are we talking about this now?"

The old woman gave no answer. For a few moments she fell into a deep silence.

Hanafi repeated his question, "If Sutan Batuah is afraid of me, and we have not heard from him in almost two years, why are you bringing up this business with Rapiah?"

"It's so difficult to talk to you about these things, Hanafi. There are many reasons. First, there is the debt we owe. Even though the other party is not waiting for payment, as decent people we can not pretend that it doesn't exist. We have certain obligations. And also, just because your uncle left our house in such a hurry doesn't mean his decision is set in stone. Maybe he's just waiting for a sign from our direction. But most important for me is that I myself would very much like Rapiah to be part of our house. I had intended to save this discussion with you until after you had recovered, but your questions have forced me to speak to you now.

"In short, Hanafi, if you still think of this old woman as your mother, perhaps you could fulfill her one wish. For the sake of our happiness—all of us—take Rapiah as your wife. If you would do that, I would be as happy as if I had won a mountain of gold."

"Just now, you said that the doctor had pronounced me well, but now you say I am still ill, which one is it?"

"I don't mean the kind of illness that the doctor treats, but a different kind: the thorn that still pierces your heart," his mother replied with a long and silent sigh.

Hanafi did not answer. Tears welled up in his eyes, and slowly trickled down his cheeks. His gaze was lost in the billowing clouds overhead, and in his mind's eye he saw anguished screams trapped in his mouth. His heart felt as if it were being sliced with the blade of a knife.

During these last few days, while laid up in bed, he had tried hard to justify Corrie's decision in order to forgive her. He had come up with a hundred reasons for her leaving as she did. His bitterness had turned back to longing, and it was then that he was convinced of the infinite depth of his love, and of hers as well. She loved him; he was sure of that, and their separation, therefore, could be only attributed to the feelings and opinions of other people.

Hanafi had held on to this hope throughout his convalescence but now his mother's words once again broke his heart as they reminded him of how Corrie had humiliated him.

He compared Corrie and Rapiah. Corrie was educated; she could equal him in every field of thought, and sometimes even surpass him. He liked that, as long as she didn't remind him of the inferiority of his race. Rapiah, on the other hand, had a limited education. Surely she would know her place. Under no circumstances would she assume to take a position that was equal to his if she were his wife.

Hanafi no longer wanted a wife with whom he could share his dreams, so if he must marry, Rapiah it would be. It would please his mother, as well as settle the family debt once and for all.

As these thoughts went through his mind, tears streamed down his face as if from an inexhaustible spring. His mother cried with him, because she knew he had just accepted his fate.

"Just remember my son, if you keep dreaming for the bird of paradise, you will forget the pigeon in your hand. There will be no peace in your life if you refuse the food on your table, and want only the forbidden fruit. Even if that woman truly loves you, she will not sit at the same table with your relatives whereas the one I am offering to you is practically my own daughter, who will know her proper place when she is living under your roof. The one you dream of would always think that she had lowered herself to marry you. She would feel that you are eternally indebted to her and that you must always look up to her and show her the highest respect. But the one I would choose for you would feel that she is the one who is indebted to you. She won't think of herself as being bought and sold to settle your debt with her father because she knows that in the Minangkabau tradition her father's estate must come to you, not to her. What she will take to heart is that you have been generous in accepting her: a simple village girl. Knowing how proud you are, I am sure that's the only kind of marriage that will make you happy.

As long as you repay kindness with kindness, you will have peace in your life. You always say that your mother is an ignorant village woman. But for once, think carefully about my words. With a clear heart and a clear mind, judge carefully the wrong and right of it."

"Do you know her temperament, Mother?"

"If I didn't, how could I think of suggesting her for you? Did I not say that she is virtually my own child? You are much too proud. If you hear one word of reproach, you lose your temper. Think about this: well-educated women are difficult. If both husband and wife are smart, small things can become big things. Tongues have no bones; they lash out too freely and too quickly. If both sides are unrestrained, such a marriage would make for a life in hell."

"I agree with you there, Mother. You are quite right. You don't need to explain that kind of life to me. I know all about that from school and from reading. We would never hear the end of it if we started talking about that, because the philosophy of the European and that of the Malay are as far apart as the sky is from the earth. What I mean by my question is whether she is patient and knows her proper place?"

"Rapiah is patient. Even if you yell at her sometimes, she will not lose her patience. Hanafi, I am giving you an unpolished diamond. Trust me."

Hanafi fell silent. "Patient and knows her place…." That's all he wanted. If it weren't for the debt to his uncle he would have resigned himself never to marry. But because he was being forced—yes he, Hanafi, was being forced—he had to make the best of it. The last thing he wanted was to marry a woman whom he didn't love yet had a mind of her own! That kind of woman, he would divorce in a day. Isn't it easy, in the East, for a man to treat his wife as he wishes, he thought to himself.

"You said her father had lost all hope," Hanafi said to his mother. "Maybe he has abandoned his plan for the marriage. Now, if we were to revive the arrangement, would it not seem like it was we who are asking for his daughter, and not the other way around, as it should be according to our infallible Minangkabau tradition?"

"Don't worry about that; you can leave that to me. We aren't sure that your uncle has lost hope. As I said, he may be waiting for a sign. I do know that if you don't change and are disrespectful towards him, he will not like you. But if you are willing to give me your word that you will honestly try to see the good things in our customs, to be not so quick to scorn but rather to be willing to praise what's worthy of praise, I promise you that I will arrange everything. And that means finding a way for your uncle to resume his pursuit without losing his dignity. In the meantime, why don't you get to know your own people, Hanafi? Mingle with your own people for a while so that you can judge fairly. We are not all bad, and I would say that there are things about us that other peoples—even those peoples whom the world respects so much—could benefit from if only they knew about them."

"Well then, Mother, make the arrangement," Hanafi said with resignation in his voice. "I don't have much of an expectation, no lofty dreams. Just make certain that tradition is observed, that they come to us and not we go to them. We have to maintain the old way for the sake of the future. But you must know that this woman can't expect *liefde* from me. Love is not a factor here. It is *plicht*, a debt, that makes me accept her. For years I built a dream castle, which seemed so strong and beautiful, but just as I was about to step into it I realized it was only a castle in the air. I put one foot inside, and the whole thing came tumbling down. Now, there's only the wreckage around me. For that reason, fantasy is gone. There will be no more fantasizing, no more *idealen*. I live now because of *plicht*; my body and soul have been ransomed."

Hanafi's mother was overcome with joy. She didn't comprehend the Dutch words her son spoke but she understood that he had accepted Rapiah as his wife. Her wish had been fulfilled.

In keeping with her promise, she immediately arranged to bring a female calf to the *dukun*, along with some clothes and twenty-five rupiah. That's what she had vowed to do if the *dukun* could cure her son.

8

A Diamond in the Rough

Two years had passed since Hanafi had that conversation with his mother about taking a wife. And before he could fully understand the meaning of her words, he was married to Rapiah.

The wedding was almost called off because of a conflict that arose at the last minute between the two parties. It started with Hanafi who maintained that a modern bridegroom had to dress in modern style. He refused to wear the traditional Minangkabau costume: a "freak show" as he described it. If the bride's family insisted that he wear the costume, he would call the whole thing off. That was his final answer. After much argument and shedding of tears, the family finally agreed that he could wear his black smoking jacket, with black vest and white tie.

Then, another argument arose, this one about his head gear. Hanafi refused to wear the *destar saluk*, the traditional headdress for a Minangkabau groom. His female relatives wept from despair, begging for him to wear at least this one symbol of Minangkabau identity, if only during the wedding ceremony. But Hanafi would not give in. To wear the headdress with a smoking jacket, he contended, would look utterly ridiculous. Only after his mother begged him on her knees, while weeping and beating her chest, did he change his mind, but only begrudgingly. He said cynically, to everyone who would listen, that he had been "sold off," body and soul. Little did he know that the family elders and the bride's party had been equally obdurate and that unless he had consented to wear a headdress they themselves were going to call off the wedding.

But Hanafi still wasn't satisfied with the arrangements. He then demanded that the bride dress in the modern way, too. He suggested a style common to the Sundanese area of West Java where brides wore little if any adornments in their hair, sometimes only a turtle-shell comb or a gold pin.

The bride's household was thrown into an uproar when hearing this demand. While it was the bride's immediate family members who had the most reason to be angry—after all, it was they who would later be embarrassed—they kept their anger to themselves and, as is the Minangkabau way, let others, the more distant relatives and family friends, make their views known. In such a situation, giving up an inch easily means losing a mile and problems that were anthills are turned into the Himalayas. In short, everyone had been working so hard to prepare for the wedding, with many of the family not sleeping for days on end, nerves were very frayed. When the women were sitting together, even the smallest insinuation or the tiniest of slights was all that was needed to fan and ignite their agitation.

On the day when a messenger delivered this particular request, a number of female relatives of the bride-to-be were sitting on the front veranda of the bride's family's house, preparing costumes for the bride's attendants. Their discussion immediately turned to Hanafi, whom they called the "half-baked Dutch groom." "If he keeps this up, we'll have to show him his proper place," one of them said. "Just because he's been 'outside' for a long time doesn't mean he can turn our customs upside down."

"As high as something flies, it must always fall back to earth," another said, quoting an old saying.

Coincidentally, the woman who had just said this was not of pure Minangkabau descent; she was Minangkabau only on her father's side.

"I wouldn't describe a person's returning to Minangkabau as 'falling back to earth'" came another woman's reprimand.

"That's not how I meant it," the first speaker said defensively. "I was simply using an old proverb to make a comparison."

Another woman was about to add her own comment but then Hanafi's message arrived and the commotion that arose when the women heard Hanafi's request was like a wasp's nest that had just been disturbed. The infuriated women immediately spoke their mind and the poor messenger could do nothing but swallow the barrage of acerbic comments from the bride's household.

It took the group a long time to compose the appropriate response; there was so much to say and so much to settle but, in the end, they decided to keep it simple and brief: "For the sake of the wedding, we will comply with your request."

And all the while, Hanafi kept harping that he had been sold off. When he arrived at the bride's house he made a big fuss about the customary seating arrangement which he was expected to follow. "I don't want to feel like a Buddha statue in a temple," he said, "being bowed to by everyone."

For the moment, it looked like the wedding might not go ahead after all.

When the elders of the two families arrived, they greeted one another with deep bows, a signal of their hope of maintaining peaceful relations between the two parties. After that the polite but formal deliberations began. Hanafi and his party were forced to remain standing for quite some time until these deliberations were over.

At one point he began to grumble that the elders were deliberately stretching out the greeting ceremony just to punish him. "How many hours are they going to make me stand here, watching their foolish comedy?" he muttered under his breath.

His uncle, Sutan Batuah, was able to prevent him from doing anything rash by scolding him: "There are customs we must follow,

Hanafi. Now you're here and you will do as you're told. If you have any complaints, we can talk about them tomorrow. I may have only graduated from primary school, but I think of myself as an educated man. I hope you can lower yourself to have a discussion with me."

After chastising Hanafi in this way, Sutan Batuah then paid his formal respects to the elders. Bowing deeply, he whispered, "The obstacle has been removed; the bull has been tamed. We now have peace." He then took Hanafi's hand and, almost forcefully, led him to his appointed seat.

That was how Hanafi began his married life.

From the beginning he had said that he married only because he was forced to; as a consequence, therefore, he couldn't be held responsible for all the turmoil within the family that his actions might cause. Almost every discussion with him ended with him shrugging his shoulders.

Two years passed. Hanafi treated Rapiah as a wife forced on him: he would fulfill his duties as a husband, but Rapiah had no claim to his heart. *Liefde, sympatie, opoffering*, all those words that so intimidated his mother, he made it very clear that Rapiah had no right to them. He was careful to keep his freedom and define the boundaries around him; Rapiah had no say in the matter. She had to agree to whatever he said. Sneeringly, he would remind her of the duty of a Muslim woman to her husband, but then he would say that he had too much honor to mistreat a woman—to "*misbruik*" her—in such a manner.

Rapiah, who knew what *misbruik* meant, bowed her head, thankful for her husband's kindness. She was young, not much more than an adolescent, but already her humility could be an example for all women. She looked up to her husband and admonished her own upbringing and limited education. She felt grateful that her well-educated husband had chosen her as his wife.

Rapiah's mother, however, could endure no more than a month in Hanafi's house. Her sorrow came not only from seeing how Hanafi treated Rapiah, but also from how Hanafi often told her, his own mother-in-law, that a Dutchman would never put up with other people—that is to say, relatives—living in his house. It's parasitism, he said in Dutch.

When Rapiah asked what the word meant, Hanafi replied, "A parasite is a person who lives on the blood of others, like a leech."

Rapiah's mother understood the insinuation. She returned to Bonjol with a broken heart, but she didn't say a word about the matter to Sutan Batuah.

Hanafi's mother disliked seeing how Hanafi treated Rapiah and, after a time, began to feel closer to her daughter-in-law than to her own son. Once or twice she brought up the matter with Hanafi, but instead of him changing for the better, he became even more harsh with Rapiah and accused her of complaining about him behind his back.

Rapiah found solace in her mother-in-law and in her son Syafei, who was now almost one year old. Her daily chores, her son, and the kitchen made up her whole world. When Hanafi went to the office, she relaxed inwardly, and the sound of her voice resounded through the house; but as soon as Hanafi returned she fell silent. It was not that she didn't like her husband; she was simply afraid of him. When Hanafi's European friends came to visit, Rapiah would hide in the kitchen with her mother-in-law.

To make matters worse, when Hanafi was socializing with his friends he acted as though his wife did not exist. Except for a time shortly after their marriage, when Rapiah had first moved into his house, he didn't introduce his wife to anyone, and he dismissed all inquiries about her whereabouts with the comment, "Oh, she's just a country girl, still afraid of Europeans."

Even towards his son, Hanafi showed almost no regard or affection. He saw Syafei as Rapiah's son, not his own.

Many people were aware of Hanafi's callousness, even some of the Dutch women in Solok, but Hanafi was ever-ready to respond to their comments or to defend his behavior with a long theoretical elaboration on duties and feelings, which, in the end, was so complicated that the women often went away shrugging their shoulders.

There was one Dutch woman, however—the wife of the Assistant District Commissioner, Hanafi's superior—who one day took him to task in front of a large group of people at the tennis court.

On that occasion she began by asking him: "Do you actually know what a man's duty is to his wife, Hanafi?" Not giving him a chance to speak, she then continued: "When you talk about a wife, you're talking about a person who gave to you her most valuable possession and who, as the mother of your son, suffered immense pain and possibly risked her very life to give you a child. Do you have any understanding of a man's duty to the woman whom, in the presence of God and his fellow men, he came to call his wife? Your theories and philosophizing are nothing but a cover to silence the voice of your conscience. Deep down you know you have done wrong and that you have acted cruelly towards that gentle and helpless creature you call your wife. You say you know Dutch culture, but what you have done is an insult to Dutch culture. You don't even deserve to polish our shoes if that's the way you are."

Hanafi was shocked to hear the woman's criticism. He had always thought of his superior's wife as a weak woman. Talking to her, he suddenly realized, was a different matter from talking to his mother, whom he could intimidate with his theories and philosophy.

He now acted with greater circumspection: "Having always thought of you as a wise and educated person, I will seriously consider your arguments, though I must say they could very well be taken as insults. But let me just clarify one thing for you and that is my marriage with Rapiah is not, in the European sense, a real marriage. I was forced into it against my will. I can't explain all the details, but I do think it's very difficult for an outsider to be objective about what is going on in another person's household."

At this, the Dutch woman snapped, trembling with anger. "You may or may not take kindly to what I'm saying and, frankly, I don't give a damn if you take it as an insult. I am not speaking to you as the wife of your boss. I am speaking to you as a woman, one who feels great sympathy for the woman you call your wife. You claim to be educated and civilized but the way in which you treat her...." The woman took a breath to calm herself. "Granted, an outsider might not know all the facts about another person's family life. I don't know what happened before you married Rapiah and I don't want to know or need to know. What I do know is that you married her and that she has given you a son. By any standard anywhere in the world you do, therefore, have an obligation to her. You say that you understand and live in accordance to Dutch values but your attitude towards your wife is, as far as I can see, something I've only read about in *The Tales of 1001 Nights*.

"Don't think I don't know about your wife. She is a diamond, I can tell you that. She might be unpolished but even an unpolished diamond has a luster that everyone—except for you, perhaps—can see as clear as day. It's your duty to polish that diamond, Hanafi. Aren't you supposed to be the civilized one? If you ask me, Hanafi, I'd have to say that, being the person you are, you don't deserve to have a diamond as valuable as your wife.

"You keep saying she was your mother's choice. Even so, how could you have permitted yourself to pick the bud from the stem just before it bloomed? A woman is a virgin but once. Before she gives her virginity away, men flock around her and worship her like a goddess. But once she's lost her virginity or is divorced, she's thought to be as worthless as a pile of rubbish. This is very different from men who, for certain women, are even more desirable the more often they divorce and marry. 'Hmm, he must be very good,' they say.

"And all that talk of yours, Hanafi, about 'inner purity' and 'nobility of soul,'—which I supposed is what you meant by '*innerlijke aristoratie*'–is nothing more than words. Every minute of your waking hour you say you want a wife who has 'nobility of soul,' but if you ask me, I'll be straightforward and say that Rapiah has more 'nobility of soul' than you could ever dream of having."

After this very public incident Hanafi's friends and acquaintances began to avoid him. He was shunned at the tennis club and, on the street, if people could not avoid meeting him, they gave him no more than a formal nod. In time Hanafi had only two or three people whom he could call friends.

His new predicament served only to fuel his antipathy towards Rapiah. He blamed her for it, accusing her of complaining to the Assistant District Commissioner's wife. Most every day he'd blow up in anger towards her. Regardless of the real cause, it was she who had to take the blame for his misery. Yet she never defended herself: because she knew her place. She simply bowed her head, even as tears streamed down her face

Though she hated to see what was happening, Hanafi's mother remained silent too. She thought that by saying something she would only make matters worse. Yet matters did grow worse, all the same. Hanafi became more and more abusive towards his wife. In fact, he no longer even treated her as a wife but as a servant he had been forced to take into his household.

Gradually, out of their mutual sorrow, a strong bond grew between Rapiah and Hanafi's mother. They grew so close that Syafei sometimes seemed to confuse "mother" and "grandmother." The two of them were happy whenever Hanafi was at the office or playing tennis; then the house was an oasis of peace, but not when he was home. Even Syafei had become afraid of his father.

9

Betraying Mother

The sun was sinking low over the horizon and would soon disappear. As the day had been unusually hot, the tennis players had left the court to retire long before their usual time. Hanafi, however, had not been among them. After he had been shunned by his former friends, he no longer played tennis, and his social circle had dwindled to include only three people: a woman clerk from the post office, and a schoolteacher and his wife, people who were outcasts themselves. And over time, the four grew closer, perhaps because of their shared fate.

That evening, they were having tea in Hanafi's garden, and the conversation had turned to their plan to form a new tennis club, one that, if necessary, might include some educated natives who could not gain admission to the Dutch-run club.

But while his friends were engrossed in their discussion, Hanafi was lost in his own thoughts. In his mind, he was in the past with Corrie, sitting with her in that very garden, joking and quarrelling as they waited for their friends to arrive to play tennis. He saw the two of them again, reading poetry, looking at pictures in magazines, and talking about the past, the future, and the endless list of other topics that always exist between two close friends. These scenes from the past appeared vividly before him as though in a dream.

In reality, however, it was Suze, the woman from the post office, who was now sitting in the chair opposite him. When Corrie left, Hanafi had lost his only true friend. He thought he could fill the void with Suze. "Everyone needs a friend," he told himself,

"someone to confide in, and to share life's joys and sorrows with."
But he soon discovered that he could not confide in Suze half the
things he had used to confess to Corrie.

Nevertheless people begun to talk about the two of them.
That's how it was in a small town: an anthill became a mountain.
Simply for the reason that they were often seen walking on the
street together in the afternoon, after Suze finished work at the post
office, people immediately assumed there was something going on
between them.

Hanafi offered the trio a second cup of tea and then hollered for the
houseboy, "Buyung, Buyung!"

There was no answer.

"Buyung! Where are you?"

There was still no answer.

"Rapiah!" he yelled louder.

"Damn it!"

He then bolted from his chair and started toward the kitchen,
which stood behind the house some distance away. When he got
there he found his mother and Rapiah so absorbed in their tasks
that they seemed oblivious even to his presence.

"I just yelled my head off for Buyung and no one answered me,"
he barked, directing his anger at Rapiah.

Rapiah was preparing coconut milk and, without stopping what
she was doing, answered him calmly, "We are too far away to hear
you, and Buyung is out taking Syafei for a walk."

"Every time my friends come, he always goes as far away from
the house as possible. He's doing it on purpose."

"The child was restless and needed to go out," Hanafi's mother
explained, also without taking her hands from their task. "And we
had to ask Buyung to take him because the two cooks are busy
preparing a meal for their master."

"Who is going to bring the tea, then? Me?"

Hanafi then stomped out of the kitchen, grumbling as he walked back toward the veranda. A few paces away from the front door, he began shouting again for the houseboy. A few moments later, Buyung finally appeared at the nearby intersection, pushing Syafei in the perambulator. The toddler was smiling brightly, turning his head from side to side as he took in the sights.

"Take him inside," he shouted, almost before Buyung had entered the gate. "Where did you take him? Aren't the grounds here big enough? How many times do I have to tell you that you are not to leave the house when I have company? I pay you to serve me, not to play. Do you understand that?"

"I was told to take him …."

"Enough! Now take him inside and bring us some tea."

Buyung took Syafei to the kitchen and told the two women that he had been ordered to serve tea. But it so happened that they had just run out of sugar, so once again he had to go out, this time to a nearby store.

Almost as soon as Buyung left, Hanafi reappeared in the kitchen doorway. Syafei was in the perambulator, crying.

"Where is Buyung now? Did I tell him to take a nap?" He then glanced at his son and added: "And Rapiah, do something with that child!"

The two women were still busy making coconut milk. They had wrapped the grated coconut flesh inside a piece of stout cloth and were now twisting it in opposite directions to extract the liquid.

As though he could not see that Rapiah's hands were full, Hanafi repeated his order: "That child is still crying, do you want him to lose his voice?"

"Can't you see your slaves are busy preparing food for their master?" Hanafi's mother asked. "Why don't you try doing a woman's work for once, or a houseboy's for that matter, so you can see how hard it is. Maybe then you'd be more considerate. If you're worried about the baby's voice, then why not take care of him yourself? And Buyung is not taking a nap; he's gone out to buy sugar for his master."

The old woman tried to be as calm as she could, but from the quaver in her voice it was obvious that her blood was boiling with anger.

Without replying, Hanafi picked up Syafei and started bouncing him in his arms as he carried him to the veranda where his friends were sitting. Perhaps sensing his father's insincerity, Syafei began to cry even louder.

"Oh, look, we have a new babysitter," Suze said in jest while clapping her hands. "Is the mistress too busy reading?"

"No, I'm sure the mistress is getting ready to go out," the teacher's wife quipped. "After all, it is that time of the day."

"So this is my family life," Hanafi grumbled as he paced up and down trying to pacify his son. "Two women in the house and a houseboy, too, and there's still nobody to take care of the child. When I have a few guests who just need some tea, the whole household falls apart. Meanwhile, everybody is criticizing me. What, do they think I live in paradise here?"

Syafei was only an infant, but even infants can feel when their parents are fighting. The little boy, who was not used to being carried by his father, began to cry violently, screaming and yelling with all his might as he twisted his body from side to side like an eel trying to free itself from the clutch of a man's hand.

Just then, Rapiah stepped into the main part of the house to fetch something. Normally, she wouldn't have dared to show herself to Hanafi's Dutch friends, but when she heard her son's loud, piercing cry, she immediately forgot her shyness and rushed to the veranda. With her shabby clothes, rolled-up sleeves, and soot smudges on her hands and face, she burst in upon Hanafi's polite company.

Hanafi, who was already upset with his son's demonic crying, and with Buyung who still hadn't come with the tea, now had to endure embarrassment before his friends whom, even before this time, had begun to refer to Rapiah as Hanafi's mother's cook.

He finally blew up. As he shoved Syafei into Rapiah's arms, he started cursing her, right in front of his guests, shouting all kinds of insults and obscenities, making even his friends feel uncomfortable.

Rapiah said nothing. With her head bowed and tears streaming from her eyes, she retreated back toward the kitchen. But Hanafi was still unsatisfied. Even as she disappeared from sight, he continued to swear at her, using words no decent person should hear.

As this was happening, Hanafi's mother entered the house and was able to hear and see everything that happened. When Rapiah and Syafei came in, she went with them to the kitchen, where she took them both in her arms and cried. Syafei began to quiet down, sobbing softly as though he understood his mother's helplessness, and her shame at being insulted publicly. All was quiet in that kitchen except for the soft sighing and sobbing of the three of them crying together.

When Buyung finally appeared on the veranda with the tea, Hanafi said nothing, remaining silent, perhaps, from trying to hold back his anger, perhaps from the sudden realization of how much pain he had caused the three most important people in his life. Who knows which? He sat there in a confused silence.

His three friends also fell silent, and there was a look of tension on their faces. When he offered some tea, they moved their hands mechanically towards the teacups, and drank the tea sip by sip.

The schoolteacher finally looked at his watch and said to the ladies, "I really should be going, I have to prepare the children's report cards."

His wife immediately spoke up as well: "Yes, it's getting late. We'll see you another day."

Suze had intended to stay behind, but Hanafi stood up to shake her hand. "See you soon, Suze," he said. As he took her hand, she quickly pulled hers away and raised her upper lip to give him a disdainful look. But to this he paid her no heed.

After his guests were gone Hanafi drew a long sigh and sank into the lazy chair near where they had been sitting. His mother, in the mean time, had come into the house, and was now standing by the window. For a long time, she gazed upon him as he reclined in his chair, as though in contemplation. Twilight had now descended.

Rapiah was in the kitchen helping Buyung bring the food to the dinner table.

With her eyes now dry, though swollen from so much crying, Hanafi's mother approached him, thinking that perhaps the time was now right to talk to her son, since he seemed to be reflecting upon his life. "Maybe he will listen to me now," she thought, as she sat quietly in front him and looked at his face. "Your wife is a humble woman, Hanafi, all the more reason that you shouldn't treat her like that."

"Oh, Mother," Hanafi muttered, "if you want to blame someone, blame yourself. Weren't you the one who gave her to me, against my will?"

For a while she could say nothing, because no words could pass through the lump in her throat. "I thought you were feeling remorseful for what you had done just now," she finally said. "But this is what you are actually thinking. Oh, Hanafi, it's fate, it must be fate that this poor old woman should have an only son like you. It's fate."

"Mother, you know that it's that wife you gave me who has poisoned my heart. She has driven my friends away from me, and will eventually drive me away from you. She has no sense of etiquette, and yet you keep defending her whenever I try to teach her a lesson."

"God have mercy, Hanafi. At least say the name of Allah with me, so you may find your way in His world. My sin against you is only in choosing the wrong wife, though everyone who knows her knows that she is a very patient woman. Whenever you fault her or curse her for no fault of her own, she accepts it with a humble smile. And then when I, your own mother, say even a single word about the way you are treating her, you say I am meddling in your affairs. Is this what you learned in all those years of schooling, Hanafi? Do you not know the difference between gold and dross?"

"I know both gold and dross, Mother. The problem is, you still think of me as a child. Do you think the governor writes letters of recommendation for children? My years in civilized society have not been useless."

"Then tell me what you find wrong with your wife, so that this old country woman can understand what makes her inferior to, let's say, that Dutch woman from the post office who thinks she has a claim on you?"

"Don't bring Suze into this, Mother. She may be inferior to Rapiah in appearance, but in everything else—even if she's only a MULO graduate—Rapiah isn't worthy to shine her shoes."

Hanafi's mother shook her head and muttered to herself, "How can you think that way?"

"How can you compare a country girl to a Dutch woman, Mother? If all along you only wanted to bind me for the rest of my life to a girl like Rapiah—who is afraid of the Dutch, who knows nothing about anything except the kitchen and can talk only about things of the kitchen, and who won't learn modern etiquette and modern ways of life—well then, if that's the kind of woman you had wanted for me, why did you send me to school at all?"

The old woman's tears began to flow again. How could she answer her son? He seemed deaf and blind to all that was good and honorable in his own people. For him, everything native was contemptible.

For a while neither said a word. In the silence, they could hear Rapiah singing. Usually, when singing a lullaby for Syafei, she sang softly, so as not to be heard by others, especially Hanafi. When Hanafi was in the house, no one could hear her, even when standing in front of her bedroom door. But now her singing rang clearly through the house; it could be heard even from where they sat in the garden. Swept along by her emotion, Rapiah had apparently forgotten that others might hear. Her song was a sad song, meant not so much to lull her son to sleep but to soothe her own heart.

If not for the moon in the sky above,
the stars would not tilt to the west.
If it were not for your being, my love,
this heart would not be so distressed.

Pandanus Island lies far out at sea,
beyond what is called Two-Geese Isle.
Though one's body in the grave might be,
good deeds live on and raise a smile.

Before giving thought to a kingly estate,
a minister's dwelling might be in store.
Before giving thought to your own fate,
behold the waves that crash on the shore.

Above Bower Island smoke can be seen;
people are burning debris and other stuff.
Embracing a mountain might be a dream,
but ones arms are surely not long enough.

Deep are the roots of the mahogany tree;
cotton husks have a strength of iron gauge.
Two turtledoves, we might be said to be,
but there is no freedom in a locked cage.

Mangos from a stone are not to be found,
jimsonweed won't grow upon a palm.
Your behavior like this has no grounds,
not for those who depend on you for alms.

Jimsonweed won't grow upon a palm;
sweet basil won't grow if barren of leaf.
Wretched is this soul, in need of balm,
for loving a man who gives only grief.

Sweet basil won't grow if barren of leaf;
on the distant mountain, flowers bloom.
As months become years, time seems brief,
yet ever more great is the pain of my wound.

On the distant mountain, flowers bloom;
yet even this far away, their scent is pure.
The heartache I suffer spells my doom;
the yawning grave, the only true cure.

If even this far, the flowers' scent is pure,
let us pick them and make a bouquet.
Death would be welcome to this languor,
a better choice than this meaningless play.

Hanafi fell silent with a far away look. Was he listening or was he, perhaps, contemplating his own unhappy fate.

After Rapiah's song was over, Hanafi's mother spoke again. "When you went to school in Batavia, Hanafi, I got by on scraps of rice. Your uncle, too, had to tighten his belt. For a woman from the country like myself, coming up with one hundred rupiah a month was like extracting blood from a stone. If it wasn't for our family's land and your uncle, who barely had enough to get by from his own small salary, it would have been impossible to pay for your schooling. And now, when I think—and everyone who knows us will agree—I have given my son a priceless jewel, I find out that is not what he wishes to receive. Oh, Hanafi... May Allah the Merciful forgive your sins, as I have forgiven you by His grace."

Hanafi burst out laughing.

"Oh, Mother, keep on praying. Maybe you'll get a vision, and it will make you understand the truth of the matter because, from my point of view, it's you who has done me wrong and not the other way around. Maybe you didn't mean to but the damage has been done. Just look at my life! I am miserable, and it's all because I have done what you wanted me to do. You made Corrie feel uncomfortable, so she's gone off to Batavia. And now, because of Rapiah's lies, my friends have shunned me. If it wasn't for you, I would have followed Corrie to Batavia. We would probably be living a happy life by now. Furthermore, after I have done what you wanted me to do, you make me even more miserable by defending Rapiah every time I try to explain things to her. Now she's ended up being spoiled.

"And as for your immeasurable loss in sending me to school, isn't that the way that it's supposed to be: that a parent pays for her children's education? Besides, as I've told you before, I am prepared to pay everything back, with interest compounded. Is that not enough?"

"My son! Do you know what damnation is reserved for those who sin against their mothers?"

Before Hanafi could reply, he screamed. A dog had sprung out from behind the almond tree and lunged toward his arm. Hanafi tried to snatch his hand away from the armrest, but it was too late; the dog had sunk its teeth into his hand. It had bit him so hard that when he tried to pull away his hand, he almost lifted the dog off the ground. Finally, after the dog released its bite, it scurried away, its tail between its legs and its head lowered almost to the ground.

A crowd of townspeople then came rushing into the grounds. "There he is, there he is!" the people screamed. "Don't let him get away." With sticks, stones, and machetes in their hand, they then took after the dog.

Hanafi's mother took her son's hand and examined the wound. "Rabies," was all she could say.

Hanafi sat in shocked silence. His face went pale as he looked at the bite wounds on his hand.

Hanafi's mother called the doctor to the house immediately. He informed her that the dog had terrorized the town all morning and Hanafi was its third victim. The dog was indeed rabid, he added, and if they wanted to save Hanafi's life he would have to leave for Batavia as soon as possible. No rabies treatment was available in West Sumatra.

Because the next ship for Batavia was due to leave Padang the following evening, Hanafi would have to go to Padang on the first morning train.

Hanafi's mother could not sleep that night. She busied herself, instead, between intermittent bursts of tears, packing clothes and other necessities that her son would need for his journey. Every so often she'd check on her grandson but whenever she saw him, sleeping peacefully in his bed, she'd find herself overcome with sadness. Softly she would weep over him and then return to her packing and unpacking of Hanafi's suitcase, counting and recounting his shirts and trousers to make sure he had enough clothes. She also gathered from his study some papers, pens, and pencils and packed them too. After this was done, she again returned to Syafei's room where she began to cry again.

Hanafi's mother didn't know why she was crying so much; being apart from her son was not something new. After all, they had been apart for years when he attended school in Batavia. Moreover, back then she had to live at home alone; now she had Rapiah and Syafei to keep her company. Hanafi was going away for three weeks to be treated for rabies in Batavia. In less than a month he would return as healthy as before. So why was she crying, and why was her heart so heavy? Was it because she had cursed him? But she had not cursed him. If anything, she had begged Allah the Merciful to forgive her son.

Hanafi wanted no big ado for his departure. "It's only for three weeks," he said. "You can see me off at the train station, but I don't want anyone going with me to Padang." Secretly, he was glad to have been forced to take leave of his family. The air in his house had grown intolerably stifling, and in Batavia...there was Corrie!

Rapiah also cried without understanding why her tears flowed as she watched the train leave Solok, carrying with it her husband to a distant place. She loved him, she knew that, but because of all that had happened during the past few months, she too felt secretly relieved that he would be away for a few weeks. "Who knows," she thought, "maybe he will have changed for the better by the time he returns."

Not entirely conscious of what she was doing, Rapiah suddenly embraced her son tightly, and with tears streaming down her cheeks, kissed him over and over again in front of everyone in the crowded station.

"Let's go home," Hanafi's mother said to her daughter-in-law as she dried her eyes on the end of her shawl. "He'll be back before you know it, even before the pot you used to cook his last meal dries up, and certainly before it's washed."

Rapiah spoke to her mother-in-law as if she were speaking herself: "I don't know why, Mother, but I feel something is wrong. I feel that this separation is going to be for more than three weeks."

"That's just because this is the first time you have ever been separated from your husband," the older woman replied in consolingly. But as she spoke, she felt her pulse suddenly quicken. She knew her words were said merely to pacify Rapiah's heart, as well as her own. For she herself had had that same premonition.

10

Together Again

Much had happened in Corrie's life during the past two years. Less than a year after she returned to Batavia from her vacation, her father passed away, after a brief illness. Nothing could alleviate Corrie's grief when she received the telegram from the Assistant District Commissioner. She suddenly realized then that her father had been her only real friend in this world, and she ceaselessly regretted her decision to return to school.

She knew that in his heart, her father would have preferred her to stay at home with him, because other than herself, his only child, he had no real friends either. And yet he had forced himself to let her go. He didn't want her to go halfway in her education. He wanted the best for her.

At first Corrie had planned to go to his funeral in Solok— she had even packed her bags—but then she realized that in her condition, it would be too much for her to see her father's grave. And besides, what friend did she have in Solok to whom she could pour out the grief in her heart? So it was she had sent a telegram to the Assistant District Commissioner instead, asking him to make the arrangements for her father's funeral. He was to do whatever was most fitting and proper, regardless of cost.

As for the family estate, her father's trustee in Padang informed her that the house was to be sold and the furniture and other household effects auctioned off, the proceeds from which were then to be held in trust until she reached the age of twenty-one. Until that time, she would be given a monthly allowance sufficient to pay for her tuition, daily necessities, and a little extra for "needles and thread." The trustee explained that her inheritance was insufficient for her to live off the interest alone; to meet her financial needs, he would have to draw a small portion of the principal as well. "But don't worry," he told her, "if you study hard and get a diploma, you will have no problem getting on in life, even without your inheritance."

The trustee had been charged by her father with the responsibility of looking after her well-being and had been given the authority to appoint a guardian, if that was deemed necessary. He emphasized that legally this meant she had to live under his authority until she was twenty-one…or married.

How infuriating this was for Corrie! It was bad enough that her own father had made all decisions regarding her schooling, her money, and her life. Because she loved him and never wanted to hurt him, she did not protest. But this was entirely different. Now her life was to be ruled by a stranger! She felt compelled to rebel. But what could she do? Had the decision been up to her, she would have quit school immediately.

"Until she was twenty-one…or married…." It seemed that marriage was the only way that she could gain her freedom. But marry whom? There were many men who had proposed, so many in fact that they had begun to spoil her enjoyment of life. Often, when she met someone new, they would chat and see each other a few times and then, before you knew it, this new acquaintance would either fall on his knees before her or assail her with lovesick letters. Bah! Why can't a man and a woman just be friends? Must every relationship end with marriage?

It wasn't that she didn't want a friend to whom she could confess her heart. And she didn't dislike being wooed either, or praised, or told how beautiful she was. On the contrary, she loved the attention. But as soon as she detected a glance, a touch, or a word that she considered beyond the pale of friendship, she withdrew irretrievably like a snail into its shell. She wasn't sure why she did this. Perhaps it was fear, possibly disgust with the thought. All she knew was that she would never marry a man who had crossed that invisible line.

One by one, she examined her suitors in her mind. Logically, she could find no serious flaw with many of them. A few even seemed perfect. Yet she could not imagine herself spending her life with any of them. Her father had once told her that sometimes a person's feelings can't be changed, not even by the person they belong to, let alone by someone else. Maybe that was it.... But then, suddenly, Hanafi's name came to mind.

Hanafi, what was wrong with Hanafi? Was it cultural differences between the two of them, which she recognized, were other people's opinions? Was that why things had turned out the way they did? If it weren't for other people, if it were just herself and her heart... Yes, she knew in her heart that she was fond of him. In fact, when Hanafi had crossed that boundary of emotion no man was permitted to breach, she had not only allowed him to enter that forbidden zone, she had welcomed him. Back then, however, she had to consider her father's advice. Had he not told her that he would not approve of a match between her and Hanafi?

Yes, that was it, she saw it now: the course of one life was determined by other people's opinions. In former days and in small towns such as Solok where one could not help but meet the same people every day, perhaps that was the most wise course of action. In such a provincial place, a marriage that rejected common notions of propriety could be made to be unbearable indeed. But what about now, in this metropolis? What was to stop them here, in Batavia? Even if people were to shun them, what of it? Batavia was a large and bustling town where there was no lack of entertainment: there were markets and fairs, not to mention motion picture shows, parks, promenades and all kinds of other attractions that were open to

Westerners and Easterners alike. As long as a man and woman were happy with each other, who cared about other people's opinions?

Oh, if only Hanafi was in Batavia. But then she suddenly remembered: Hanafi already had a wife! That put an end to her daydream. She was convinced that she would not, that she could not, marry for the rest of her life.

So what was she to do now? If her father were still alive, she knew that she would not consider leaving school, that she would abide by his wishes and pursue a diploma, not only because she loved him but, even more importantly, because she knew that if she truly did not want to graduate from school, he would never impose his will on her. But now, because of his death, she was being forced to stay in school, regardless of her own wishes. As such, she could think of nothing else but to break free from the bondage.

"One more year and I'll be twenty-one," was all Corrie could think of in the days that followed. It was no wonder, therefore, that she failed her subjects and was made to repeat her fourth year. But this only increased her impatience and made it even more difficult for her to concentrate.

From her own experience, Corrie came to understand one of her character traits: if a person wanted her to do something, he or she had best let her do it of her own accord. Under pressure, she might bow to a person's wishes, but whatever she had been asked to do would not be done well.

As a diversion—and with her principal's permission, to be sure—Corrie began to take piano lessons. Every afternoon, she would now ride her bicycle from Salemba Avenue, where her boarding school was located, to her teacher's house in Pasar Baru. After her lessons finished, at seven, she would often take the long way home, stopping at the city's more pleasant sites to catch the breeze. Among her favorite spots was the boulevard that hemmed the western edge of Gambir Park. There, the city air seemed cooler and the traffic quieter. Sometimes, she would dismount from her bicycle and walk it along the sidewalk. When finding an empty bench she would sit and contemplate her sad life.

"One more month and I will be twenty-one," she thought one evening as she rode past the park. Yes, one more month and she would be free. But what then, she asked herself. Thoughts of the future only intensified her loneliness. Her only friends, the other young women at boarding school, would soon go their separate ways, each with a plan of her own. One was going home to her parents' tea plantation, another had an uncle who had invited her to work at his large trading company, yet another would announce her engagement as soon as she graduated. But what about her? What home did she have to go to? What uncle of hers had a large trading company? Where would she live? What friends would she have?

As these thoughts were going through her mind, she turned the corner to South Gambir Boulevard, when suddenly, before knowing what had happened, she found herself tumbling from her bicycle to the ground. She had been struck by another cyclist, a native man who had also been knocked to the ground.

She watched, dazed, as the man picked himself off the ground. When seeing her he suddenly grabbed his bicycle and jumped on it, as if to flee, but before he could get more than a few meters away, another man, this one a gentleman, it seemed, caught hold of the rider and forced him to get off. "Come on, now, apologize to the lady," she heard the man say. "If she's hurt, I'll see that you pay for it with your head!"

The man then escorted the rider back to where Corrie was, prodding him from behind as they walked. By this time Corrie had picked herself up and checked her bicycle for damage. She had bent over to massage her knee. "It's all right, sir" she said when she saw the frightened look on the face of the native man as he was being pushed towards her. "It was my fault as much as his. I didn't have the light on, so I couldn't see very well," she explained.

"If you have suffered even one small scratch, Miss du Bussée, this man will pay for it with his life!" the man exclaimed. He then took off his hat and bowed.

Corrie stared at the man. "Hanafi! What are you doing here? And why are you calling me "Miss du Bussée'?"

She looked at the man who had run into her, and then whispered to Hanafi, "Let him go. I should actually thank him for running into me."

"You can go," she then said to the other rider, "it really was my fault."

After the rider had left, Corrie and Hanafi proceeded to one of the benches on the edge of the wide field.

"I think it's better now," Corrie said after massaging her knee a little more. "So, tell me, when did you arrive and what are you doing here? Tell me what has happened with you?"

Corrie's voice and her gestures were revealing of the sudden wave of happiness that had come over her. Gone was the thick fog that had clouded her mind. Now, in the evening's clear air, there was only the face of her dear friend Hanafi.

"I was bitten by a rabid dog," Hanafi told her. "For the past three days I've been going to the Pasteur Institute for treatment."

"Three days you've been here, and if I hadn't gotten into an accident that almost cost me my neck, we might never have met!"

Hanafi looked away, staring at the lights of Deca Fairgrounds as if mesmerized by their glow.

"It's not that I didn't mean to look you up," he said after the long silence. "In fact, I felt obliged to, if only to extend my condolences for your father's death. But Corrie, when I got married I received a postcard from a 'Miss C. du Bussée' that was addressed to a 'Mr. Hanafi.' In turn, when this woman's father passed away I sent a card addressed to 'Miss C. du Bussée'.

"Oh, Corrie," he sighed, "on paper, terms of address don't matter, but in real life it's you I want to see, not 'Miss C. du Bussée'."

Corrie extended her hand to him. "What's past is past," she told him. "I admit I was wrong, Hanafi. Can't we be friends again?"

Hanafi gazed into her eyes for a moment before he took her hand.

"What I wanted from you then, what I asked of you before, was much more than friendship. If that is what caused the rift between us, then let me take it back. What can I say?" He shook his head. "I guess, it was not destined to be."

Corrie spoke evenly, "Only God knows whom our soul-mate shall be. I feel, Hanafi, that if your love for me was true, there would have been no need for you to force me, no need to demand from me what I could not—or could not yet—give to you. Real love is in the giving not in the taking, especially if the demands of one party are such that they only serve only to drive two people apart."

Hanafi paused before answering, "You are right, Corrie. I treasure our friendship too much to let this matter get in the way."

"Thank you, Hanafi. I would be very sad indeed if the relationship we have had since childhood were to be ruined because of it. I want you to know that aside from you there is no one I can truly call a friend. Of course, there are my classmates, but in a month or so, after I've left school, we will go our separate ways. And as for the young men in this city, you simply wouldn't believe it. After a few casual conversations, they want to drag me down the aisle. I'm the one you should feel sorry for, Hanafi."

"You're leaving school?" Hanafi asked. "And then what, Corrie?"

"And then I don't know. I'm just tired of school. Do you not feel a little sympathy for a creature such as myself who no longer has a home, who has no friends, except perhaps you, who has no dreams, who doesn't know where she's going? Oh, Hanafi, I can't tell you enough times how much I would appreciate your friendship and to share with you a relationship where we could forget that I am a woman and you are a man."

"Poor, poor Corrie," Hanafi said soothingly, "Perhaps if you found a job..."

"Oh, I'll find a job," Corrie immediately replied. "That's not the difficult part. But did you ever realize that in this world there are some people who go on living only because they have to? I now understand that a person could die just from being sick of living."

Hanafi leaned back his head and gazed at the sky as if to lose himself in it. He thought of what Corrie had just said about going on living only because one has to. She had asked if he knew what that meant. Imagine such a thing! Did she know that during the past two years, that was exactly how he himself had lived? Compared to that, her burden seemed light: she was free to marry whomever she wished and not have to answer to others. She owned her life whereas he was bound by obligations, to his wife, his mother, and his son. Everyday, all that he heard about was duty and obligations.

He wanted to pour out these things to her. But not tonight, he reasoned. Not yet, he thought, for she herself was so full of grief.

"It's getting late," he finally said. "What time do you have to be back at the dormitory? And are you able to ride your bicycle or should I hire an automobile?"

"My knee still hurts, but I am sure it will be fine," Corrie assured him. "You know what would be lovely, though, if you could escort me to Salemba. Maybe you could walk my bike. If my knee really starts to hurt, then we can hire an auto or buggy."

"Better yet, why don't you sit on your bicycle," Hanafi suggested. "I'll push you so you won't have to pedal? It's not good to put pressure on an injured knee; it might get worse."

"All the way to Salemba?" she asked.

Hanafi's voice trembled as he spoke. "Salemba is nothing. I could walk with you to the sky's very edge."

Corrie remarked lightly, "Well, alright, but you'll probably fall unconscious from the exhaustion long before we get there."

Little did Corrie know, her joke had cemented Hanafi's determination.

As they talked and made their way towards Corrie's dormitory, lightness returned to each of their hearts. They were so at ease with each other, it was as if the unpleasant incident in Solok had never happened.

At one point Corrie remarked that it would make her very happy if Hanafi could meet her at school to accompany her to her piano lessons and then meet her again, after her lesson, to accompany her home.

"That way, no one would dare run into me!" she laughed. "Oh, but what am I saying. You don't have a bike."

"But I could buy one," Hanafi answered. "It wouldn't cost more than thirty rupiah."

"But you're not staying in Batavia. You're going back to Solok in a few days? What would you do with the bike then? That would be a waste of money."

Hanafi couldn't bring himself to tell her the thought that had just crossed his mind.

"Well, I could sell it, and if I lose a rupiah or two, so what? I can think of it as the rental fee."

"Oh, you don't know how happy you've just made me. My lesson finishes at seven o'clock and I don't have to be back at the dormitory until half past eight. That means we have an hour and a half to go around the city. Won't that be lovely?"

If it was up to him, Hanafi thought, he would gladly spend the whole night riding around Batavia with her.

With Corrie perched on the bicycle saddle, Hanafi pushed her bicycle all the way from Gambir to Salemba, never once stopping to rest.

After arriving at Corrie's dormitory they said their polite goodbyes.

"It's too bad that we're here already," he said. "I wish you lived a little farther, say in Chinatown maybe."

"What, pushing me for an hour isn't enough for you? If my knee wasn't hurt, I wouldn't have let you push me for so long. But it's almost half past eight. I have to go in."

"I keep forgetting, you're not a free woman; you live under the rules of the dormitory."

"That's right, Hanafi, but in just one more month, then I'll be free."

Both smiled as they parted.

The next day, at half past four, Hanafi appeared at the front gate of the dormitory with his new bicycle.

"Marvelous!" Corrie exclaimed when seeing him in the distance. "I feel alive again."

11

Soul Mates

After waiting for more than a quarter of an hour, Hanafi finally saw the apple of his eye emerge from the Pasar Baru side street where Corrie's piano teacher lived. He suggested they take a different route back to her dormitory: "Why don't we go via Gunung Sari? If we turn on Jembatan Merah, we can take Jakarta Avenue back."

Corrie looked uneasy at the suggestion. "I'd rather not take Jakarta."

"Why not?"

"It's too quiet. I don't feel comfortable."

"But it's still early, and the moon is so bright."

"I've been along it with friends during the day, but at night, I don't know..."

"There's nothing to worry about. I know the street used to have a reputation for being unsafe, that robbers were used to hold up buggies that went that way, but there's a police station there now and armed policemen patrolling the street."

"In that case, it would be lovely. It might be nice at night, away from the hustle and bustle of the city."

"From there, if we cut through Ketapang and Petojo, we'll come out by Gambir Park."

Corrie frowned. "If it weren't for the school rules, I would be willing to go as far as Tanjung Priok Harbor. After being cooped up all day in my room or at school, I just can't get enough fresh air."

After agreeing on the route, they pushed off, chatting as they pedaled their bicycles. At the Jembatan Merah bridge, Corrie suggested they make a stop. The sky was clear, and the evening still early enough that they did not need their lights. For a while, they simply stood on the bridge and gazed at the shimmering light of the moon on the water. In the distance they could see thousands of fireflies swarming over an overgrown field.

Hanafi was first to break the silence. "How about going to Nieuw Zandvoort beach on Sunday?" he suggested.

"But will you still be here this Sunday?" Corrie asked. "I've just been thinking how sad my life will be once you go back to West Sumatra."

"I'll still be here this Sunday."

Corrie seemed confused. "But I thought you were only going to be here for two weeks."

"I was," Hanfi told her, "but I've asked for an extended leave of absence."

"Didn't the doctor say you had been cured? You have to be careful with rabies, you know. And you'd better warn me first if that dog left you with any souvenirs!"

"Don't worry, I don't have rabies. I extended my leave for something else."

"And what's that?"

"I'm moving to Batavia for good," he told her.

"But what about your job? Are you going to quit your job in Solok?"

"No, Corrie, at least not yet. I'll just be glad when the matter is settled."

"What are you referring to?" Corrie asked.

"A few days ago I put in a request for a transfer to the Civil Service office here. The section chief said they don't normally take people from provincial offices, so I have to wait for their decision. If there is an opening, I will have to officially resign my old post before I can apply for the job here. I don't know why it has to be so complicated, but that's how things are."

"That would be wonderful, Hanafi. But what about your family? You'd be bringing them with you, wouldn't you?"

Corrie sighed involuntarily, then dropped her gaze to the purling water below the bridge.

For a moment Hanafi also fell silent before he answered in a slow, almost reluctant, voice: "I don't think they'll be coming to Batavia, Corrie."

"They're not?"

"It's complicated, but it would be best if they stayed in Solok."

"But that's not right, Hanafi. A married man's foremost obligation is to his family. You mustn't take that lightly."

"That's why it's complicated. Over these last few days, my heart has become torn between duty and feeling. Corrie, you don't know how much my heart is torn."

"Hanafi, I am from West Sumatra too and I know how it is with the men from there: you marry a girl from your home village. Without much thought, you then leave her to travel in a faraway land where you take another wife! That's the tradition, at least as I see it. Maybe I can accept such behavior from an unschooled country boy. But you are not like that, Hanafi. You yourself have said you are not like that. I think it would be immoral for you to do something like that."

"Maybe to be branded immoral is my destiny, Corrie. In Solok, just about everybody has ostracized me. The Assistant District Commissioner's wife even insulted me in public, all because I can not fulfill my duty to a wife who was foisted on me."

"But you married her, Hanafi, out of your own free will, did you not?"

"Strictly speaking, I did. But just so that you know, Corrie, I have to tell you that at that time, after you had left, I nearly went crazy. I had a fever that burned for days; I couldn't think clearly even after I recovered. To this day I don't quite know what happened. My body felt limp, my mind exhausted. Whatever people told me to do, I did. And while I was in such a state, my mother kept telling me how much I owed my uncle for my schooling, not only in terms of money, but also in terms of kindness."

"Then what happened?" Corrie inquired.

"According to my mother's reckoning, the so-called debt I owed my uncle could only be erased if I married his daughter, my cousin Rapiah, even if the marriage lasted only for a day."

Sympathy entered Corrie's voice: "How terrible it must have been for you."

Hanafi looked into Corrie's eyes. "So is it now my fault that I can't adhere to my people's customs? No one ever told me that my uncle was supporting me. My mother never told me that she had pledged me to my uncle as payment for that debt. In their minds, it was my uncle's right that I would become his son-in-law once I had finished school." Hanafi scoffed, "It's wonderful being Minangkabau, isn't it Corrie?"

Corrie shook her head. "Having been raised and educated in a Western fashion, that must have come as a terrible shock for you. But what I don't understand," she reasoned, "is why you can't repay your uncle from your salary, in monthly installments, for example?"

"I wish it were that easy. A monetary loan can be repaid with money," he explained, "but kindness, as my mother calls it, can only be repaid through kindness."

Corrie lowered her gaze to the water. "You know, Hanafi, the more I think about it, the more difficult your life seems to me. But you have to also see that arranged marriages are common throughout the world, in the West as well. Kings and queens can't marry just anyone they want. Money marries money, high-society ladies marry only men of noble lineage. A civilized person must accept his lot with grace. He must try his best to find happiness from it and to make better what can be made better. I think that's how you should be, Hanafi. Even if you don't love your wife you must respect her and care for her if for no other reason than she is your wife."

"I've tried that, Corrie, for two years and what good has come of it? Instead of getting closer, we have drifted further apart. Lately, we have even stopped asking why. We have different tastes is all," he said, "different outlooks and different dreams. Trying to change Rapiah is like trying to get a cow to eat meat. The animal won't do it, even if it is starving."

"Is Rapiah stubborn, like you?"

"No, she's not," Hanafi said honestly. "If she were, there might be some hope. But on the contrary, she agrees with everything. Everything I say, no matter what, she quietly accepts, and always with the same acquiescent expression on her face. If she then did as I told her, it would not be so bad, but she doesn't.

"I don't know what it is, but everything she does irritates me, and when I tell her about it, she just smiles. What do you call this kind of behavior? I swear she's going to drive me crazy," Hanafi complained, "yet people keep saying that she's an 'unpolished diamond.'

"Well, that's easy for them to say, because they don't have to wear it; but I do, and it's digging into my flesh. She's afraid of anyone who wears a formal shirt. And that's in Solok! How do you think she will survive in Batavia?"

"I see your point," Corrie told him. "I suppose a man who stays married to a woman he cannot respect doesn't seem very moral either. Fortunately for Malay men, they can easily divorce their wives if they want to. Isn't that right?"

"That's what my mother says about marriages: easy come, easy go."

"But your son?"

"That's more complicated. In the Minangkabau tradition, a boy's maternal uncles have more right over him than does his own father, especially if the boy's under a year of age."

"You are caught in a difficult position," Corrie said. "Morally speaking, I think it would be better to let your wife go, so that she could start a new life, rather than keep her in an unhappy marriage. Maybe then she could find a 'diamond polisher' with whom she would be happy.

"As it is, it seems that you are just making each other miserable. But I really don't want to meddle in your private life. The break up of a marriage is a terrible thing. And who knows, maybe your wife doesn't want to be divorced.

"Whatever the case, I hope I haven't put any evil thoughts into your head. I am sorry if I have."

"It's nothing you've said that has made me consider divorce. For some time now it has been my opinion that divorce is the only way out of the misery that is poisoning everybody: my wife, myself and my mother as well. On the day of our divorce there will be streams of tears, no doubt, but in the end I am sure everyone will thank me for it.

"If I divorced from my wife, there's something else that would proceed a lot more smoothly," Hanafi added.

"What's that?" Corrie asked.

"I have applied for European status," Hanafi announced. "The head of the Civil Service Department, a friend of my father's, is helping. If that comes through and Rapiah is still my wife, and Syafei my son, we would have to be remarried at the City Hall. That would create a major problem. For myself, the way things are now, I am convinced that Rapiah and I will never be happy together and if we were to get married under Dutch law, it would be much difficult to divorce her later.

"And then there's Rapiah's family to consider. Her father, who graduated from primary school, is very old-fashioned. Imagine what the rest of her family, the ones who live in the village, are like. If Rapiah were to obtain foreign legal status, I am sure it would take the village chiefs and elders more than a year of endless deliberations before they could decide what to do with her.

"I guess what I'm saying is that Rapiah is a big obstacle to my plans, and there is simply not enough love between us to resolve the issue."

A clock was heard: eight strokes and then a single chime.

Corrie shouted in surprise, "Hanafi! It's a quarter past eight."

"We'll have to go back by Gunung Sari," he told her, "there's not enough time for a detour through Sawah Besar."

They did not speak as they pedaled their bicycles, each lost in his own thoughts. When saying goodbye in front of the door to the dormitory, Corrie's hand trembled and her voice shook. She didn't know what she was feeling just then. When she reached her room, her heart was still pounding. That night her sleep was disturbed, much like the time in Solok, the night before she went to Hanafi's house.

Again and again she asked herself why it so affected her to hear Hanafi's life story. Would she be happy if he were to divorce his wife? No, that was unthinkable. While it was true that she wanted him to move to Batavia, she could never possibly hope for another person's divorce. No, Hanafi was a close friend, like an older brother to her; yes, like an older brother.

The next evening, they again rode around the city but not a word was mentioned about their discussion from the previous night. The following Sunday they went swimming at the beach, but during their time there neither broached the subject. Corrie didn't ask Hanafi about his return to Solok, his application for a job in Batavia, let alone about his wife. She did, however, remind him that she would soon be twenty-one: "It's my birthday this coming Thursday," she said, "and I'm going to be twenty-one. We're having a little party at the dormitory. Would you like to come? It starts at six."

"Did you invite many people from outside of school?" Hanafi asked.

"No," she told him, "you are the only one. You'll be like a rooster in a coop of hens," she laughed. "But don't get any ideas. If you do, I'll drive you out with a broomstick."

On the evening of Corrie's birthday party, she greeted Hanafi at the front entrance wearing not her usual school uniform, but an evening gown. She smiled to see the look of surprise on his face.

"I almost didn't recognize you," Hanafi said in near awe.

"That's a woman's art, Hanafi. For this chignon alone, I spent four *ringgit*, and for this dress... Oh, it's better that men don't know these things. My friends aren't coming until seven," she informed him. "The party will be in the main hall. I've ordered food from a caterer, so you don't have to worry about going hungry tonight. There will be a violin concert as well, by the Wiener Orchestra. But for now, let's go sit in the garden."

She took his hand and was about to lead him away when she noticed a bouquet of flowers in his other hand. "Oh, Hanafi, you brought flowers! I love gladiolas. I don't know where my brain is this evening; I didn't even notice them. They are beautiful. Thank you, Hanafi. Red is my favorite color. It's yours too, isn't it? And look at the number of blooms! It's rare to find so many on a single stalk. Before we doing anything else, we must put them in a vase. Wait here," she said, when taking the flowers from him and hurrying off towards her room.

Moments later, Corrie returned, panting slightly. "We don't have much time before the others arrive," she said. "After that, there will be no time to talk."

They strolled to a bench beneath a canopy of lush and dangling vines where they sat down.

"Congratulations," Hanafi said. "My wish for you is that your life will lead you to an even brighter and nobler path than the one you have traveled so far." He pulled from his pocket a small box. "And here's a little something from me to you."

Corrie's face lit up when she opened the box to find a diamond ring inside.

"It's beautiful," she sighed as she slid the ring on her ring finger and extended her arm to admire it from a distance.

"You have good taste, Hanafi, and it fits perfectly. When did you measure my finger?"

"Every day, Corrie!"

"Oh, you're bad! Look, the musicians are here to start the party. We had better make haste."

"You should congratulate me too," Hanafi said. "I got the job I applied for, with a salary of three hundred rupiah."

"Oh, congratulations, Hanafi. That's wonderful. And you even got a raise."

"I was due for one anyway," he told her, "and I had a glowing letter of recommendation from Solok. I guess there's someone who doesn't hate me. As for me and my wife, we are divorced now which is, I truly believe, the best solution for both of us."

Corrie felt her heart quicken within her breast, and her blood rush to her head. Speechless, she stared at the ground as though hoping to find words to say there. "It's too bad," she finally said softly, as if muttering to herself. "But under the circumstances it probably is the best solution. Life is so short, who wants to be miserable? Although I don't agree with divorce in principle, sometimes it's better than staying together, if that means poisoning each other's hearts." She sought another course of conversation. "But anyway, tell me about your new job. What do you do? And when do you start?"

"I start tomorrow. I'll be working in the archiving department."

Corrie went on, asking this and that, realizing herself that her questions were without purpose. She asked them only because she wasn't sure what it was she really wanted to say except, perhaps, that she enjoyed talking to him.

They suddenly they heard voices: "Corrie, Corrie, where are you? Everyone's here, except for the birthday girl." Three young women appeared from behind the arbor. "Oh!" they said almost in unison when they saw Corrie and Hanafi sitting on the bench. Corrie knew well the meaning of their "Oh!", and she felt her face blushing. But she was glad.

Throughout the rest of the evening, Corrie kept Hanafi close to her side. Once in a while, she let the other women dance with him, just to be courteous. In jest, she told her friends she had to keep him on a short leash because she didn't want her "brother" to get snared by all the beautiful women.

They answered her with an ironic "hmm," and everybody laughed.

From that time on, Corrie accepted that her feelings for Hanafi were more than those for a brother. Had he repeated his proposal then, she was sure she would have announced their engagement that very night.

Hanafi felt this. He could sense that Corrie had become more receptive to his intentions. And that night he could barely restrain himself from declaring himself. But there was something else that had to be taken care of first. He was still waiting for the government's decision regarding his European status. Once his status had been made equal to hers, he would certainly return to declare his intentions.

12

The Wife his Mother Gave

In Solok, all was quiet at Hanafi's house. The front door to the house was always closed; the lamp in the veranda was never lit. From the street, the place looked abandoned, as though its owners had left. In the morning and evening, Buyung the manservant would take Syafei out for a ride in his preambulator, but that was the only sign of life at Hanafi's home.

Hanafi's wife Rapiah and his mother had taken to staying indoors, sequestering themselves in the kitchen. They never seemed to leave the house. Their visitors knew to go directly behind the house to find them. No one was ever seen at the front door to ring the bell or announce themselves.

The day was a normal one. The two women were working in the kitchen. Syafei was sleeping soundly in his cradle in the back veranda.

Rapiah smiled as she watched her mother-in-law prepare the day's curry. "You're making so much," she said. "You'd think we were having a party."

"And there's more to come," Hanafi's mother announced. "I still haven't made my beef salad or Mengala chicken." She looked at Rapiah. "If you are going to fast, I think it's only right that you have good food ready when you break the fast. It doesn't matter to me if you eat it or not. Once the food is on the table, I feel satisfied."

"This is the fourth Thursday I have fasted," Rapiah remarked. She turned to see if her son was still asleep. "That's how long the boy's father has been gone. And I intend to keep on fasting every Monday and Thursday until he comes back safely."

"That's very virtuous of you, Rapiah, but you must take care of yourself," she warned. "You don't want to become skin and bones."

"I know I have lost a little weight, but it's not from the fasting. I feel fine," Rapiah said.

"You only think you are fine because you are not paying attention to yourself. You have to remember that you are feeding two mouths. Look at Syafei, how pale he is."

Rapiah nodded. "I've been thinking of weaning him. Other children are weaned by the time they're one, so I think Syafei should be too. But somehow I just don't have the heart to do so. It's strange, Mother, his crying seems sadder and sadder as the days go by."

"That's because he's not well."

"But there's something else. When I check him in the middle of the night, sometimes I catch him sobbing in his sleep, with tears coming from his eyes. And then as suddenly as he starts, he stops and then goes back to sleep."

"Little children sometimes do that, Rapiah. It's normal."

"But I can't help worrying that something has happened to his father. I have been having bad dreams."

Rapiah's mother-in-law shook her head. "Dreams are from the imagination. You are thinking about Hanafi too much. It's taking its toll on both you and Syafei. In truth, I must tell you, Piah, that life in this house is more peaceful without him."

Rapiah blushed. When she then poured the coconut milk she had just extracted from desiccated coconut meat into the wash basin instead of the pot on the hearth, Hanafi's mother could not help but shake her head in pity. "Rapiah," she sighed. "Look at where you poured the coconut milk. Why do you lose your mind over Hanafi like this?" she asked. "Frankly, if he weren't my own son, I would have told you to ask for a divorce."

Looking down at the pool of milk in the wash basin, Rapiah suddenly broke down in tears.

"You must not cry," her mother-in-law told her. "There will be no benefit from your fasting, if your heart is burdened with grief. Don't worry, he's been gone for a month now, he will be back soon."

Rapiah spoke through her tears: "For the past week my heart has felt so strange. Something is happening but I can't tell what it is. I know we shouldn't believe in superstition, but people say that if your hair comes undone while you are eating it means you are going to lose your husband to another woman. Is that true?" she asked her mother-in-law.

"Humbug!" her mother-in-law spat. "If we believed all the things that people used to believe, we'd never have any peace of mind. We're supposed to believe that if a flame from the hearth licks the inside of a pot, a visitor will come. Well, let's just see if that happens. And as for your hair coming undone, that's because you haven't been paying attention to yourself. You have hardly even looked at yourself in the mirror since Hanafi went away. If you combed your hair and put it up as neatly as you used to do, it wouldn't come undone."

"A toad came into the house, three times," Rapiah moaned.

Her mother-in-law looked incredulous. "And what is that supposed to mean?"

"It means that someone is casting a spell that is intended to separate a husband from his wife."

"Oh, my child, no wonder you are thin. You keep thinking everything is bad." Hanafi's mother tried to appear cheerful, but even her smile could not conceal the worried expression on her face. Deep down, she too believed in such omens. And she too had had a premonition that something had happened with Hanafi, something that would bring sadness to his family. But this she did not want to reveal.

It was Thursday, the day when the mail arrived from Batavia. A month had passed since Hanafi's departure, during which time he had never even once sent a letter to his family. The only news his mother and wife had of him was obtained by way of friends who heard that he had sent postcards to his friends. They themselves hadn't even received a postcard.

That day, Hanafi's mother woke up with a feeling that she they would receive a letter from her son, and that it would contain bad news. To take her mind off her premonition, she busied herself in the kitchen, attempting to entertain the notion that perhaps Hanafi himself would return home that today.

"Don't worry," she said to her daughter-in-law. "The mail comes today. Who knows, maybe Hanafi himself is coming."

"We have waited for four Thursdays. I have a strong feeling we will get a letter from him today, but my feeling tells me that the letter will bring bad news."

Before her mother-in-law could answer, Syafei began to cry and Rapiah immediately ran to attend to him. She sang soothingly as her rocked her son in her arms.

> *Do not use spinach in the curry,*
> *curry tastes much better with fern.*
> *Hush, my child, and do not worry,*
> *for your father will soon return.*

> *A longhouse with silver trim,*
> *stands tall on teakwood beams.*
> *Apparent pleasure, a happy grin,*
> *can hide a broken heart's screams.*

> *Behold the twisted stump of a tree,*
> *the laurel that once stood in the vale.*
> *Accept one's fate for what it may be,*
> *even if it would seem beyond the pale.*

The Pagu River forms a large pool,
if its course at Lubuk Kabau is sealed.
Experience becomes a useful tool,
when painful memories are healed.

Firing your gun, you make your way,
hunting for game the whole day long.
I call out your name, as if to pray,
hoping in earnest you'll not be gone.

In gingham clothing, the effect is grand,
one that is magnified by jasmine flowers.
We know not whether to sit or to stand,
when uncertainty has us in its powers.

Behold the rice in the field as it ripens,
and the white cotton bolls on the plain.
Anxiety lessens as laughter heightens,
though dark clouds hide coming rain.

Twilight had fallen, the lamps of the house had been lit. The front gate stood open as the two women sat on the veranda, waiting for the postman to come.

"He usually comes at six," Hanafi's mother said, "and now it's half past and time to break your fast. Why don't you go and eat something."

"If there's mail from Java, it's usually a little later. I'm sure the postman will be here soon," Rapiah said. "I won't be able to eat or drink anything anyway, until I know if there is a letter from Hanafi." She looked towards the walk outside the gate. "Oh, there he is now. He's walking slowly, as if he knows how anxious we are. Look at him; he keeps looking this way. I told you so, he's heading this way. And he has a letter in his hand. Hurry up, Mr. Postman. Is the letter from Batavia?"

Unable to wait for the postman to deliver the letter, Rapiah ran to meet him. She snatched from him the piece of paper he held in his hand.

"A notice for registered mail," Rapiah remarked. "We have to pick it up from the post office." She could not hide her disappointment. Not only was the notice addressed to Hanafi's mother and not to her, she wouldn't be able to retrieve the letter until the next day.

"What did he say?" Hanafi's mother asked.

"I don't know," she answered. "This isn't a letter. It's a notice telling us there is a letter from Hanafi waiting at the post office. We have to pick it up tomorrow. And you have to sign for it."

"But how can I do that, Piah? You know that I can't write. You do it for me," Hanafi's mother suggested.

"But I can't," she said. "You have to sign for it. It's registered, so it must be very important."

Rapiah sighed, now certain of the bad news to come.

Hanafi's mother also sighed as she wondered why the letter was addressed to her instead of Rapiah.

"So what shall we do now, Rapiah? I can't write."

"But you know how to sign your name. We'll go to the post office together," Rapiah told her, "and you can write your name in the presence of the postmaster. I think you are allowed to do that."

"It's all so complicated."

"The worst part is that we won't know until tomorrow."

"Be patient," Hanafi's mother advised. "Try hoping for something good. Better that than thinking it is bad. Allah the Merciful does not let anything happen to His servants that will not benefit them in the end, no matter how bad it seems at first."

Though the older woman's voice was calm, the paper in her hand was shaking. "Let's eat," she said as she got to her feet. "Think of your son: he's still living off your body."

In the dining room, an array of dishes filled the table, but when the two women tried to eat, they felt as if their throats were sealed.

They couldn't swallow a single grain of rice. Finally, wordlessly, they rose and put away the dishes.

Neither of the women could sleep that night. Rapiah listened to her mother-in-law's deep sighs, even as she struggled to explain away her disturbing premonitions. "I'm just being superstitious," she said to herself. "There's no proof whatsoever that anything bad will happen. Just because Hanafi has been gone for a month doesn't mean he's not coming back. It's very possible that he had to stay longer. After all, who can predict how long a disease needs to be treated?"

Suddenly, her thoughts were interrupted by Syafei's scream, a cry so loud Hanafi's mother came bursting into the room. As two women reached his bed, they could see the little boy flailing his arms wildly. Rapiah swept her son in her arms. As she rocked him and kissed him, her mother-in-law turned over the boy's pillow, straightened his sheet and blanket, and searched the corners of his bed.

"Something must have bit him," she said, "but I don't see any insect."

They searched his body for signs of an insect bite but couldn't find any.

Gradually Syafei's screams dissolved into sad, whimpering sobs. To his mother's ears, he seemed to be expressing what she herself could not bring herself to say.

"He can feel what we feel," Rapiah cried.

Hanafi's mother couldn't answer for she was crying as well.

13

Breaking Free

The next day, right after Rapiah had cleared the breakfast table, she readied herself to go to the post office.

"Why don't you go by yourself, Rapiah?" her mother-in-law asked. "Why do I need to go?"

"You know why," she reminded her. "I told you yesterday. You have to come because you have to sign for the letter. And hurry, it's eight o'clock."

"There is no need to hurry," Hanafi's mother said. "It's not even half past seven. The post office isn't even open yet."

"But I just saw the postmaster go past," Rapiah argued. "He is a kind man. I will ask him if we can get the letter before the post office is officially open."

"I don't know why you have to take an old woman like me to a place like that," her mother-in-law grumbled. Even so, she began to get ready to go.

"What are you afraid of, Mother? It's just a post office."

"Maybe it's because I'm from the country. People from there are afraid of the Dutch, afraid that they'll curse us if we do something wrong."

"Not all Dutch people are like that, Mother. We have probably heard more cursing from my son's father than we ever will from that postmaster."

Hanafi's mother didn't look sure. "I hope you are right. When Hanafi is angry, he always knits his brow and says 'paradam, parodom,' or something like that. In those times, all of Allah's earth seems bleak to me. Is that how the Dutch speak?"

"Not at all, Mother. Decent Dutch people don't swear, especially not in front of women."

"It's strange how Hanafi only does it around his own family. He never speaks bad to his friends." Hanafi's mother looked at Rapiah for greater certainty. "Are you sure the postmaster won't swear at me?"

"Yes, I am sure, Mother. When we meet him you will see for yourself."

When the two women arrived in the post office, they found that Rapiah was right.

"Please sign here, Madam," the postmaster said with a smile when handing her the form.

Hanafi's mother clenched the quill and dipped it several times in the ink bottle.

"I think you have enough ink in there now, Madam. Here, sign here. You can use the letters from the Quran to spell your name."

As soon as the quill touched the paper, her hand wavered. "Spell it for me, Rapiah," she whispered. "I've forgotten the letters. There wasn't much school in the old days, you know."

"Mim ... alif ... ra ... ya ... alif ... mim. That's it."

"That's good. Even I can't write like that," said the postmaster with admiration in his voice. "Now, Rapiah, you sign here, and then I'll sign there. There, that's it." He lifted the packet from Hanafi. "Hmm, it's quite heavy. Maybe there is a lot of money in it." He then handed Rapiah the letter. "Good day, Madam. Good day, Rapiah."

Once the two women were outside the post office, Hanafi's mother drew a deep breath. "He's so kind,"

"Generally speaking, the Dutch are kind, Mother, as long as we don't do anything wrong."

"But Hanafi was raised in the Dutch way. Why does he seem to have taken up only their bad ways, and none of the good ones?"

Rapiah did not answer, but only quickened her steps.

"Slow down, Rapiah. You're walking as if you're late for a train."

Rapiah smiled, and then stopped to wait for her mother-in-law.

When they got home she tore open the envelope.

"Read it out loud," said her mother-in-law. "And keep your faith strong. Whether it's good or bad, we will give thanks to Allah who is always generous to His servants."

For a moment, Rapiah simply stared at the letter in her hand.

"Go on, read it. Whether it's good or bad, we will bear it together."

> *Most beloved mother,*
>
> *In truth, I ought to address this letter to Rapiah, but because it was you who gave me that woman, it is to you to whom I wish to return her.*

Rapiah held her side, feeling a sudden pain.

> *Let me be brief about what happened. When I arrived in Batavia I met a former superior of mine who is now one of the top men in the Civil Service Department. He told me there was an opening for a clerk in the Batavia office and that if I wanted the position, I had to apply for it immediately, because the office already had many applicants and wasn't going to wait before filling the position.*

This position would open the way to the top. I could eventually become a reference clerk; it would just be a matter of time.

So without much thought I immediately applied for it, and sent my letter of resignation to the old office. I have now been working here for fourteen days as a full-time employee.

The starting salary is just a little more than what I was making in Solok but there is much greater opportunity for advancement, especially now that I have applied for European Status.

If that status is granted to me, Mother, it will be as if I have no native family. I will no longer live beneath the emblem of our family house.

You must tell the people in the country that I hereby relinquish my hereditary title of Sutan Pamenan. In all family matters, please regard me as non-existent. Because I have, with all my heart, decided to relinquish all ties to family and tradition, what the family does no longer concerns me. Thus, what I do should not concern them either. I only have one link left with the family and that is you, Mother. That will never change.

Rapiah is a different matter. She is a country girl and a man's status rises and falls with that of his wife. In Solok, where there is only a handful of Dutch people and most are not even members of the Dutch elite, Rapiah already felt awkward and afraid to socialize. Batavia is much larger. Here, even housewives are educated, presentable, and competent in many fields. The cooks here in Batavia are ladies compared to the girls in our village. Thus, when I become Dutch, I will surely need a wife of comparable status.

I don't blame everything on Rapiah; she can't help being who she is. All I ask is that you let me stop myself from betraying you. I will not once mention the pain and sorrow that I have suffered while bound to the wife you chose for me. I only trust that you will understand and, in so doing, will allow me to return to you the gift you gave me.

It will be no use for Rapiah to wait for my return, and she should not even think of coming to Batavia...

Rapiah stopped reading as the manservant Buyung pushed a perambulator into the room. Syafei was crying.

"Take him out to the garden," Hanafi's mother said, her voice trembling. "Be patient," she said to Rapiah. "Finish reading it first."

Rapiah looked at her son. "In a moment, darling, in a moment mother will be out to take care of you," she whispered hoarsely. Now, with her eyes glistening with tears, she continued:

...She is still young and can surely find another husband. I will not stop her from doing that. In fact, I hope she will soon find someone who is compatible with her background. It is obvious that she and I are not meant to be. I ask you, Mother, to give to Rapiah the document I enclose with this letter.

I don't know when I can bring you to Batavia. With my small salary, I will have to live simply.

Pray for me, Mother, that I will soon reach my goal. If Rapiah wishes to return to her father, please don't stop her. In fact, I hope you will show this letter to her parents; I am so busy that I do not have time to write a separate letter.

Finally, I request that you send my clothes to
Batavia. As for the furniture and the other things in
the house, you can do with them as you wish, either
sell them or take them to Koto Anau.
In closing, I ask for your understanding.

Yours humbly, your son,
Hanafi

Rapiah then took out the enclosed document addressed to her. "A legal notice," she sighed.

For a while the two women were silent as tears ran down their faces.

"Rapiah, my child," Hanafi's mother finally said, "I have often said to Hanafi that he should never forget you are the daughter of my blood brother. To my mind, sometimes it's not clear which one of you is my child and which one is my child's spouse. Ever since you married Hanafi, I have grown closer and closer to you and now feel as if you were the child I delivered from my womb.

"You have seen how Hanfi treats his mother. He has made not the least effort to bridge the gap between us. And now, with this decision of his, he has severed all ties with me, especially if he becomes Dutch! He has completely cut himself off from our people, both in body and in spirit.

"You have lost a husband, Rapiah, and I have lost a son. Now I am asking you if you will take his place. Come with me to Koto Anau. Let us go back to the village and start anew. We will spend our time praying to Allah the Most Generous that He will show us the way of righteousness.

"Will you come with me, Rapiah? If you miss your mother and father, we could also go to Bonjol. We can go wherever we please. There is no one to stand in our way now. You and I and Syafei, the three of us will spend the rest of our lives together. And when I go to my final rest, you are the two who will mourn for me."

Rapiah bowed her head. She felt as if her heart had stopped beating. Her mother-in-law's words were for her like a beam of sunlight breaking through the fog. She felt that she would never want to be separated from this noble soul. And she understood that her mother-in-law, Hanafi's mother, had made her offer not merely out of pity for her having lost a husband, but because the old woman herself needed comfort in her abandonment.

Rapiah dried her eyes with the edge of her sleeve. "But Hanafi said he will send for you to go to Batavia."

"What's an old country woman like me to do in Batavia," the woman asked. "To be ridiculed even more? Even here in Solok, people say that I am ignorant and old-fashioned. In Batavia, *Mister* Hanafi, who is now about to become a Dutchman and who associates only with the Dutch and what he calls society's upper crust, will surely be ashamed of his country mother. Maybe he's right," she said. "Maybe I am stupid and backward. If that's the case it would be best that I stay in the village. I would not want to get in the way of him achieving his goals.

"I won't curse him for his resolve. I long ago accepted all the suffering that he might cause when I carried him in my womb. I freely gave the milk of my breasts when it was his milk of life. I willingly made the sacrifices that were required to put him through school. I have always given freely, never asking for anything in return. Although it hurts to be rejected by my own son and to be thought of as a hindrance to his goal, I will still pray that Allah—praised be His name—will bless him and give him his dream." Her voice cracked. "But now I have no one else, Rapiah. If you care for me, please come with me."

Rapiah took her mother-in-law's hand. "Mother," she said, "if you truly want me to take Hanafi's place, I willingly accept your offer and will go with you wherever you want to go. And if one day you should find yourself missing him and want to move to Batavia, Syafei and I can go to my parent's home in Bonjol."

Hanafi's mother shook her head. "Don't talk about me going to Batavia again, Piah. Maybe it's better for Hanafi and I to be apart. There is no use trying to mix oil and water. It is true that he is the flesh and blood of my own womb…. Maybe it was the way I raised him, maybe his upbringing was wrong, maybe he grew up in the wrong environment, I don't know, but now he has separated himself from me. Even though he has the same eyes that we do, he does not see what we see. And he does not feel what we feel." She looked as if she were about to faint. "I never thought I would lose my only child, Piah. Your father is my only sibling. We share the same father and mother. Both of us have but one child, which is why I want to take you with me, Piah. We'll go tomorrow. I have some old furniture at the house in the village. There's nothing we need from this house."

Rapiah scanned the room. "But what are we going to do with all these things?" she asked.

"We can send them to an auctioneer," Hanafi's mother suggested but then hesitated. "But, but maybe not. Maybe we should take everything with us to the village, the flower vases and everything." She turned her head away, addressing her distant son. "Oh, Hanafi, I can not believe Allah the Merciful will not one day bring you back to the mother who bore you." Now she spoke to Rapiah: "I am certain that Allah the Almighty will not abandon him; He will bring Hanafi back to the right path. We must be patient, Rapiah. And let us start our new lives together."

The two women kept on talking, discussing what they were going to do. In the end, however, they chose to place everything in God's hand. Together, they accepted the responsibility of bringing up Syafei, an innocent child who should not be made to suffer for his father's mistaken ways. When they called Buyung, the manservant came in pushing Syafei in the perambulator. Hanafi's mother bent over the sleeping child, and softly whispered in his little ear: "May God shower you with his blessings, my grandchild. May you be the balm that heals our broken hearts."

14

Happy Together

Three months had passed since Corrie's twenty-first birthday. After leaving school, she had moved to a house that she rented in Pasar Baru. She did little each day except practice playing the piano. She had no thoughts of finding a job. Why should she worry about tomorrow, she thought. She had enough schooling, and for now she could live on her savings. She was certain that when the time came, doors would open wherever she went. Her trustee himself had said during their meeting that she could work in his office if she wanted to. But with a smile she told him that for the time being she simply wanted to be free, because she had lived "in bondage" all her life.

Every afternoon, Hanafi came for tea to Corrie's house, which he nicknamed the dove-cote. Sometimes they would ride their bicycles around the city and on Sundays they would pedal to the countryside and enjoy the fresh air. Most days, however, they simply perused the newspaper that Hanafi always brought with him. Together they would read the local news, leaving the political and editorial columns untouched. Sometimes the whole newspaper lay folded, unread, as they talked about all that had happened in their lives, and shared their hopes, sorrows, and their plans for the future.

One day, Hanafi arrived with an unusually tense expression on his face. As usual, he carried a newspaper, but his movements were jerky, and his hand trembled when he shook Corrie's.

"What's happened, Hanafi? You look so serious."

"There's some important news," he said as he opened the newspaper.

"Forget the newspaper," she told him, "just tell me what's so important."

"Read it yourself," he said as he pointed to a short official announcement.

Corrie's eyes scanned the announcement: "The Government hereby declares that Hanafi, a clerk at the Civil Service Department, has hereby obtained European status and that henceforth, may use the name Han, or Christiaan Han...."

"Oh, you are a European now! Congratulations," she said to Hanafi. "The name 'Christiaan', it has a nice ring to it. I can call you Chris, or Christy, or Chrissy. Such a sweet name!"

Suddenly Corrie fell silent, her gaze fixed blankly at the flower pot in the corner.

"What are you thinking?" he asked her. "Aren't you happy that my life is finally changing?"

"Of course I am, Hanafi, I mean 'Han.' How could I not be happy for you? But I was just thinking, I was separated from my father by God's will and every time I think of him, it still affects me deeply whereas you, here you are, cutting yourself off from your mother by your own choice."

"I am not separating myself from my mother," he told her. "It's true, I have severed all ties with my people and their traditions, but the spiritual bond between a mother and a son is one no one can break. In my heart, I shall never lose her. If, because I aspire to a better life, she were to disown me, I would of course be forced to consider myself cut off. But even if that happens—what can I say, Corrie?—I'm willing to sacrifice even that for you."

Hanafi then fell on his knees by Corrie's chair. "The only obstacle between us was race," he said as he reached for her hand. "Now you can forget I am a Malay. In law I am now of the same racial status as you. From this point on, Hanafi is gone. Let us now erase his past. Will you be my wife?" he asked.

Instead of answering him, Corrie ran her fingers through his hair, took his hand and then led him back to his chair. "You must give me some time to think," she told him. "I have just begun to taste my freedom and it will be hard to give it up. Give me some time to think it over."

Hanafi shook his head. "We don't have to marry right away. You can have your freedom for a year, or two, or even ten. I will wait for you. All I want is your heart's decision, which is something for which there should be no need to wait for; if it is not there now, it is not likely ever to be there. But if you say yes, Corrie, then I will wait for you as long as it takes. I want you to know, Corrie, I have placed my future and my destiny entirely upon you. Will you not marry me, Corrie?"

Corrie attempted to lighten the atmosphere: "And if I say no, will you throw yourself into the river? If you do, don't do it in a deep river with a strong current because it will be hard to rescue you. Choose a shallow stream, with not too much current and lots of people around."

Corrie's gaiety brought tears to Hanafi's eyes. "So you think this is all a game? Women can be so cruel," he muttered. "They play with men like a cat plays with a mouse."

"Forgive me," Corrie said soothingly. "I didn't mean to insult you. Even though I am now twenty-one, in my heart I feel like a child and sometimes the mere sound of the word 'marriage' frightens me."

"If you are not ready," he told her, "I will wait. I will wait even until your hair turns white, as long as you give me your promise."

Now she really did laugh. "When my hair turns white I doubt if I will like myself! And I suspect you won't either. If and when I consent to be a man's wife, I want my betrothed to be enthralled by my looks. I don't want it any other way. Which is why," she then said, "I don't think you will have to wait that long for my decision.

"A friend of mine, a classmate, is now vacationing at her parents' coffee plantation in East Java. She once told me that I could visit whenever I wanted. I think now would be a good time for me to take her up on her offer.

"Let me go there, Han, and while I'm away let us not write to each other. I will come back when I have made my decision."

Hanafi look forlorn. "How many days, Corrie? How many weeks will that be?"

"I don't know," she told him simply. "It could be a week or it could be a year. If you are really willing to wait, then wait."

Hanafi didn't answer. He gazed at her as though he could penetrate the secret in her heart. "I feel reluctant to promise to keep such an open-ended promise. What if, after all this, you say no?"

"That kind of thinking is not good. It's not right, Chris." She gave his new name special emphasis. "When I say I need time to think, you must accept it as that. Please don't ever think that I am toying with you. If I didn't want to marry you, I would say so now."

Hanafi knew from the way Corrie spoke that he must not press her. He knew that if he applied pressure at the wrong time, his turtle dove would surely fly away, this time never to return.

"You are right, Corrie," he said. "If you really wanted to, there is nothing to stop you from saying no to me now. At the same time," he asserted, "I want you to know that waiting for your answer will be like hell on earth for me."

"Both of us need time to think, Han. You too must think carefully about whether you are prepared to take me as your wife. The older I get the more I notice my bad qualities. I am stubborn, like you. But I am also, I must admit, very flippant, this way one minute and that way the next. I have been pampered since childhood and have never had to live in need; which is why, I suppose, people say I have a big head. If someone wants to marry me, he has to accept me as I am and not expect me to become the perfect wife.

"Corrie, we have been friends since we were little. A love that grew from that would surely accept things as they are. I love you not because of your looks, but because I enjoy loving you, for... being you."

"That's good, Han, because I know what can happen to a husband and wife. Before the couple marry, they are willing to overlook the other's flaws because both are sure they can correct them later. But afterward, they find that it is not so easy. I have seen both men and women get so carried away by their passions that they can't think rationally. But for me, I don't know, it seems like I am different from other women. If I honestly look into my heart, it seems that what I truly want from marriage is a friendship, or something that is more like a brother-sister relationship, instead of that between a man and a woman. In my relationship with you thus far, that is what has been truly dear to me. To be honest with you, Han, I feel a little deflated to think that you are no different from other men, in that way."

Hanafi was silent for a moment. "Are you afraid of men, Cor?" he asked.

"I don't know. With other men, yes, I guess I could say that. I feel disgusted even at the slightest touch. That's not the way I feel with you. With you, I don't shrink from holding your hand."

Hanafi drew a sigh of relief. For a moment he thought that Corrie was the kind of woman who had no interest in men. But her last words reassured him. And he remembered that afternoon in Solok, when she lost herself in his embrace.

Hanafi and Corrie ended their discussion by agreeing that Corrie would go away to her friend's house at the coffee plantation near Probolinggo. They would write no letters while she was away. When she had made her decision, he would hear from her either through a letter or in person.

For the next three days they prepared for Corrie's departure. Arrangements had to be made with her landlord, they had food to pack and clothes to pick up from the cleaners. On the fourth day, they stood together on the platform at Gambir station. They spoke little, each feeling uncertain of what the future might hold.

Corrie's indecision was genuine. She could not say yes because her heart was undecided. On the other hand, her affection for Hanafi was so great that she could not think of one reason to prevent them from becoming husband and wife. She certainly could not deny the sadness that overcame her whenever she had to part from him.

As the train slowly pulled out of the station, she looked out the carriage window and waved her last goodbye. She could still hear Hanafi's shaken voice. "Till we meet again, Cor." "Yes, until then," she replied, her voice also trembling.

With her eyes shut, she sank into her seat. She felt at that moment that what she was leaving behind, the man who was now standing on the railway platform, was no less than a part of herself. And she felt certain then that when the time came for her to want to marry, there could be no other man.

Less than a month later Hanafi received a letter. His happiness was indescribable. The letter read:

Christy,

As soon as you receive this letter, ask for a one-week leave of absence. Come to Probolinggo and stay at the Hotel Semeru. At the hotel, ask the telephone operator to connect you to the office of the administrator at the Gunung Wayang coffee plantation, and then ask to speak to me. I am planning to introduce my fiancé to my friends here.

Corrie

Hanafi was able to obtain a one-week leave of absence with no difficulty and the very next day he was on the train heading to the eastern end of Java. It was a two-day journey. And as soon as he arrived, he went to find the telephone.

The operator had no difficulty establishing the right connection. And he was soon talking to Corrie. But she did not sound happy. "I'll meet you tomorrow at the hotel," she said. He tried to carry on a conversation, asking her this and that. But all she said was, "I'll explain everything tomorrow."

Although he was exhausted by the long train ride, and his bones felt like they had been shaken loose, Hanafi could not sleep that night. "What could have happened?" he asked himself. "Why was she so curt?" And he began to wonder if she wanted to call the whole thing off. "But she couldn't," he assured himself, "because in her letter she had called me 'my fiancé,' and she had asked me to come all this way."

By early morning, Hanafi was already out in the hotel's front yard, pacing back and forth. The only sustenance he could manage was a cup of coffee and a little slice of bread, which he had to force down his throat. He checked his watch every minute, each time thinking that it had stopped. He was tempted to go fetch Corrie himself but the hotel receptionist told him that the only way to the plantation was by car. At about ten o'clock a large sedan with shiny bronze trim drove into the hotel's front yard. As soon as he saw Corrie stepping out of the car, Hanafi ran to meet her. Passionately, he took her hand and gazed deeply into her eyes but Corrie seemed more concerned with practical matters.

"We are not going to spend the night here, we have to get ready to leave for Surabaya," she told him, then ordered the porters to unload her luggage.

"But...."

"I will tell you everything on the train. Now you have to pack your things and pay the bill. I wish we could spend the night here—I am so exhausted—but we can't wait. We'll stop in Surabaya."

Soon afterward, they boarded the train for Surabaya. The second-class carriage was almost empty. And Corrie drew a deep sigh of relief as she settled on her seat. "Oh, at last I can breathe," she said. "I asked you to come all this way because I had planned to announce our engagement at the plantation. My friend and I were planning to pick you up at the hotel and then we would all celebrate our engagement with a nice dinner at her place. Everybody was excited. But when her father found out who I was being engaged to, that's when things fell apart. In short, he objected to having you at his dinner table. He even changed his attitude toward me, when he found out that you were a Malay who had become Dutch. He lent me his car and his driver to meet you in Probolinggo, but would not let his daughter come. That's what happened to our engagement party."

Hanafi looked away, and fell silent for a moment. "What do you plan to do now?" he said softly.

"I suggest we go back to Batavia and get married there quietly."

"I agree," he told her wholeheartedly. "Forget about the plantation. Let's not worry about what other people think: the whole wide world is before us."

"Still," she said, "it would have been nice to have an engagement party, wouldn't it? It happens but once in a lifetime. Neither of us have a family, and she was my only close friend. After her father cancelled the party, we planned to have a little toast at the hotel, just the three of us. She had some money saved but..."

"Don't be sad, Cor. We have each other. Who cares what the rest of the world thinks? We'll have happiness as long as we have each other."

"I hope you are right, Han. I truly hope so."

15

Becoming Husband and Wife

In Surabaya, Hanafi and Corrie spent the night at a small guest house, where they registered as Mr. Han and Miss Han, as if they were relatives. They asked for separate rooms and carried on as though they were a brother and sister stopping over in Surabaya on their long journey to Batavia. And while the other guests went to the dining room already dressed for an evening out in the city and so full of excitement they seemed to be calling out to everyone, both young and old, to come along, Hanafi and Corrie did not set foot outside the hotel's gateway. Corrie did not even show herself in the dining room. She said she had a headache and asked for dinner in her room.

By daybreak the next day, they were already at the train station, and not long afterward were on their way to Bandung onboard an express train. The carriage was full and, again, Corrie made motions of suffering from a headache. Throughout the journey, she leaned against the headrest and kept her eyes closed. Hanafi, on the other hand, ran to a newsstand whenever the train stopped at a major station. Each time, he'd come back to his seat carrying a book or two in his hand, but none of them could hold his attention. He ended up tossing them into the overhead luggage rack before he had read even the first ten pages. "There isn't one interesting sentence in them," he grumbled.

At the sound of his voice, Corrie opened her eyes. "Of course not, Han. Who can read in this heat? Why don't you open the window to let in some air?" Hanafi could barely hear her; her voice was so weak that it made him think of a dying person struggling to utter her last words.

He pushed down the window, and a gust of wind blew directly against her face, but she remained motionless as the wind tossed her hair about her face. Hanafi was at a loss for words.

"Corrie, why don't we switch places?" he finally said. "You'll catch a draft where you're sitting."

Corrie moved to Hanafi's seat, across from hers, and again looked out the window as she sank listlessly into the corner.

How differently things would be for other women who were on a trip with their fiancé or newlywed husbands, she thought. Surely a woman in such a situation would see beauty in everything. The sight of a water buffalo standing mutely in a freshly cut rice field, with the cowherd dozing on a nearby footpath would be enough to assure her of the peace and happiness that life on earth holds. A small, dark stream meandering through a grove of nearly barren *dadap* trees to empty itself into a paddy field would make an unsurpassed picture of a tropical paradise. Even the song of a bamboo flute played by the blind men in the train stations on their journey would sound melodious and deeply moving to such a woman.

But what about her? She didn't know what she was feeling. Her chest felt heavy, as if a weight was pressing against it. No scenery could hold her interest. All she could think was the end of the journey. Even the express train felt too slow for her.

She asked herself if she regretted her decision. She could find no answer in her heart. She loved Hanafi, and her love was not lessened after what had just happened. But she also realized that in truth she had accepted him because of pity, and she could not shake the thought that her life would have been much easier if she had not met Hanafi.

Normally, newly-engaged couples could not resist embracing and kissing each other, even in front of a crowd of people. Corrie, however, found it hard even to look Hanafi in the eye. Somehow she felt embarrassed about their relationship, and preferred to give the impression that they were just relatives.

When their train pulled into Bandung station shortly before eight, darkness had fallen. As soon as they left the station, they looked for a taxi to take them to a hotel. In the taxi Hanafi reached for her hand but she drew back.

Hanafi looked at her sadly. "Do you regret your decision?"

"If I regretted it, I would have called it off," she told him.

"But you're acting so strange."

"I'm just exhausted, and I have a headache."

"It's just that we're not acting like an engaged couple. And I can't help thinking that..." He paused, then blurted, "Just reassure me of your love, would you?"

Before she could reply, the taxi had turned into the hotel's driveway. The change of scenery somehow made Corrie breathe a little easier. "A marriage based on love alone is easily broken," she confided, "because love runs out. From the very beginning, when you first wanted me to be your wife, what I felt most toward you was compassion. And in my opinion a marriage based on compassion has a stronger bond than a marriage based on anything else."

"Only compassion?" he asked.

"You shouldn't expect anything more."

Hanafi drew a long sigh. When they got out of the taxi, the porters fought over their luggage.

"Do you have two rooms?" Corrie asked of one.

"We do, Ma'am," the man answered, "but the Master better check in quickly at the office before someone else takes them."

While Hanafi hurried off to register their names at the hotel office, Corrie waited in the lobby. As soon as he returned Corrie told the bellboy that she would like her dinner brought to her room.

The next morning, as they as rode in a buggy on the way to the train station, Hanafi tried to bring up the previous night's conversation but Corrie gave him only a sad smile. "Please, Han, you must understand," she told him. "I'm thinking about my life and my future. A woman is a maiden but once. After she marries, it's different; unlike a man, who can always go back to being a bachelor again, even after marrying many times. The commitment I am making is a serious one. So I just want to be alone with my thoughts for a while."

On the train from Bandung to Batavia, they kept their thoughts mostly to themselves. Hanafi sat gloomily throughout the journey, lost in his own imaginings. When they arrived at Gambir station, Corrie said she was going to stay at the Hotel Hollandia on Gunung Sari Street, and firmly refused his offer to accompany her there.

"No, Han, over the next few days you have to find a house to rent. Find a modest one on a side street that's wide enough for a vehicle to pass. When the house is ready, then you can let me know."

"Shouldn't we look for the house together, in case you don't like my taste?"

"Oh, I think you know what I like, and what's appropriate for us. You also have a better idea about what is a reasonable rent, since you are the one who will be paying it. But I will arrange the furniture, and we will share the cost fifty-fifty."

"Fifty-fifty, Cor? Why?"

"Because I want it that way. In these matters you have to let me have my way."

Hanafi shook his head, but didn't dare protest. "Very well then, but I still would like it if we could look for a house together."

"People don't know we are getting married, Han. What will they say if they see us looking for a house together?" As she spoke, Corrie extended her hand to Hanafi. "I will be waiting for you at the hotel."

She then jumped into the waiting taxi. "To Gunung Sari," she told the driver.

As he watched Corrie speed away, Hanafi had to reassure himself with the thought that she would become his wife in a matter of days. Surely the dark clouds would disappear once they were married. And with that comforting thought he got into a taxi and headed home.

The next afternoon, he went to see Corrie at her hotel. "We have a house," he announced. "It's on Ketapang which is fairly wide and the rent is only seventy rupiah."

"That's good," she said with apparent satisfaction. "And I too have been busy. I bought some furniture at Franzen—nothing fancy, of course, and it comes to eight hundred rupiah. We can each pay half."

"That means we are equal," Hanafi declared. "I like it that the wife doesn't just stay in the kitchen."

Corrie knew that Hanafi meant those words as a rebuke to Rapiah, his first wife in Solok. He often made such remarks whenever he spoke of his 'country wife,' and they always offended her.

"Tomorrow we have to pick up our order at Franzen," she said abruptly. "After you deliver the furniture, you can arrange for the electricity and water connections. Once that is done, you can move in and start living there. The sooner we put together our house the sooner we can go to the Registrar at City Hall. But, remember, you have to bring two witnesses, and we have to make cards for our wedding announcement. From City Hall, we will head straight to the station and take the train to Sukabumi for our honeymoon. I don't want any more ceremony than that."

Corrie spoke matter-of-factly but Hanafi was so excited that he failed to notice her lack of enthusiasm.

"Very well," he said happily. "Tomorrow I will move into our house, and then the day after tomorrow ...."

"If you want, we can go to the Registrar at City Hall."

"And then by the afternoon, we will be in Sukabumi. And you will be my wife, my sweetheart, mine for life. Hurrah!"

He took Corrie's hand, and was about to put his arms around her but she flinched at his touch. "We're in a restaurant, and…we haven't been to City Hall yet."

Hanafi withdrew sullenly. Before he could say a word, Corrie called for a waiter.

"Would you like some tea?" she asked him.

"Yes, please."

"Two teas, please," she told the waiter.

"What time should I come here tomorrow, Cor?"

"It's up to you."

"Well, if it was up to me, I wouldn't want us to ever be apart, not even for a second."

"Unfortunately life is not a bed of roses, Han. But alright, let's make it seven o'clock tomorrow. I'll wait for you here on the veranda. But remember, until then I am still Miss du Bussé!"

"Very well, tomorrow at seven. But, wait, I can't. I have to go to the office first. The new secretary doesn't come in until half past eight and he's the person I have to talk to if I want a two-week leave. I'll have to explain to him what I want the leave for."

"All right, you can tell him, but don't tell anyone else, except for the two witnesses."

"What, are you ashamed?" Hanafi asked.

"No, I'm not ashamed. I just think it's better if people stay out of our business. It's bad enough that society demands we must have witnesses, and announcements, and that the marriage has to be approved by someone else, or else people will look askance at us. Wouldn't it be better if a man could simply marry a woman, and that other people have no choice but to accept their decision?"

"I agree," Hanafi remarked. "I like that idea." He then dropped his gaze, speaking softly, "For a moment I thought you were ashamed of marrying me."

"Oh, don't talk nonsense. Remember, I still have a choice."

Hearing that, Hanafi fell silent, but again, he managed to banish his doubts with the thought that soon Corrie would be his wife.

"There's a wonderful film showing at Deca Park tonight," he said as if in invitation.

"Maybe after we get back from Sukabumi," Corrie told him. "I'm still tired from the journey."

"But it's such a beautiful night. The stars and the moon will soon come out. The fresh air will be good for your headache."

"But watching a film isn't good for a headache."

"How about a drive then, to the outskirts of town?"

"That's an idea. It might do me good to get away from the hustle and bustle of the city for a while."

Hanafi at once went out to look for a taxi. When he returned with one, Corrie joined him and they were soon speeding towards Priok. Inside the cab, he tried several times to snuggle close to her, but she warded him off, just like before, until he finally gave up. When they parted, they were like a brother and sister in the midst of a quarrel.

Two days later Hanafi and Corrie stood in front of the Registrar at City Hall with two clerks from Hanafi's office as witnesses.

Corrie wore a simple bridal gown; Hanafi wore his dinner jacket. From City Hall they went to the post office to mail their announcement cards. Corrie then went back to her hotel. She changed, paid her bills, then packed her suitcases and brought her things to her new house on Ketapang. From there the newlyweds went to Gambir station.

"Corrie, my wife..." Hanafi said to Corrie, "I can't begin to speak of my happiness. It's greater than if I had won a whole mountain of gold."

"I'm sorry if I don't look as excited as you are. I'm still overwhelmed by everything. When I think of what a milestone in my life this is, I can't help thinking about the past and about those loved ones no longer here with me. I wonder if my father would be happy or sad if he could see his daughter now?"

"He wouldn't be sad," Hanafi told her. "He once admitted that to me."

"He would be happy as long as he knew his daughter would not be mistreated."

"But how could I ever mistreat you when you are all I have ever longed for? Before I had you, my life was miserable, lonely and empty. No, Corrie," he reaffirmed, "I will never mistreat you."

"I hope that is true," Corrie intoned. "And I hope that God the Almighty blesses us and strengthens our love, so that we love each other until our dying days. I know I have bad qualities," she confessed, "more bad ones than good ones, I suspect. I hope that you can help to correct my flaws but at the same time," she added, "respect my right to be different and accept my faults, with understanding and forgiveness. As the Dutch say, '*met beleid, begrijpen en vergeven.*' Perhaps, then our bond will last."

16

In the Storms of Life

Other than the one letter that he sent to his mother, Hanafi sent no news to his family in Sumatra. Two years passed and when his relatives finally came to learn that not only had Hanafi married a European, but also that he had become one himself, they ceased to consider him to be a member of their family. For Hanafi's part, this was a pronouncement he would have been happy to accept. He was now a Westerner by law and he wanted to have nothing more to do with native people, not only his estranged family in West Sumatra but also in Batavia, where he had not made a single native acquaintance since his move to the capital.

This did not mean that Westerners embraced Hanafi as one of their own. On the contrary, although he had made every effort to be included in their social circles, he forever remained an outsider. At his office, his European colleagues would do no more than greet him formally when they met. And at the Government Employees' Tennis Club, he and Corrie were shunned soon after they joined. Nobody actually spoke ill of them to their faces, but whenever the other members gathered after a game to chat or to plan an excursion, he and Corrie were always excluded. If they tried to insert themselves within a gathering, one by one its members would excuse themselves until they were left alone. And if ever they invited someone to join them in seeing a film or another attraction in the park, the answer was inevitably, "Sorry, we have already made plans."

Eventually, he and Corrie simply withdrew from the club's social circle. On weekends, to buoy their spirits, they would take excursions out of town. Sometimes they rented an automobile; other times, they took the train. Invariably, they always spent a lot of money on these trips, but somehow they were never able to enjoy themselves. The thrill was gone.

Gone, too, was the girl who had once captivated everyone with her beaming smile. Ever since her marriage to Hanafi, Corrie—who had once been known for her boundless energy—had become a dour woman, a wife with no ambition of her own. She still had her looks, and Hanafi could enjoy her beauty to his heart's content, but the gleam in her eyes had dimmed. If she ever laughed, lines appeared around the corners of her mouth, which meant that she was laughing not from joy but from sorrow. Needless to say, the young couple no longer bantered like they used to. If he invited her to the beach, for instance, she was more likely to resist than accept his invitation. "Places like that are so full of pretentious people," she'd say. "But if you really want to go, I'll go."

There were times when Hanafi could almost not bear to witness his wife's spiritless bearing. He found himself so angry he wanted to break into a rage but, at the same time, he would find himself at a loss for words.

"What has gotten into you?" Corrie once asked him when seeing his silent rage.

"What has gotten into me?" he returned. "What with the way that you have been acting, you're likely to send me to the madhouse."

"Well, if you think I have neglected my duty as a wife, we can talk about that."

"No, Corrie, you haven't neglected your duty. And that's the problem! Because that's not what I want. What I want is the old Corrie, the girl who would challenge me and argue with me, the girl who flirted with me and drove me mad, the girl who made me laugh. That's the Corrie I want!" he told her. "What has happened to her?"

"Do you really have to ask? The answer is obvious. That girl's name was Miss Corrie du Bussé; now I am Mrs. Han. The old Corrie wore short skirts; now my hem must always be below my knee. Before, I was free and my world was limitless; now my world has a boundary because I have to submit to my husband."

"That's nonsense, Corrie. You're not the only woman with a husband. All married women were once free, and yet they don't act like they have been taken advantage of."

"So maybe I'm different from other women. Are you going to blame me for that?"

"I don't know who, or what, to blame. But if you love me, Corrie..." He paused. "I really wish you could be more like the way you were before, bringing sunshine wherever you go, instead of dark clouds."

"I don't think that's possible. And please don't think that I am just putting on an act. In fact, if you saw me laughing or jumping about, that would be an act, because that's not how I feel. That's just how it is. And about love for a husband, tell me, have I neglected or taken too lightly any of my obligations to make you question my love?"

"But I want more than your obligations."

Corrie shrugged her shoulders.

Hanafi, looked deeply into Corrie's eyes. "When we were friends, we used to keep each other on our toes. We had clear-headed discussions about so many things."

"As far I know, I am still clear-headed when I speak. In fact it is you who often gets agitated and mumble incomprehensibly. And besides, what do we need to have clear-headed discussions about?"

Hanafi was growing more agitated. "About the way you behave, for one! You say that you are not acting, but it sure looks like you are."

"So you really want to know why I've changed?"

"I do," he pleaded. "Please tell me."

"I've changed because my world shrank after I married you."

"That's music to my ears," he answered cynically.

"Well, you asked."

"So, the world crumbled because you married a Malay."

"That's right, my world crumbled because I married a Malay. That's the truth, and you know it. The only question is, how are you going to deal with it? So far all you've done is blame me."

"When did I ever blame you for the fate we share?"

"Never explicitly, but whenever you speak to me harshly, like you are now, I can't help thinking that you are punishing me, for what has become of us."

Hanafi searched for the right words. "I am sorry if I have been harsh with you," he sighed. "But why must we care about other people's opinions? If they don't want to be our friends, so be it. As long as we love each other, there is still a whole wide world for us out there, even for us, two outcasts."

"But I can't bear living as a pariah," Corrie answered. "Ever since I was a girl I've always been the center of attention. Wherever I went, my friends followed me. I decided which games we played; I was always the referee if ever there was a fight. No one made enemies with me. And that's also how it was at the school. But now, even my friends from Salemba have turned their backs on me. You keep saying that as long as there is love, we don't need to heed other people. That may be true for you, but I don't have the strength to live like that. Maybe that's my weakness, I admit it. I can't bear this burden, and that's why I have changed."

"Oh, Corrie it's all my fault. What a sin I have committed in wanting you as my wife. It's all my fault, it's all my fault."

Corrie shook her head. "No, Han, it's our fault."

"I wish there was some way I could cast off this curse," he cried. "Let's go out, Corrie, get out of here. Let's laugh and have fun like we did before. All other people can go to hell."

"That's easier said than done. No matter what we say, society is an important part of a person's life. We can vow a hundred times not to care what other people think, but the heart does not always listen to the mind. If a person rejects us, it hurts. And even if we have a hundred other friends there to console us, the rejection of that one person who turns his back on us still leaves a wound. How much greater is the pain when not one but, instead, two or three friends reject us. And the way it is with us now, there are not just two or three, it's everyone! Everyone acts as if we were vile. Don't tell me that you haven't noticed. On the contrary, I believe their rejection hurts you very much. You show it in the harshness of your words, when you get angry with me, for no reason.

"But then," she added, "Maybe I act the way I do because that is my own way of dealing with the pain..."

Hanafi was not sure what to say. "But if you still love me," he began, "and don't blame me entirely for your own suffering, is it possible that you could try a bit harder to make our lives more bearable? Now that we have no one else, would it be so difficult to show a little cheer when we are together? I am now your earth and your sky, Corrie, just as you are mine. We are both orphans and outcasts. Shouldn't that make us closer? Why are we living this way, like two people who tolerate each other only to fulfil their duties?"

"You are right," Corrie told him. "We should help each other, especially now. But you must change too," she said. "Perhaps, if you continue to talk to me as you are doing now—gently and calmly—our relationship will improve. I need you to be more patient with me."

Hanafi reached for Corrie's waist and drew her close to him. He kissed her again and again. "Oh, Corrie," he moaned, "my dear and precious wife. I am so sorry if I have ruined your life. But I want you to know how much I love you no matter what. I promise that from now on, I will not say one harsh word that might hurt you. Poor Corrie, my Corrie. We must be strong if we are to stand strong in the face of the storms of life. Together we can sail our ship to a safe haven, distant from this suffocating world."

Corrie held her husband tightly and kissed him tenderly, as tears streamed down her cheeks. "Let's hope, Hanafi, that God will give us the strength."

Hearing this, Hanafi broke down, and they held each other as they cried.

But alas, less than a week later they were to face yet another trial, one that threatened to break forever the fragile bond between the ill-fated husband and wife.

17

An Unjust Accusation

One day, less than a week after her tear-filled discussion with Hanafi, Corrie was seated on the back veranda of their house when she found herself startled by the sound of a woman's voice. "*Daag*," came the Dutch greeting.

Corrie turned her head to see an older woman everyone knew as Auntie Lien. Immediately, her face lit up and her lips curved into a smile, for she counted Auntie Lien as her only friend. "Hello!" she called happily, in return.

Aunty Lien was said to possess prophetic abilities and during the day, when Hanafi was at the office, she often came to the house to divine Corrie's fortune. Corrie herself had little faith in fortune telling; moreover, she did not even think of Auntie Lien as a person with whom she could relate in a serious way. The simple fact was that the elderly lady was her only contact with the outside world and she welcomed the diversion.

The two women went inside and Corrie took a seat on the sofa. Auntie Lien was about to follow suit when she suddenly slipped on a *dukuh* peel and might very well have fallen backward if Corrie had not caught her hand.

"Dead son of a horse!" the woman blurted out.

The woman's outburst caused Corrie to burst into laughter.

"What did I say? Dead horse? Eh, eh, eh...," the woman blathered. "You want to see me dead, young woman? You are too much, you know."

Corrie, still choking with laughter, called for the maid. "Mina!"

"Mina!" Auntie Lien parroted involuntarily.

When the maidservant came running in, Corrie stood and was followed by Auntie Lien. She pointed at the *dukuh* peel on which Auntie Lien had slipped and reprimanded the servant: "The floor is filthy, Mina,"

"The floor is filthy, Mina." Auntie Lien mimicked Corrie's again.

"I could kill you sometimes," Corrie said.

"I could kill you sometimes."

"The devil...." Corrie said.

"The devil...." Auntie Lien repeated.

"I must teach you a lesson," Corrie said as she took off her woven sandal and waved it at the girl.

Auntie Lien again followed Corrie's cue and removed a heavy leather sandal from her foot. "I must teach you a lesson," she also said, but before either could throw their sandals at her, the girl ran away, laughing.

"Go get 'er, Auntie! Go get 'er," Corrie whispered excitedly.

With her sandal held high in one hand, Auntie Lien chased Mina around the back yard. Soon, the dog next door started barking, darting along the sparse bamboo fence to join the fray. Mina ran into the kitchen and locked the door. Auntie Lien banged at the door as the dog barked even louder. Finally, Auntie Lien gave up the pursuit, but continued to yell frantically as she walked back toward the house.

By now Corrie had fallen to the sofa, convulsing with laughter. But when she saw Auntie Lien faced off with the dog, she willed herself to regain control. "Auntie Lien," she shouted. "That's enough, now. Come inside."

Auntie Lien came into the house panting hard. Slumping into the rattan chair beside the sofa, she looked at Corrie and shook her head. "Oh, you are too much, young lady. To think of it, making an old woman run around like that!"

"I'm sorry," Corrie apologized, "but that was just what I needed. I haven't had a good laugh like that in months. Now I feel much better."

After the two women had caught their breath, Auntie Lien took out a package wrapped in a faded handkerchief. Inside was a deck of dirty, dog-eared cards, a little larger than regular playing cards.

"Before you start, Auntie, let me bring you something to a drink. What would you like: port, sherry, or whisky?"

"That's too high-class for me. A cup of coffee will do. And if you don't mind, would you let me chew my betel nut?"

"You know the rule," Corrie remarked. "Betel nut is strictly forbidden in this house. You can have anything else—cakes, pastries, whatever snacks you want— but not betel nut."

"Well, what about cigarettes? Could I get some smokes off of you?"

"You can smoke a whole carton if you want," Corrie declared. "I'll go and get them for you."

Corrie went into another room. When she returned, she brought with her an almost full carton of cigarettes and an ashtray.

"These are good ones," she said to Auntie Liem, "they even have gold-colored filters. They're three and a half cents each! My husband smokes one after a meal, or when we go out to a show. Try one."

"Why didn't you ever offer me one of these before?" the woman asked.

"I didn't know you liked to smoke."

"If I can't chew my betel nut, smoking will do."

Auntie Lien then took a cigarette, lit it, and drew two or three drafts before exhaling the thick smoke through her nostrils. She then dealt seven cards on the table and asked Corrie to pick one. After Corrie had chosen a card, she placed another row of seven cards on the table. Again, she asked Corrie to pick a card, from which she started another row.

"Look, a seven of clubs followed by the ace of hearts. You're not sure about something. Nine of spades, jack of clubs ... Hmm, this could be good or it could be bad."

Corrie immediately broke up the rows of cards. "Time to stop, Auntie Lien. I don't like to hear anything bad, only good things. So that's it for today, I don't want to look at any more cards. They lie anyway. Once they said there was a man hoping for my favors but so far no one has come to my house, begging for me on knees."

Auntie Lien puffed on the stub of her cigarette, put it out, and then lit another one. She looked slyly at Corrie. "Well, young lady, if that's what you really want, maybe I..."

Corrie cut her off. "What are you suggesting? I am a married woman and I don't want to hear anything of that sort." Glancing at the woman's bag, she changed the subject. "Now, what else did you bring for me to look at today?"

"Oh, I almost forgot to show you," the woman declared. "I thought you didn't like to buy things."

"Well, I've changed my mind," Corrie told her. "Now I want to wear nice things; the money is no problem."

Truthfully, Corrie had very little interest in jewellery but a feud with her next-door neighbor had changed her mind. It was a silent feud, for neither woman had exchanged a word with the other, but it was hostile all the same. Corrie's neighbor's husband was also a clerk in a government office, just like Hanafi, but from the day Corrie had moved into her house, the woman had given her nothing but dirty looks.

The woman seemed to be forever being trying to outdo Corrie. When, for instance, the kitchenware vendor came to Corrie's house and the two of them could not agree on the price of an item, even after haggling, the neighbor called him to her house and proceeded to buy the merchandise at whatever price he asked. If Corrie bought a kilogram of beef, her neighbor would buy two. Whatever it was that Corrie bought, the woman would buy the same but more and always at a higher price.

To make matters worse, the woman gossiped tirelessly about Corrie and Auntie Lien. Auntie Lien, she thought, was a procurer and only a woman of questionable honor would so frequently invite her into her house. Although such remarks infuriated Corrie, she felt that it was below her to answer these accusations, which came to her through Mina, who had in turn heard it from the neighbor's cook. Meanwhile, as Corrie herself could see, her neighbor had problems of her own. Almost every day, the grounds outside the woman's home would fill with vendors—sellers of house wares, firewood, meat and so on—who would wait there to be paid. Usually all they received was yet another promise for payment "tomorrow." It would have been very difficult indeed to keep these kinds of people from spreading tales about the state of the woman's finances.

The neighbor's cook then informed Mina that her employer was having to send her to the pawnshop almost every week to pawn furniture and other household wares. As the pawn slips she held grew ever higher in number so did their redemption value which increased at a monthly rate.

Obviously, with all this information, Corrie could have easily retaliated against the woman's poisonous words if that were her proclivity. But she did not like to gossip. She decided that she would seek vengeance through much more subtle means. Aware that the source of her neighbor's animosity was envy, Corrie hatched a plan that would reveal the woman's true nature. She would start to wear golden jewellery and gems; she knew that the neighbor would be hard-pressed to follow her lead. Because Corrie had quite a bit of savings, she was able to buy as much jewellery as she wanted.

Auntie Lien pulled out a large pair of diamond earrings, which flashed the sunlight. "These are one and a half carats each," she said.

"But they're so big," Corrie remarked. "Wouldn't they be too heavy to wear?"

"Heavy? Compare them with the weight of your hat and you'll see which one is heavier."

Corrie looked at the gems more closely. "It's too bad they have a yellow tint."

"If they were pure blue, like the ocean or the sky, they'd cost you three or four thousand at least. It's because of their yellow tint they're only six hundred."

"You think they suit me?"

"The Dutch say pearls bring tears. Take off the ones you're wearing and try these on." Auntie Lien motioned with her hand as she lit yet another cigarette. "Go ahead, try 'em on and take a look in the mirror."

Corrie took off her earrings and put on the ones Auntie Lien had brought. She shook her head from side to side, and laughed.

"They're not too heavy. Except that I don't normally wear this kind of earring. You don't think it's too much of a change?"

"Take a look for yourself, the mirror doesn't lie."

Corrie went back to the mirror, smiling rather sheepishly as she shook her head. "Are you sure they suit me?"

"Anything you wear would suit you, young lady. The way those look on you, they look like they're worth thousands."

"Come back tomorrow. I will wear these for a day. If I like them, I'll buy them tomorrow. How's that?"

"Very good, Miss, I'm sure you'll like them. They're the real thing. And the price is just five hundred."

"I thought you said six hundred?"

"Oh, did I? I meant to say a little under six hundred. I guess I'm getting old and a little senile."

Corrie looked at the clock. It was a quarter past two. "My husband will be home soon," she told Auntie Lien. "You have to leave before he arrives." She then called Mina and told her to set the table. As she spoke, she pressed two one-*ringgit* notes into Auntie Lien's hand. "Here's some money for the buggy," she whispered.

No sooner had Auntie Lien left when Hanafi came into the house through the back door. Of late he had been coming home with a cloudy expression on his face. Corrie was used to that and had stopped asking him why. Today, however, his face was red with anger, and he did not utter a word until he had taken a seat at the table.

"Unless my eyes deceived me, that old woman who just left was Auntie Lien."

"No, your eyes didn't deceive you."

He looked at Corrie sternly. "What was she doing here?"

"Nothing. She comes occasionally just to pass the time."

"So, she comes here often."

"Once a week."

Hanafi's eyes bulged with anger. "So, my wife is now a good friend of Auntie Lien? Do you know what she does? She is a pimp!"

"I don't know what she does outside of this house but in this house, at least, she has never comported herself that way. I can tell you that much."

Hanafi raised his voice. "I'm warning you, Corrie. If you play with fire, you're going to get burned; if you play with water you're going to get wet. I don't want that woman in this house."

"She comes here when you're at the office. You don't even have to see her."

"It doesn't matter. I have the right to decide who can and cannot come into my house."

"Our house."

Hanafi shot up from his chair, and went to the drawing room, pacing up and down as he tried to think of what to say. Then, when his eyes caught sight of the cigarette butts in the ashtray, he nearly had a shock. He turned to look toward Corrie but before he could say a word, he noticed the new diamond studs in her ears. How had she acquired them? His mind reeled with the thought.

"Corrie," he said with a trembling voice, "I have seen your savings book and know how much money you have in the bank.

You could not have paid hundreds of rupiah for such expensive jewellery, not with your own savings, that is. Have you had any other visitors in this house?"

Corrie was about to swallow a spoonful of rice but when she heard what Hanafi had said, when she realized the meaning of his accusation, her throat suddenly closed. She took two or three gulps of water and, after calming herself, wiped her mouth with a napkin. Involuntarily she bit the edge of the napkin with her clenched teeth. "What did you say?" she asked with a quaver in her voice.

"I'm saying that you have been up to something, something vile, here, in my own house," he shouted while standing before her. "Don't try to deny it; there's enough proof."

"Just what are you accusing me of doing?"

"I am accusing you of adultery."

Corrie stood up. "Take that back!" she demanded. "If you want to talk to me in a civilized way, you will take back your accusation. Otherwise it's impossible." She threw up her arms. "You're so arrogant, and so deceived! You're behaving like a judge who has made up his mind before the trial."

"Then you'll excuse me for pronouncing my verdict prematurely," he told her, "but I do have eyes and ears. I don't need to question the accused; I'll find the evidence soon enough. If it pleases you, very well, I'll retract my accusation for now, but you are still under suspicion."

Without saying another word, Hanafi walked into the bedroom and did not come out again for the rest of the day. In the living room, Corrie tossed herself onto the sofa and wept inconsolably.

That night, Corrie remained in the living room, laying awake all night. As her tears dried, her pain turned into anger. What was wrong with Hanafi? How could he not look at the facts? How could he level such an accusation against her? If he was going to be that way, she decided, she would adopt an equally uncompromising stance. If he wasn't willing to ask her for an explanation, she was determined that she would not offer him one. And if by the following day he had not asked her for an explanation, she resolved that she would rather divorce him than remain remarried to a man like that.

In the morning, Hanafi greeted her with nothing but his knitted brow. When he left for the office, they still had not spoken.

As she sat alone, Corrie realized that she herself had had reservations about Auntie Lien. She had heard things from her neighbors, and now her own husband said the same thing. Maybe there was some truth in the rumors about Auntie Lien. If her husband had warned her in a respectful manner, she would have surely stopped seeing that old woman at once. But now that he had behaved so arrogantly, she intended to keep seeing Auntie Lien just to spite him.

At around ten o'clock that morning, the older woman came to the house and Corrie politely showed her in. Once they sat down, Corrie returned the ear studs, saying that she did not think them appropriate for a married woman. She did not say that her husband thought they were the gift of a wealthy gentlemen caller, because of which the very sight of them now repulsed her.

Auntie Lien asked drew a draught of smoke from a cigarette. "Why don't you like them?"

"I just don't feel like them, Auntie. And the price is too high."

"Well, the price is no problem. Let me tell you the whole story. Actually, these earrings aren't the kind of stuff I usually sell. They're from Baba Cie, a rich landowner from Tangerang who wanted me to sell them for him. But if you would like to receive them, as a gift…."

Corrie was perplexed. "Who is Baba Cie? And what kind of gift are you talking about?"

Auntie Lien tittered. "Oh, my, you're still so young, you don't know the pleasure worlds of Batavia. Baba Cie is a young man, a Dutch-school graduate. His father is a captain, one of the heads of the Chinese community, and even though he's still alive, he has already giving his son a piece of property, the money from which Baba Cie can use however he wishes, even for just having fun. Those earrings mean nothing to him, young lady. And you know, if you made him happy, you could ask him for most anything and he would give it to you."

"Auntie Lien!" Corrie stood up. "For three months, you have come in and out of this house and I have treated you as a guest. I have let you do as you please but don't ever think, even for a second, that I will allow you to insult me in this way. I don't want to start a row. Let's just say that I feel you have humiliated me, and I don't want you to come anymore. I can't tell you how my husband would react if he were to learn of this."

"No need to get angry," Auntie Lien replied. "If you don't want to do it, you don't have to; there's no need to get angry."

Corrie's voice grew insistent. "Please go home now, and don't come back again. You can skip this house the next time you pass by."

Corrie then walked into the dining room without showing Auntie Lien to the door. Now was the time, she thought, for her husband to be there to defend her honor, not to accuse of her of something she hadn't done.

At that very moment, Hanafi stormed into the house, through the back door. His eyes immediately fell on the ashtray with the fresh cigarette butts in it.

His eyes shot angrily about the room. "So, am I am too late for the show?" he asked his wife. He pulled a pistol from his jacket and slammed it on the dining table. He then grabbed Corrie who struggled to free himself from his arms.

"You coward," she shouted at him. "What are you going to do to a defenseless woman?"

"Nothing yet. I want to catch you red-handed first. Then you'll see what I'm capable of doing."

"So you are still accusing me?"

"More than accusing!"

"Very well, if that's the case, prepare your evidence and your witnesses for the judge, so we can be divorced by the court of law. And let's make it quick. Because I don't want to live with you for even another minute!"

Corrie stormed into the bedroom and started packing her suitcase.

"Before you go, tell me his name," Hanafi said as he followed her. "So I can settle things with him man to man."

Corrie might have used that opportunity to explain the real situation but she was so enraged that all she could think of was leaving.

"You're such a clever man," she said. "I'm sure you can find that out by yourself."

Hanafi suddenly looked defeated. He was now convinced that his suspicion was true. "So this is what's become of us," he said half sighing. "And this is the woman for whom I have sacrificed everything."

"So now you regret taking me for your wife. Oh, my heart bleeds for you."

"Well it damn well should. I've given up everything for you: banished myself from my own upbringing."

"'Banished yourself', you say! In case you hadn't noticed before, I'm the European who married a Malay. And look at me now! My looks and my money are gone. My own people look at me as if I was a pile of dung. That is what I call banishment. Yet you still think you're the one who has suffered the greater loss."

Hanafi found himself unable to do anything but look on as Corrie arranged her things into the suitcase.

"Banished himself, banished himself," she muttered, as if to herself. "After I accepted him as one of my own people!"

"But what's the use of my European status?" Hanafi asked. "My own people now shun me; Europeans are disgusted at the sight of me. And we're not just talking about upper-class Europeans," he complained, "even the lower-class ones, the ones out in the country, won't associate with me."

"But that's your own fault. They were happy to welcome you before, even the upper class."

"Oh, forget it," he barked. "I have to get back to the office. I didn't ask permission to leave. If you want to talk about it, we can talk about it this evening."

Hanafi then left the house without saying another word. Corrie continued packing. When she finished, she had three large suitcases. She then sent Mina to look for a taxi, while she wrote a note to Hanafi.

Han,

> *This is our punishment for choosing the wrong path, for betraying our parents, and not heeding their wisdom. Regardless of what has happened or is yet to happen, don't place any hope that we can ever live under one roof again. The gap between us is as wide as that between earth and sky.*
>
> *I ask that you don't come to visit me in my hotel, or wherever I may stay.*
>
> *I will neither claim nor expect to receive even a single cent from your salary. I repeat, not a single cent. But if you wish, you can return to me the money that I spent on the furniture and other household items. Please deposit it in my account at the Spaarbank.*
>
> *We are divorced as of now—for life. If you feel it necessary to bring the matter before a judge. you can make the arrangement. As for me, I don't see the need for that. I no longer wish to be your wife. And that's that.*

Corrie signed her full name, "Corrie du Bussé," and then placed the note on the dinner table. When Mina returned shortly after, she found her mistress sobbing. Corrie told her that she could work for her if she did not want to stay with Hanafi. And then she left.

But as she turned to look at her house one last time from the taxi, she cried. It was true that she could not recall one happy moment in the two years she had lived there, but all the same, her heart was there. It was her first house as a married woman. It was where she had left her girlhood behind. And it was there that she had begun walking down life's path which, for her, had turned into a trail laced with land mines and thorns. As she emerged from the side street, she felt she was now on the road to a new life. But where should she go?

18

Living a New Life

When Corrie left her home she had no idea of where she would go. She didn't want to stay in a large hotel where there were lots of guests, but she did not know where else to go. Therefore, when the taxi driver asked her, "Where to, Ma'am?" she answered him hesitantly: "Let's just drive around for a while." By driving around the city, she hoped that she would come across a place she liked. About one hour later, it so happened, in the Tanah Nyonya area of town, a sign hanging outside a large house caught her eyes: "Homestay for Women."

She ordered the taxi driver to stop and, after making enquiries with the manager, an elderly woman, she was shown a modest suite at the back of the house: a bedroom and an attached sitting room. "This is it," Corrie thought, "this is where I'm going to stay."

From her first day at the homestay, Corrie knew she would not make many friends. The few frail, older women gave her the impression that she was merely a newcomer who had yet to pass their scrutiny. From the two younger boarders, both working women, she got the impression that her presence in the homestay had been forced on them. They had to accept her whether they wanted to or not.

Corrie did not mind this situation. Given her uncertain future, she actually preferred to be alone. Eager to immerse herself in work, she started looking for a job immediately after she was settled.

Three days later Corrie found a job at a bank. On her first day at work, however, she had hardly sat down at her desk when the woman next to her spoke to her without introducing herself: "So, Mrs. Han, who would've thought we would meet here? What a coincidence!"

Corrie looked at her, puzzled. "Pardon me, but..." she began.

"Oh, of course you don't know me. I know you from Mrs. Jansen, your next-door neighbor on Ketapang. But then, I suppose, you and Mrs. Jansen don't visit much."

The sound of her neighbor's name stabbed Corrie like a dagger. She knew right then that she would not work there for long.

"Oh, yes," the woman continued, "Mrs. Jansen never stopped telling me how sorry she felt for you. But it's true, unfortunately, that any woman Auntie Lien takes to visiting must eventually fall."

Corrie considered what the woman meant by "fall." Although the tone of her voice was sympathetic, there was nevertheless an insinuation that Corrie had somehow fallen into Auntie Lien's clutches. That came as another blow for her. And yet she realized that if her own husband was so quick to accuse her of adultery, how could she not expect others to do the same, especially Mrs. Jansen, a woman who despised her?

Suddenly, her anger at Hanafi flared up. Not only did he fail to defend her honor when it was under attack, in her mind he also was responsible—that accursed husband of hers—for everyone else's presumption about her supposed "fall."

Her lips trembled. But what could she say? The more she tried to explain, the worse things would look. She had no choice but to keep quiet. And so she cast down her eyes as she arranged the papers on her desk.

For three more days, she endured the woman's condescension. Her rapport with the other office mates was not particularly amiable either.

On the fourth day, she was called into the director's office. The director had a cloudy expression, and without any preamble asked her to sit down. "This is not easy for me to say," he began, "but it needs to be said. There's a lot of talk about you and your life, which is said to be less than reputable. Personally, it is of no concern to me, one way or another; I was young once, too. But I have to answer to the board of the bank, which is made up of people who may have different opinions regarding the matter. In short, if the rumors are true, there is no place for you in this office. If they are not, then you must be prepared to answer some questions from the board."

Corrie sat as motionless as a statue, overcome by the humiliation. But then her dejection turned to anger. It infuriated her that other people should have the right to pry open her private life. She was convinced it was all Mrs. Jansen's doing.

She wiped her tears and then lifted her head to meet the director's gaze. "Sir," her voice was shaky, "under no circumstances will I grant anyone, except a judge, the right to pry into my personal affairs, much less my problems, which are hard enough to bear as they are. It should satisfy you and the bank's board to hear me say once and for all that I am innocent. I will not say another word regarding the matter. And regardless of whether or not you believe me, I don't think I can work here any longer." Corrie then stood up to say goodbye.

"Wait a minute, please." said the director. "I want you to know that I believe in your innocence, wholeheartedly. I am not blind. The slander came from an anonymous letter that was posted to the chairman of the board. So if you will just be patient and give me time to defend you, I'll fight for your position here."

"Thank you, sir, for believing me. I will never forget your kindness but I still don't think I can work here."

"I understand it would be difficult, but try to reconsider. It's not easy finding a job nowadays."

"I know that but I also believe that for someone who doesn't mind hard work, there will always be a job somewhere."

"So, are you sure you want to resign?"

"Yes. In fact, I knew that I would have to from the very first day."

"In that case, take fifteen rupiah from the cashier, five rupiah per day for three days' work."

"You're very kind, sir, but I don't think I can accept that, as I wasn't hired as a day laborer."

The director extended his hand. "I'm sure you will find a living somewhere; the kind of determination you show always opens up doors. But for now—what can I say?—this world is a vile place. Best of luck to you, and if you want to, you can mention my name wherever you are applying for a position. Who knows, it might help."

The director's kindness lifted her heavy heart.

"Thank you again, sir," she smiled. "I won't refuse a helping hand in this difficult time."

From the director's office she returned to her desk to finish up her work, and then went straight home. Once she got to her room, she searched the "help wanted" section of the newspaper. One agency in Kali Besar had an opening for a business secretary who was fluent in foreign languages. And although she had never written business correspondence in a foreign language, she was fluent in several. So she went to the agency and was soon sitting opposite the office manager. He was a young and friendly fellow, so friendly in fact that it made her uncomfortable.

"Don't you find it hot here in the East, and doubly so in Kali Besar?" he asked. He smiled at her as he splashed some eau de cologne onto his handkerchief. "Oh pardon me, please, how could I be so rude? Would you like some eau de cologne?"

"No, thank you," said Corrie.

"Ah, yes, about the salary. It really depends on your skill. I mean, good secretaries who are fluent in foreign languages…. Well, you can't just pick them off the street. So if we find a good one, we'd be glad to pay her in gold. But we'll talk about this later."

He then gave Corrie some letters that needed replies. Almost all were the same and there were even examples to use as references. She was soon absorbed in her new task. Before long, the clock struck one, and to her surprise, all three clerks in the office rose from their desks, and as though on cue, walked out the door.

"Human beings also need to feed their souls," the smiley boss walked in, "we must be careful not to starve ourselves." He put on his jacket in front of a mirror and, still peering into the mirror, combed his hair and moustache with a small comb he kept in his pocket. "Here I go," he smiled as he looked from side to side. He then walked over to Corrie's desk as he wiped his face with the cologne-soaked handkerchief.

"Come on," he said, "it's time for lunch. There's a guesthouse nearby that serves food." And before she could say a word, he reached for her fingers on the typewriter. "Look at these delicate fingers, I think they should be used only for pleasure, not for crass things like making a living,"

Corrie snatched back her hand. She pushed back her chair, and stared at him squarely in the eye.

"Sir!"

"Oh, don't get angry with me, I'm not a bad person. It's just that, we're both young; you don't have a husband, and I don't have a wife. We live here on this earth for such a short time: no more than, say, seventy years at the most. So, why not enjoy ourselves? Come to the guesthouse and share a meal with me. If you want to, we can go out every afternoon and evening, and Batavia will open its doors of delight to us."

Once again he reached for Corrie's hand. Corrie shot up from her chair and glared at him in disbelief. But he simply stood tall, and smiled.

How could this man act so forward, with a Dutch woman, Corrie asked herself. She was angry but also puzzled. Maybe he knew what had happened with her husband. Might he have heard the false accusations as well? Maybe he had, and consequently thought that she was a woman of loose virtue. Or maybe he thought that all women who looked for a job actually wanted to sell themselves. Then again, maybe that was just the way he acted with women.

Without saying a word she strode toward the door and grabbed her hat from the coat rack. "Whatever happened may very well have been my fault, sir," Corrie said as she walked out. "But I can tell you one thing and that is I am not the woman you had in mind, and this is not the job I had in mind. Good day!"

She then left without giving him a chance to apologize.

As soon as she had returned to the boarding house, Corrie threw herself on her bed and wept bitterly. Not long afterward, however, she heard a knock on the door. She thought it was the maid, and casually told her to come in. But it was the manager. With a start, she sat up and straightened herself.

"Don't worry," the elderly woman said gently, "you can think of me as your own mother. If my daughter were still alive, she would be about your age. And I think she would look like you, too." She sat down next to Corrie and wiped her tears. "You have been here for only four days—but I know your story. First, let me just say that I never believed it. And secondly, even if it was true, it's none of my business, as long as nothing of that sort takes place in my house. Now you have to believe that God will not allow the innocent to be accused for long. Just this morning, your husband came. He told me everything. And although he had just met me then, he was crying like a little child. In short, your husband is now convinced of your innocence. He admitted that he was wrong."

Corrie searched the old woman's eyes, and saw nothing but kindness. "But what can I say," she said sadly, "the rice has turned into porridge; there's no going back to the way it was. My husband is rash; he says and does things that he later regrets. And now, because he has accused me of such a despicable act, and with such a loud voice that everyone heard him, my name is tarnished.

"As a woman you know that honor is like a porcelain vase and that once broken it can never be mended. He may admit that I have done no wrong, but what about the others? Ninety out of a hundred people will remain convinced of my guilt. What am I to do? Go around holding up a banner that says, "I am not guilty'?"

"You may be right, my dear," the manager averred. "But you can't always worry about what people think. The world is cruel, but God has shown His mercy. For one, he has given back your husband."

"But what other people say affects me, in body and in mind, even when I don't want it to. Just imagine, in the last four days I've had two jobs, and I had to leave both because of this incident. I think the whole of Batavia has made up its mind that I am a loose woman. Everyone feels they can treat me with contempt. So how can I not help but feel filthy?

"And it was my very own husband who is the source of that filthy rumor! Even if he now admits to being wrong, it's too late. The filth will not come off so easily. Please don't tell me to go back to him. If you want to help me, show me another way. I want to get out of Batavia. I want go somewhere, it doesn't matter where, as long as I can have some peace and quiet."

For a moment the manager fell silent. Had it been her decision, she would reunite the young couple immediately, but now she realized that that was impossible. She understood how Corrie could feel no love for Hanafi at the present.

Corrie's mention of leaving Batavia brought to her mind a possible solution. "Listen to me carefully, my dear. I understand how angry you are at your husband. It was God who separated you, and it will be God who brings you back together. All of our efforts will come to nothing if they are not God's will. So listen, I have an older relative who is much like myself, unmarried and without children. She runs an orphanage in Semarang, and has been looking for a helper for a long time. The subsidy she gets from the government is large enough to permit her to hire one, but she is choosy and no one ever seems good enough.

"The only person that seems to qualify is me, but I can't leave this city, because this is where my daughter and her father are buried. But you... You are young and I have known you for only four days, but from what I've seen—and I hope my eyes didn't deceive me—I think you're different from most young people nowadays. So if I can make the arrangements, would you like to go to Semarang?"

Corrie clasped her hands together. "Oh yes, very much. That's exactly what I want: to be far from Batavia, and living with an older woman in whom I could find a mother. The salary is of no concern; room and board is all I need. I don't need many clothes, and I still have some money in the bank."

"When could you leave?" the manager inquired.

"First thing in the morning." Corrie answered quickly, unaware that her answer might have been prompted by her desire to avoid seeing Hanafi.

The older woman sensed that this was the case but she knew that if the young woman and her husband were to be reunited, it would be better that some time passed first to allow tempers to cool.

"Very well," she said, "I will give you a letter to take with you. I am sure my relative will like you."

The manager then spent much of the evening composing a long letter, telling her relative as much as she knew of Corrie's story, from beginning to end. The next morning she took Corrie to the station. After the train left, she sent a telegram, informing her relative of Corrie's arrival.

Hanafi came to the homestay early the following morning. When he heard that Corrie had left, he was frantic to go after her and it took the old woman nearly an hour to dissuade him from going. She explained that going after his wife now would only drive her further away. His best chance for their reunion, she said, was to leave everything in his wife's hands. She then promised him that she would keep in touch with Corrie. Through her letters, she would remind her of what was right, until the coldness in her heart melted. And when that happened, she assured Hanafi, he would surely hear from her.

Realizing the truth of the woman's advice, Hanafi consigned his fate to her hands.

19

Daughter-in-Law, Mother-in-Law

The glow of dawn had spread over the eastern sky, beckoning the approaching sunrise. Birds were flitting about, chirping and whistling; the hens had come out of their coop and now the rooster was chasing them around the grounds of the house. Her world was a beautiful place, Rapiah had to admit, yet she remained unmoved by its serenity. For almost an hour she had been sitting alone by her bedroom window, her eyes gazing toward the golden, shimmering light on the Bukit Barisan mountain range.

From time to time, she turned to check on her son. His face was so tranquil, and she knew by the even rhythm of his breath that he was soundly asleep. Thank God he doesn't know the storm that is raging in his mother's heart, she thought. Smiling sadly, she again directed her gaze toward the mountains.

The door separating her room from Hanafi's mother's suddenly opened. "You didn't sleep all night, Rapiah," said her mother-in-law. "And you have been sitting here since dawn. This cold wind is not good for you, or for your son."

"I didn't sleep because Syafei was restless. But you must not have slept either, otherwise you wouldn't have known."

"We old folks don't sleep much, that's normal. But I think it was you I heard tossing and turning, not Syafei."

"I try to keep my faith strong, Mother, but sometimes the devil creeps into our hearts and makes us...." Rapiah was silent for a moment. "I mean, it's been three years since he left. No news, no word, nothing. You would think that at least for the sake of his son.... His son deserves to know."

Hanafi's mother sat down beside her, and sighed. "Dear Piah, don't mourn for what has been lost. It is sad for me to say this but if you think about it we are better off without him. When he was here, with us, he was constantly always venting his anger on us. For myself, now that you and Syafei have come with me, I feel that I have found someone to take his place. Now I think you should also think about finding a replacement for him."

Rapiah stared at her mother-in-law. "Please don't say another word about that. My heart won't let me think such a thought, not even for one moment. And besides, who would want a woman like me, who already has a child?"

"Tuanku Demang for one," she suggested. "He has written to your father about it but your father has left the decision to me."

Rapiah burst out in laughter. "Are you serious?"

"Why do you laugh?" her mother-in-law asked.

"I don't know. I just pictured Tuanku Demang with his head of white hair, his gold teeth, and his cane. I should really call him 'grandfather' because his grandson, Datuk Sinarto, is older than I am." She laughed again. "Oh yes, I think he would make a perfect replacement for Hanafi!"

"According to our customs, Piah, such a marriage is not unusual. He may be old, and his grandchildren fill half the village, but he is high-born, which means that he can have any girl he wants."

"What about you then? You have been a widow for fifteen years. Why don't you take him? I wouldn't mind having Tuanku Demang as a father."

Hanafi's mother surprised herself when she, too, suddenly burst out laughing. She laughed so hard that there were tears in her eyes.

"You are too much, Piah. You know I am too old. Tuanku Demang doesn't want someone like me."

"Your hair is still black, you still have all your teeth, and people don't have to yell when they speak to you, as they do with Tuanku Demang. People have to yell so loud when they speak to him that they scare the chickens. But you, if you combed your hair and put on some make-up, you would be, relatively speaking, a young woman."

"Enough said about that, Piah; no more jesting. I don't need a husband because my only child is grown up and is able take care of himself. I'm thinking about you. It's you who needs a husband."

Rapiah placed her right index finger against the index finger of her left hand, as if to count. "First of all...," she said, but before she could continue, her mother-in-law interrupted. "First of all, I am worried about your son. And rather than marrying a young man, who will only break your heart sooner or later, it's better to take a more mature husband who will support you and your son."

"If you are tired of taking care of Syafei and me," Rapiah said to the older woman, "you can let us go back to Bonjol."

The old woman was taken aback by Rapiah's reaction and rushed to defend herself: "Don't get me wrong, Rapiah. Give me the chance to tell you what's really in my heart. What I really wish is that you and Hanafi could always be with me, forever. But Hanafi has left. That's God's will and I accept it. So all I have left is you and Syafei, from whom I never want to be apart."

"So why do you want me to remarry? You know that if I remarry, my husband will take us away from you."

"But I can't think only of myself, Rapiah. You're still young and it's not good for you to be a without a husband. That's my second point. The situation brings shame on you and it brings shame to your house. People will say that you are unwanted. And although in our tradition, it's your maternal uncles' responsibility to find you a husband and not my own, I know that your relatives in Bonjol will say something to me if you don't remarry soon."

Rapiah looked at her mother-in-law sympathetically. "Now I know why you keep bringing this up. Well, if my uncles talk to you, tell them that it's *my* wish not to remarry. If they want to talk to me, I'm ready to answer them. And besides, is it really that shameful for a woman to be without a husband for a long time, or even for the rest of her life?"

"Of course it is, Rapiah! People will say nobody wants her."

"But you yourself have been a widow for fifteen years. When Hanafi's father died, you must have been a young woman. Why was it not bad for you?"

As she had no ready answer for the question, Hanafi's mother smiled. "You are very clever, Piah. I don't think I stand a chance arguing with you. But tell me, seriously, are you still waiting for Hanafi?"

"What would be the use, Mother? Isn't he living happily with his European wife, free from the shackles of the old world, and from me? But even if I'm not waiting for him, I have no thoughts of taking another husband."

"As your elder, Piah, I feel obliged to find you a husband. But—I might as well tell you—it's your father who is bent on having you remarried. He told me that he would rather see you become a second wife to a government soldier than to see you get back with Hanafi."

"But Hanafi is his own nephew."

"...And is supposed to inherit his estate. As you know, in Minangkabau, Hanafi is considered to be more closely related to him than you are, his own daughter. Even so, he is determined to cut off all ties with Hanafi since he divorced you."

"Do you agree with him?"

"That's difficult for me to answer. How can one disown one's flesh and blood?" Hanafi's mother asked. "And yet, judging from his past actions, I also feel unsure about accepting Hanafi back as your husband."

"What if I wanted to take him back?"

"I would support you, whatever your choice is. But your father would not approve. And to go against one's mother or father is a sin that would be very difficult to bear, either here on earth or in the afterlife."

"But I am sure my father would change his mind eventually."

"Let's hope so, Piah. I pray that when the time comes for you and Hanafi to meet again, God the Almighty will have touched his heart and relieved him of his bitterness. But it worries me to harbor such a hope, because I'm sure that it is of no use. Your father is a proud man and will not take back what he has once thrown out. Before Hanafi married you, he saw how Hanafi constantly belittled our religion and our culture. It broke his heart, and he did not want to accept him as his son-in-law. To change his mind, I promised him that I would, with you, do everything I could to correct his ways. But alas, instead of getting better, Hanafi became worse, even going so far as abandoning his own wife and child.

"How could I possibly persuade your father to take Hanafi back now? It's like I just told you, Piah, he wants to marry you off as quickly as possible, as revenge. And if you don't find someone soon, he might think that it's my doing, that I'm protecting my son from his revenge. It puts me in a difficult position."

"It's difficult only because I haven't spoken to him," Rapiah advised. "But I will. Before I came of age, it was right for my father to make decisions on my behalf, to make me do things that seemed right in his eyes. But now that I'm a mother, I think he should consult me first."

Hanafi's mother was impressed with Rapiah's determination; she was no longer the child she once had been. "But aren't you afraid of going against your father's wishes?" she asked.

"I would never willingly betray my parents," Rapiah answered. "But I don't think my father will force me to make that choice. He is an educated man and he supported me wholeheartedly when I went to school. All I want is to speak to him. I don't want to rebel or to bring shame on him or our family. But I can not believe that he would be willing to sacrifice his daughter just for the sake of revenge. That's why I want to speak to him and to my uncles." She took Hanafi's mother's hand. "Please don't worry. I will not suggest that my decision is due to your influence."

"I'm glad to hear that your heart is strong. As Hanafi's mother, I can't help feeling happy when I hear that you have no desire to replace him. But what about your son?"

"Hanafi himself was very young when he lost his father, and he managed to get a good education without a stepfather."

In the depth of her heart, the old woman truly was relieved. No matter how Hanafi had behaved, she still hoped and waited for his return. Hanafi, Rapiah, and Syafei... The three of them were her family and she could find no joy if one of them was separated from her. She believed completely that the four of them must always be together, in joy and sorrow. When the time came for her to leave this world, it was to these three people she wanted to express her final farewell.

Little did she know that Hanafi and Corrie had already been divorced for almost a year. Koto Anau was a small place; people tended to stay close to home and visits by outsiders were rare. All of Hanafi's relatives, the ones in Koto Anau as well as the ones in Bonjol, imagined that he was still living happily in the glitter of the big city with the woman of his dreams.

When Syafei awoke he immediately climbed down from his bed and ran to find his mother. Although he was not yet five, the little boy could sense his mother's emotions. Knowing that she was sad, he leaned his head against her side as if to melt away her pain. But far from being consoled, the boy's love only seemed to deepen his mother's sorrow. Rapiah forced a smile and ran her hand softly through his hair.

"When you get older, do you want to go to a Dutch school?" Rapiah asked.

"Of course," Syafei answered.

"What do you want to be when you grow up?" his grandmother then asked.

"A lieutenant!" the boy announced.

"But soldiers have to go to war," his mother told him.

"I know that, Mother. That way I can kill my enemies with my sword."

"Killing another person is not a good thing to do," Rapiah advised.

"What if it's your enemy?" the boy asked.

"But how do you know who the enemy is?" his mother asked in turn. "If you are a soldier and get sent to war, the people you have to kill might not be enemies; they might not even be people you know. Is it right to call people you don't know your enemies?"

Syafei thought for a moment. "Well the people in the country better not be against us then," he reasoned.

"What do you mean?" his mother asked. "Who are these 'country people' you speak of?"

"Malay people."

Rapiah frowned. "Well I'm Malay and your grandmother is Malay too."

"You're Malay?" Syafei thought about this for a moment. "Well, if that's the case, then you must be the queen of the Malays."

Hanafi's mother shook her head. Where had her grandson gotten such ideas, she wondered. She gave Rapiah a look of concern. "I don't know where he got them but your son seems to have some of his father's ideas planted in his mind. Before he goes to school," she told her, "you must teach him to pray. Even after he starts school, you mustn't neglect his religious instruction. I made a mistake with Hanafi by not giving him any religious instruction. So ever since he was small, he had set himself apart from his people. I just hope you don't make the same mistake."

Rapiah stroked her son's hair gently with both hands. "Just who do you mean by Malay people?" she asked again, this time with a playful voice.

"All those children with shabby clothes."

"Those people are just like us," she told him, "not a wee bit different. The only difference is that they don't go to school, so they don't dress the way we do."

"They're dirty and they don't wear shirts."

"They're dirty because they don't wash. Speaking of dirty, isn't it time for you to wash up? Go to the well," she ordered, "so you won't be like the dirty children."

Syafei quickly snatched his towel and soap and then sprinted off to the well.

His mother called after him: "Don't forget your toothbrush!"

Syafei immediately turned and ran back into his room.

"He's the spitting image of his father," Hanafi's mother commented as she followed the boy with her eyes. She then looked at Rapiah. "Be careful that you don't let him follow in his father's footsteps."

"A person's character can change, Mother, as long as he receives the proper guidance. If we bring up Syafei correctly, Allah willing, we'll be able to count on him in our old age."

"I hope so, Rapiah. You're so patient and faithful, I'm sure Allah will grant you your wish."

20

From Darkness to Light

After Corrie's sudden departure, Hanafi could not bear to stay at their house in Ketapang. After a nearly fruitless search, Hanafi finally found a place to live, at the home of a Dutch colleague. While his office mate welcomed him with open arms, the man's wife was not as sympathetic. Although she was never rude, it was obvious to Hanafi that she tolerated him only for the one hundred rupiah a month she received in rent. So it was that even after months of living there, he did not feel free to wander beyond the small terrace outside his bedroom. To get to the backyard or the bathroom, he would detour around the house, instead of going through it; he knew he was not welcome there except at dinnertime.

When the couple had company, they never invited Hanafi to join them and as he had no visitors of his own, he spent most every evening in his room, alone with his thoughts. He tried reading but no book could hold his interest for long. From his bed, he would stare longingly at his colleague and his wife, chatting under a tree in the backyard. On two or three occasions he had asked the houseboy to serve him his tea in the backyard, with his landlord and landlady, but when emerging from his room, fresh from an afternoon shower, he found the teapot and cup on the small table by his door. Without asking, he knew the houseboy was simply following his employers' instructions.

Other times, overcoming his reserve, he carried his cup to his friend's little table in the garden. "May I join you?" he smiled. "No matter how good the tea is, it's always better with company."

"Please, have a seat," his landlady said politely but on those occasions, as soon as he had sat down, the conversation stopped. His friend and his wife answered his questions with little more than a "yes" or a "no," or worse yet, with no more than a nod of the head. When his friend tried to restart the conversation, his eyes would dart nervously towards his wife, until, finally, he would be silent once more.

Hanafi realized he was putting his friend in a difficult position. And moreover, his own freedom was being curbed. Whenever he left the light on past eleven in order to read because he could not sleep, the next morning at breakfast, he would inevitably hear his landlady mention the rising cost of electricity. Going to the cinema was not a simple matter, either. If he went to the late show, he would hear her say something about the boarder next door, also a bachelor, who had no regard for his hosts' reputation, because he came in late every night. That, she insisted, would surely tarnish his hosts' good name. On the other hand, if he went to the early show, she would reproach him for being late for dinner, even after he had said he would not be eating dinner at home.

"Of course you can have your dinner wherever you want," she would say. "It's just that, someone who has accepted money to provide room and board doesn't feel appreciated when the boarder refuses to take what he has paid for. And to send dinner to your room is too much trouble for the houseboy. So I would appreciate it if you could come to dinner on time."

So just to see a film, Hanafi had to wait until Saturdays, the day that his landlord and landlady went out. He knew he had to move again. But where? He had asked several Dutch families, and none would take him. To board with a native family was out of the question. He was now Dutch. How could he be comfortable in a native household, where they did not even know the difference between a spoon and a fork?

The five o'clock whistle from a nearby factory blew. Hanafi was lying on his bed, contemplating his fate. Like ships on the ocean, images from his past floated before him: the house in Solok and its front yard, his mother sitting on the cot with her betel-nut case beside her. He could almost hear Rapiah's voice as she played with Syafei, who crawled about the kitchen.

"Oh God, I can't believe I miss them," he moaned. He wiped his eyes, cradling his head in his hands.

In his hometown, people had treated him like a king. Whatever he wanted he received, and whenever he gave an order, people hurried to obey. But here, he got in people's way no matter what he did. Wherever he went he saw only long faces, and whenever he opened his mouth, he was either ignored or misunderstood.

Then he thought of Corrie. Twice he had written her in the year since their divorce, and twice his letters had been returned, sealed just as he had sent them. Corrie's former landlady, whom he had come to view as a surrogate mother, told him that he needed to be patient, that the path to Corrie's heart was still blocked. Was there even a glimmer of hope that she would ever take him back, he wondered miserably.

He summoned Corrie's image to his mind. No other woman, he thought, had such feisty yet alluring charm. But alas, her heart had turned to stone. Then he thought of Rapiah. Did he love her? No, he could not love such a passive wife, who had been offered to him like a bowl of sweets on a platter. Only Corrie, with her high spirited manner, was able to capture his heart. In realizing this he also came to see that he had abused Rapiah's affection and, suddenly, he felt pity for that poor country girl.

He had wronged both Rapiah and Corrie. Would there ever be forgiveness for him? Rapiah had accepted everything with fortitude, though that did not mean she would readily accept his apology. And Corrie had rejected him outright.

And what about Syafei, the boy who legally was no longer his son since he obtained his European status? Who would the poor fellow take after, him or Rapiah?

There was a knock on the door. "It's half past five, sir," the houseboy called.

"Tell your master and mistress I have a headache. If I feel better, I'll join them for dinner at eight. If not, don't wait for me."

"Yes, sir," the boy answered and went away.

Hanafi remained on his bed, and did not turn on the light even after darkness fell. He missed his hometown. And although he knew he would never have the liberty he once had, he could not shake off the thought of going home.

There came another knock on the door. "The mistress wants to know if you would like dinner in your room," the houseboy asked through the door.

"No, thank you, Emod. Tell them I'm sorry I can't join them. I have a bad headache, and I'm not eating at all."

At about nine Hanafi's landlord knocked at his door, and then walked in before Hanafi could answer. He held out his hand. "Here, I brought you some aspirin." He turned on the light and poured a glass of water from the carafe above the wash basin. He then sat on Hanafi's bed and drew aside the mosquito net.

Hanafi sat up, took the tablet and for a moment looked into his friend's eyes. "Thank you, Piet. You're a real friend."

"I try, but please understand that I'm a married man."

"Don't worry, I understand. In a marriage, it's the woman who usually holds the upper hand. But, tell me, there is one thing I would like to know. What is it that I've done to your wife that makes her so upset?"

"As far as I can see, nothing," Piet answered.

"So why does she treat me as if she's holding a grudge against me?"

"I suppose, Han, it's because we human beings have little control over our feelings. Mr. A may not have done anything wrong against Mr. B, but somehow Mr. B hates Mr. A. If someone asks him why, he'll say, 'I don't know, I just can't stand him.' Our sympathy and antipathy often take hold of us for no reason whatsoever. All we can do is be understanding."

"But still, I don't think I've done anything wrong towards you or your wife, or anyone else for that matter."

"Maybe not my wife and I," Piet said, "but are you sure you didn't wrong anybody else."

"Who?" Hanafi asked.

"Well, I'm wont to interfere in other people's affairs."

"This is about me and my wife, isn't it?"

"I didn't want to bring it up," Piet told him, "because it's none of my business. But now that you've brought it up, let me tell you first of all that I'm neutral. But my wife, along with many people, thinks you have committed a wrong against your wife. That's the source of her grievance."

"But that's none of her business." Hanafi shouted, jumping to his feet.

"Calm down, Han. If my wife hears you, she'll be here in no time, and I'll be the one who gets in trouble. Sit down and have another glass of water. And then we can talk, if you want to."

Hanafi sat down by the wash basin and poured himself another glass of water. Quickly, he gulped it down, and then pulled out a pack of cigarettes. "So this is the way the world is, huh, Piet?" he said as he offered Piet a cigarette and lit one himself. "Your wife doesn't know Corrie; she's never met her. And she doesn't really know me, either. But when we, Corrie and I, had a fight and separated—which may not even be permanent—your wife suddenly has a score to settle with me. Is that just?"

"Of course not. But that's how things are. It's like those two Dutchmen who had a fight at Café Juliana in Senen. You heard about that: beer bottles being thrown, chairs being broken, and both of them ending up in the hospital. You know what started the fight? One was pro-English, the other pro-German. And probably, neither of them has any family or even knows anybody in England or Germany. Yet that's the way it is.

"But let's go back to you and your wife. When you married her, certain people felt offended. Don't ask me why; I don't know, and I don't care. And when you divorced her, they said you abandoned her."

"Can't get married, can't get divorced."

"What can I say, Han?"

"I've already heard what people have had to say—at least from the people who dislike me—and don't care to hear anymore. I want to know what you say, as a friend. I know you've said you're neutral, but surely you have an opinion when it comes to something like this."

Piet tapped the tip of his cigarette on the ashtray several times. "Before we start, remember that I may say things you won't find pleasing. And it's you who asked me to speak."

"Go on, Piet. I know a friend will not speak just to insult me."

"All right," Piet put out his cigarette. "We started this conversation because you wanted to know what you had done wrong to my wife to make her treat you with such disdain. The answer is, as I said before, nothing. What rouses her anger is not what you have done to her, but what you have done to your wife. My wife, like many people, believes you took advantage of her. Now I know no one, including my wife, who has the right to punish you for what you may or may not have done but that doesn't change the fact that I can do little to change their feelings.

"Feelings are feelings, no one knows what causes them. Why do dogs hate cats? And why does one person say bitter melon tastes awful, while another says it tastes wonderful on rice? I am a full-blood Dutch, but I love the natives; they have many characteristics

I admire. But there are also people, like my wife, for instance, who is half native, and yourself, a pure native, who look down on these people. Why is that, Han? It's feelings... Feelings are the source of everything. It's not our place to ask where they come from."

Hanafi nodded. "But still, I wish things could be different with your wife. Other people's opinions no longer concern me, but you and I work together; we have been friends for almost a year; and now I am boarding in your house, living under the same roof and eating at the same table. She has the opportunity to look at my circumstances objectively. So why should her opinion be the same as those who know nothing about me? Wouldn't it be better if your wife could look at all the facts before she pronounces judgment?"

"I doubt it would make a difference," Piet told him. "At best you might clear yourself of blame regarding your divorce, but not your marriage. My wife, along with many people, was upset by the fact you married Corrie. They said you must have lured her into your net."

"What are you talking about?" Hanafi cried. "'Lured her into my net? Corrie and I have known each other since we were children. When we got married she was twenty-one, and I had proposed to her openly and honorably, without any lure or net."

"Calm down, Han, I'm only telling you what others say. Remember, you're the one who wanted me to talk to you openly like this. Do you know how they paint your relationship with Corrie?" Piet paused for moment. "That as a Malay you are versed in the art of love, that you know all kinds of secret spells. They say that Corrie was an innocent white woman who knew nothing of men; that you befriended her, and with your black magic, won her trust, the unreserved trust of a younger sister to an older brother. You aroused her desire and after you got what you wanted... Well, they say that after you drank the nectar of the fruit, you threw out the pulp."

Hanafi shook his head. "How heartless," he muttered.

"There are, mind you, some who judge you more fairly."

"And what do they say?"

"They say that although you and your wife might have genuinely loved each other, you still should not have gotten married. And since you're the man, considered superior when it comes to rational thinking, the responsibility falls on you to see that. The Dutch say women are passive, men active. If the man doesn't want something to happen, it never will. So, even if the desire between a man and woman is mutual, it's the man who must control himself."

"Even so, I still don't understand why was it wrong for me to marry Corrie?"

"As far as I am concerned, there was no wrong, not as long as you truly intended to honor her as your wife. No, there's no taint of sin in that."

"It appears most of the world doesn't share your view," Hanafi said.

Piet lit a fresh cigarette and drew a few drags. "Listen, Han, don't think that people here don't know about your past life in West Sumatra. They know you left a wife and a child behind; that alone was enough to upset some people. And then there's the question of race. You yourself look down on the natives. How do you think my people see you?"

"Before you go on, let's clear up one thing," Hanafi remarked. "I don't look down on my own people. It's their customs that I'm at odds with, because I was brought up in European society. I may have been born a Malay, but my character, my world view, and my customs are more in line with those of your people, don't you agree? Moreover, I have obtained European status. What more do they want?"

"You're an intelligent man, Han, but when it comes to feelings, you seem to be both deaf and blind. I can't explain it entirely, but suffice it to say that in their minds you're still a native. The more you try to barge into their world, the harder they will slam the door in your face. In their opinion, it would have been more honorable for you to remain among your own people, and look up respectfully to the Europeans. If you did that, they would accept you as a highly-cultured native. But the way you approach them now, they despise that. Those are feelings we're talking about, Han, feelings that they themselves don't know the source of."

Hanafi thought for a moment. "And what about you, Piet? What are your feelings?"

Piet swallowed a few times as though to clear his throat. "To be honest, I blamed you too, not because of race—you know I don't care about that—but because I feel sorry for you and your wife. Let me just say something about your marriage... Your divorce is another story. Neither my people nor your people approved of your marriage, yet you ignored public opinion and went ahead with your plan. To show their disapproval, people shut you out of their social circles, even your work colleagues.

"The fact is, deep down, they actually liked you, yet none of them would show their support or visit you at your home. In the end, I think, divorce was inevitable, regardless of who was at fault.

"The bond between husband and wife is a fragile one, especially under such pressure. In your case, you were both ostracized. Every misfortune only added to your pain and lessened your faith in each other. And in your anger, you blamed each other because you had no one else.

"After a time, how could there be anything left in the marriage except bitter resentment? You came to love each other less and less and, before you know it, there was an unbridgeable abyss between you."

Piet paused for a moment to gauge Hanafi's reaction, but Hanafi remained motionless and without expression. "And now that you have divorced your wife, people's anger has turned to fury, especially on the part of the women. Your people have a saying, 'Men are one in shame, women are one in feeling.' United in their feelings, the women condemn you with one voice. They say you are a callous man who took advantage of two women just to satisfy your desires.

And that is why my wife feels she has the right to be involved. If she seems cold toward you, now you know why."

"Thank you, Piet," Hanafi said. "In fact, my mother once warned me of almost the same thing. But I had always thought of her as an ignorant country woman." Hanafi looked up and puffed on his cigarette. "The question is, what can I do now, after the catastrophe?"

"Only time will tell. Maybe realizing your fault is already halfway to making amends. Try to think of the future: maybe there are still ways to right the wrong, to dress the wound. As long as it can be healed, there's still hope for a new life, even if you have to bear the scar." Piet looked at his watch and stood up. "Well, it's getting late," he said. "If you want something to eat, I'll get the houseboy to bring your dinner."

"Thank you, Piet, but I think I'll try to get some sleep now. Maybe tomorrow, along with the sun, a new life will rise in me."

21

The Bonds of Love

Hanafi stayed awake all night, summoning to mind the people in his life. At last, he grasped the meaning of his mother's words, the words of an old country woman whom he once thought of as ignorant. How profound they seemed to him now. He understood that the education one gets from school is not enough to equip one for life, unless it is accompanied by wisdom.

For the first time, he realized the debt he owed his mother. It was a debt he could not repay even if he built her a palace. He remembered how she followed his wishes, and never once responded harshly, no matter how unreasonable his actions had been.

And then there was Rapiah. No one could deny she had a heart of gold. But she lacked the womanly wiles needed to ensnare a man like him. No, he could not love her, for one could never instil that magic feeling into one's heart. But as he thought of how he had wasted the poor woman's life, and regarded her as little more than a slave, a feeling of compassion overwhelmed him.

Finally, he thought of Corrie. No one had caused him greater pain. The words she spoke on the day of their separation still echoed in his mind. "Regret," she had said; she regretted having degraded herself by going off with a Malay. Wasn't that the lowest insult, so low that he should want to lay his hand on her? But he admitted that he was also to blame. Corrie's fault, he confessed, lay only in her reaction to his grave error. Oh, how he pined for her now. But what could he do? Two letters had been returned unread.

Their days of courtship, days when love swept him to the highest heaven, suddenly came back to him. But the memory only served to remind him of his mistake, a mistake that had ruined their marriage. Knowing Corrie's temperament, he should have treated her with patience. Then they could have made a happy home together. But instead, he took a stern approach, even treating her unjustly at times, directing his anger at her when he could no longer bear the rejection they both suffered. If only he could have kept his temper; perhaps then his marriage with Corrie would not have come to such a bad pass.

He had cast aside his first wife, thinking she was worthless, when in truth, she was an unpolished diamond. His second wife, on the other hand, was a priceless jewel, already well-polished. But again, in his blindness he let her slip from his hands.

He hid his face in his hands and sobbed inconsolably. "Oh, Corrie, look at me now. Come back, come back, so we can patch things up and live together as we did before."

Yes, he still loved her. She was his first love, and he had loved her since the days when they were still in their primary-school uniform. If she were in Batavia now, he would go find her at once. And he would not stop begging her to forgive him until she did, and took him back as her husband.

More than once, he turned on the light, and began writing her a letter. But he would tear it up before he finished, because he knew he could not express in words what he felt. And besides, he was afraid it might be sent back unopened.

Finally, he jumped out of bed and threw some clothes into his suitcase.

To Semarang! He was going to Semarang to find Corrie. And what if she did not take him back? Heaven knew! All he knew was that he could not go on living without her. It was half past three in the morning, a good time to get ready, he thought. After he finished packing, and readied himself, he then sat down and wrote a note to Piet. He told Piet, matter-of-factly, that he was going to Semarang to pick up his wife. He asked him to request a week's leave of absence at work on his behalf. And if the boss could not grant his request, he instructed Piet to tell the boss that he could deal with him as he liked. Without rereading it, he put the hastily written note in an envelope, addressed it, and left it on the small table in the front veranda.

At half past four, he left the house carrying his suitcase. After walking a little way, he found a taxi to take him to the station.

For almost the entire journey, he sat with his head against the headrest and his eyes shut. But even though he had not slept the previous night, and every part of his body was exhausted, no sleep would come to him. When he arrived in Semarang that evening, his head still felt dizzy. A taxi driver told him he knew where the orphanage was, and proceeded to take him there. When he entered the gate, he saw children at tables fighting over food. An elderly woman was running from table to table, trying to keep order.

Hanafi realized at once, that she must be the woman who took Corrie in. Her name was Mrs Van Dammen. She was the supervisor of the orphanage. When she saw Hanafi staggering toward her, she took a few steps back, placing a table between herself and the stranger. Without a greeting or introduction, he asked of Corrie's whereabouts.

"And who are you, sir?" the woman asked in a faltering voice.

Hanafi realized that in the half light of the evening and with his clothes dishevelled and blackened from the journey, he must have given the woman a fright. "Oh, forgive me," he said, trying his best to sound polite. "My name is Han. I would like to see my wife, Corrie."

"There is no Corrie Han here," she said, looking from the corner of her eyes towards the gate, in case she had to make her escape.

Mrs. Van Dammen appeared to still believe that he was some deranged vagrant. But that wasn't entirely surprising, he thought. He was pale as a ghost and he was having difficulty concentrating. His eyes were constantly shifting and his voice was shaky. He made a more concerted effort to calm his voice. "I have come from Batavia," he said slowly. "I know Mrs. Hansen, who runs the homestay for women in Tanah Nyonya. I've come directly from the station, and my luggage is still in the taxi."

The woman breathed a sigh and clasped her hands together. "Thanks be to God!" she said. "Forgive me, Mr. Han, I wasn't expecting you. My relative, Mrs. Hansen, sent no word of your coming, and lately there have been many vagrants breaking into people's houses. So I was frightened when I saw you. Oh, please, let's have a seat inside!"

She wiped her eyes with a handkerchief, and turned to the tallest boy among the children. "All right, Yan, you're in charge. Remember, if they make trouble, you're the one responsible. No punching or kicking like yesterday."

After glancing over the children, she took Hanafi's hand and led him inside. She asked him to sit down, and ever so gently began speaking. "It's God's mercy that brought you here. I hope you can meet with your wife."

"Where is Corrie?"

"In the hospital," she said and then paused as she breathed. "At four o'clock this afternoon, I wired my relative in Batavia telling her that Corrie, your wife, had fallen ill. It's very serious. And now, less than four hours later, here you are. It's God who called you here."

"Yes, perhaps it is, because no one told me to come. I didn't even see Mrs. Hansen; I just up and left. But you say that Corrie is ill. What's wrong? I can only pray that when she sees me she'll get better."

"I hope that your prayer—that our prayers—will be answered," said Mrs. Van Dammen gravely.

"What's wrong?"

"Corrie contracted cholera and was taken to Paderi hospital yesterday morning, by order of the authorities. I wanted her to stay here at home because I've come to think of her as my own daughter but they wouldn't let her because of the children. They won't even let me visit her at the hospital. At four o'clock this afternoon, I received some worrisome news from the hospital, which is why I wired Batavia, asking for you to come."

Hanafi stiffened. "Is she still with us?"

"We must hope that God has extended her life."

"Please don't tell me that she has passed away!"

"Not the last I heard; I hope she hasn't."

Hanafi bolted from his chair and ran back to the taxi. "To Paderi hospital, quickly, quickly!" he shouted as he ran.

Once at the hospital, Hanafi was stopped by the attendant at the gate. He would not let him pass since it was not visiting hour. Only after much explaining was he allowed to speak to the nurse. The nurse in turn, told him she could not let him see Corrie. First of all, she wasn't sure that he was her husband. Moreover, Corrie was in danger and might not survive a visit. As it was, she was quarantined in the ward for contagious diseases.

With tears streaming down his face, he begged the nurse to talk to the doctor until she finally took pity on him. The doctor, who was now sure that Corrie would not pull through, granted him special dispensation. After agreeing to subject himself to the hospital's disinfecting procedures, Hanafi was finally allowed inside the ward.

The nurse warned him beforehand: "Your wife is in a precarious state, slipping in and out of consciousness. If she's made to talk too much, she might…."

"If I can just rest my eyes upon her, that would be enough," Hanafi replied.

The nurse took his hand and led him to the ward.

"Is there hope?" he asked.

"It's in God's hands," the nurse said. "We human beings, we just try our best. Now, you must be careful not to aggravate her condition. Here it is, Room 4-B; this is her room. Go in now. Quietly," she whispered, then waited as he went inside.

Hanafi entered the room on tiptoes. How shocked he was to see Corrie's face. Her eyes were sunken. But her shallow, intermittent breathing meant that she was still alive. Was she asleep?

He stood, as if glued to the spot, his eyes fixed on his dear wife's face. The nurse, he could feel, was now standing quietly behind him. She touched his shoulder. "She is unconscious," she whispered.

Not knowing what to do, Hanafi kept starring. And then suddenly, as if ordained by fate, Corrie opened her eyes and smiled. She raised her hand to Hanafi, who clasped it in his as he sat down beside her. "Corrie," he cried, "it's me, Hanafi, coming to take you home."

"Oh, Hannie," she caressed his hair softly. "I knew you would come. I've been waiting for you...to say goodbye."

"But you can't go, please. Don't leave me again. Tomorrow we'll go home. I'll get an ambulance, and we'll start a new life."

"Give thanks to God that we're allowed to meet again. But I must be the first to go. I'll wait for you there." Her eyes pointed to the ceiling. "This is the only parting that can lighten my burden. Han, forgive my sins."

"I'm the one who sinned against you," he wept. "You did no wrong. Please don't leave me, Corrie. You can't leave me."

"Be strong Han, every creature..."

And Corrie fell silent. Hanafi turned to the nurse, as if expecting her to do something. The nurse, seeing that Corrie had fallen unconscious, waved her hand towards the door.

Before leaving, Hanafi leaned over to kiss his wife. Again and again, he kissed her hand and lips. "What's the point of living if you leave me, Corrie? Take me with you!" he cried.

Corrie opened her eyes. "Farewell, Han, we..."

"Corrie!"

"It has come, the time has come. Farewell, my love. Live a good life and take good care of your son. Have faith in God, and remember me."

And then her eyes closed forever.

Hanafi stared in shock.

"O Corrie," he cried as he kissed her again and again. "Nurse! Nurse! Look at my wife! Help her, please. I'll be indebted to you for the rest of my life if you can help her."

The nurse placed her hand on Corrie's wrist, and then her chest. She shook her head. "It's God's will," she said. "Be strong."

"Please..."

"No human power can help you now."

"Has she...?"

"Your wife has passed on to eternal life," the nurse said softly. "And she departed well, forgiving and being forgiven. Look at her peaceful expression. She was smiling as she left."

"Corrie!" Hanafi screamed, and fell to the floor.

An attendant came, and together with the nurse, lifted Hanafi onto an empty bed beside Corrie's.

22

The Suffocating Universe

Hanafi remained unconscious for three days following his collapse after the death of his wife. Once he regained semi-consciousness, he started babbling to himself constantly about Corrie, a condition that lasted for several days, until his fever subsided. Physically, he seemed restored but he said very little, as if his mouth had been sewn shut. His only words were brief answers to questions from the doctors and nurses. He avoided the other patients, as if he was afraid to talk to or even look at them.

Somehow, he managed, nonetheless, to write to his landlord in Batavia, telling him of his illness and his stay at the hospital. In the letter he enclosed a note for his superior along with a doctor's certificate. But he made no mention of Corrie.

For fourteen days he remained in the hospital before the doctor finally released him. Although all traces of his shock seemed to have disappeared, he avoided personal contact.

From the hospital, Hanafi went directly to the Dutch cemetery, where he asked the caretaker, a kindly old man, to be shown to Corrie's grave.

"This way, please," the caretaker said as he lead Hanafi to the path outside his door. As they walked, the man attempted to engage Hanafi in a conversation. "It was Mrs. Van Dammen, from the orphanage, who arranged and paid for a first-class site for your wife," he said. "It's only the perimeter walls that still need to be discussed."

Hanafi said nothing. In fact, he had not uttered a single word since they started walking, with him staying a few steps behind. Whenever the caretaker turned his head, as if pressing for an answer, he gave him no more than a nod. But the chatty old gentleman took no offence, and he continued on. In his years at the cemetery, he had seen many in Hanafi's condition.

"This is your wife's grave," he said finally. Hanafi stepped forward and stood still, his eyes falling on the piles of flowers and wreaths strewn on the modest grave. "The flowers are from Mrs. Van Dammen," the old man said. "She comes almost every afternoon. She's a kind soul, that lady. No wonder she can be a mother to all those orphans, though there's no shortage of rascals among them. Oh, not too many people could…"

But before the man could finish his sentence, Hanafi threw himself upon the grave, sobbing like a child. For the old man, this, too, was not an unusual sight, but as always, he felt the tears smarting his own eyes. Quietly, he stepped back and walked away, so as not to intrude or perhaps so as not to cry himself.

When Hanafi finally returned to say goodbye to the kind old man, the sun was already high above the horizon.

"If it helps to console you," the caretaker said as they shook hands, "my own wife passed away ten years ago. Her grave is not far from here. And every time I visit her, I still get tears in my eyes. But, you know, we all have to pass on to eternal life some day. Your wife has left, while you still remain in this world. But if you both keep your faith, surely you will meet again."

"Thank you, sir," Hanafi interrupted. "Mrs. Van Dammen will take care of the walls. And by the way, I think two people who are in love should depart together, not one after the other." As he spoke, Hanafi turned away to hide his tears. "Goodbye, sir."

From the cemetery he took a taxi to the orphanage. Mrs. Van Dammen, who had received a phone call from the nurse, was expecting him.

But as they met, they could speak no words. Both were choked with tears.

Gaining control of herself, Mrs. Van Dammen wiped her eyes. "Your wife lived here in my house for less than a year, but it felt as if she was my own flesh and blood. She was patient, and sincere, and open-minded. All the good human qualities seemed to gather in her. The orphans here are rascals for the most part, but they changed after your wife came. They listened to her, and not because she forced them to, but because she was kind and they loved her."

The woman's words made the burden that Hanafi felt all that much heavier. "Yes, madam," he said, "she had a heart of gold. And I'm the fool of a husband who could not appreciate her."

"She forgave you a long time ago," Mrs. Van Dammen said consolingly. "She said she just wanted to stay here for one year; after that she would return to you. My relative in Batavia never stopped coaxing her and though she was won over in the end, she kept saying she wanted to stay here at least a year so that she could see the results of her work. Who could have guessed that she would have to go so soon? And after only two days in the hospital?"

"I went to the cemetery before coming here," Hanafi said abruptly. "Perhaps I could talk to you about the perimeter walls for her gravesite."

"What would you like to do with the walls?" Mrs. Van Dammen asked. "You need not worry about the cost. A few months ago Corrie gave me her bank book for safekeeping. She had six thousand rupiah in her savings. She also gave me a notarized statement, saying that if she should pass away before either of us—Oh, it was as if she knew!—that I was to withdraw her money. After payment of funeral costs, including a simple grave wall—she insisted that it be modest—the remainder was to be divided in two, half for you, sir, and the other half for the orphanage."

Hanafi shook his head. "That's so like her, to be so generous. Oh, Corrie, how happy we would have been if I knew how to appreciate you. But alas..." He paused and then turned toward Mrs. Van Dammen. "It's not that I'm refusing my wife's inheritance, but what good is money to me now? I would like to give my half to the orphanage as well. I'm sure she'd be happy with my decision."

"Thank you, Mr. Han, thank you on behalf of the children."

"You're welcome. And as for the perimeter walls, if I may, I'll leave the decision up to you. Do what you think is best. I can't stay for long. I'm going on a long journey."

"Where are you planning to go? If I may ask."

"First to Sumatra, to see my mother. After that, I don't know."

Hanafi then asked for his suitcase, which the nurse at the hospital had sent there. Mrs. Van Dammen asked him to stay with her for a while. He could sleep in Corrie's old room, she told him. But Hanafi told her he wanted to stay at an inn. After signing a statement regarding his donation, he left.

From there he went to the station, where he bought a ticket for the express train to Batavia leaving the next morning. He stored his suitcase at the station, and then headed back toward the orphanage.

"Mrs. Van Dammen," he said when he saw her, "I forgot about my wife's clothes and belongings."

"Oh, yes, I forgot too" said the old woman. "They certainly belong to you."

"I want to donate them to the orphanage, as well. The only thing I would like is the medallion that she was wearing when she passed away."

"Thank you again for your generosity," Mrs. Van Dammen told him. "Let me get the medallion for you. I won't be a moment."

Soon afterward, she returned carrying a gold medallion on a fine gold chain. It was thin, and not much larger than a one cent coin. Hanafi flipped open the locket. Inside, there was a small portrait of himself and Corrie.

"My wife wore this until the moment of her death. So I, too, will not part with it until it's my time to leave this world,"

Hanafi said goodbye to the kindly old woman, and left. But he did not go to an inn, instead, he went back to the cemetery. He immediately sought out the old caretaker. "I'm planning to go on a long journey," he told the man when finding him, "and I don't know if I will live long enough to visit my wife again. So I'd like to have your permission to keep watch over her grave tonight."

The man looked at Hanafi with pity in his eyes. "But it's only five o'clock in the afternoon. You're not planning to keep watch until morning, are you?"

"Yes, until tomorrow morning" Hanafi replied. "I'll leave for the station at dawn. Until then, I'd appreciate it if no one disturbed me."

"The express train doesn't leave until seven. Why don't you drop in before you leave, for some coffee. And what about dinner? You have to eat tonight, don't you? I'll wait for you at eight."

"Thank you for your kindness, sir. If I feel hungry, I will certainly join you for dinner."

"All right," the man said in consent. "And by the way, when my wife passed away, I didn't want to leave her grave, either. But eventually, the heart will heal. I've seen many people who…."

"Till we meet again," Hanafi shook the caretaker's hand before he could start a long story.

"Till we meet again, Mr. Han. If you need anything, anything at all, even in the middle of the night, just knock on my door. The sky is clear now, and the moon is bright. But later it can get cold, usually around one o'clock. Don't you want a blanket or a jacket?"

"Thank you for the offer, sir. If I need them, I'll let you know."

And Hanafi headed off to Corrie's grave. But he had barely sat down on the perimeter wall of an adjacent grave, when a groundskeeper toddled over with a large chair.

"My boss sends his regards. He says that maybe you'll find this useful."

"Tell him thank you," Hanafi replied. "Also tell him that I really don't need anything."

After the groundskeeper left, Hanafi moved the chair closer to Corrie's grave and sat down. Now and again he would speak to her as he wept.

The sun set, the evening turned into night. The only sound was the chirping of crickets. Pine boughs that had whispered in the evening wind now stood still in a melancholy silence. Now and again, the cries of owls, calling to one another, could be heard in the distance.

Hanafi sat with his head in his hand. He would be happy, he thought, if he could be buried right now, next to his wife. But his longing to see his homeland, and his mother, was also irresistible.

Corrie and his mother were the two people dearest to his heart. But he could never have them both in his life. It was as though fate had conspired to keep these two creatures apart, never to be united. He had been forced to make a choice and he had chosen Corrie. That choice had not changed. Even after her death he still felt that he could not return to live with his mother. In his mind, that would amount to betraying his love for Corrie. Yes, he would go to Sumatra, but only for a while, just to visit his mother and ask for her forgiveness, and also to see his son. And then he would go away somewhere; somewhere, but he didn't know where.

As the night grew even more still, the newly risen moon cast eerie shadows on the tall pine trees and the gravestones. The air grew cold. And Hanafi could feel the chill penetrating his shirt. He peered at his wristwatch; it was only half past nine. And then he saw in the distance, a figure coming his way. In the bright light of the moon, he could make out the shapes of two men. One was balancing a chaise lounge on his head, the other toting a basket on a pole slung across his shoulder.

They approached Hanafi. "I'm the night watchman," said the man with the chaise lounge. "The boss waited for you to come to dinner since eight o'clock. Now, he sends you this." The man put down the chaise, and then opened the hamper his companion was

carrying. Inside was a meal, complete with eating utensils, a thick
blanket, and a large thermos.

"Oh he shouldn't have..." Hanafi felt genuinely grateful. "Thank
you. And tell your boss I will stop by tomorrow morning at six, to
thank him in person."

"Yes sir," said the night watchman and then left. As the dew
settled, Hanafi's clothes grew damp and cold. He was exhausted and
felt chilled to the bones. He opened the thermos and gulped down
the hot coffee until he could feel some warmth in his stomach.
Then he took the blanket and lay down on the chaise.

The next thing he knew, he was awoken by the light of dawn
shining on his face. Somehow, he felt as though he had spent the
entire night conversing with Corrie. He must have fallen asleep and
had a dream, he reasoned. Tossing aside his dew-soaked blanket, he
then got up.

He stepped over to the grave and knelt. "I must beg your leave,
Corrie. I must go see my mother," he whispered. "After I see her,
we shall see each other again, somehow. Until then, your medallion
will represent you and it will not leave my neck. Have you truly
forgiven me?" he asked. "You have no idea what torment you put
me through when you left me. Farewell," he said, "until we meet
again."

Hanafi prostrated himself, touching his lips to the ground.
Taking a handful of earth, he wrapped it in a handkerchief and
then got up and made his way down the path toward the caretaker's
house.

"Good morning, Mr. Han," said the old man, who was standing
in front of his door. "Weren't you cold?"

"Not at all, thanks to your generosity. With your chaise, your
blanket and the hot coffee, I stayed as comfortable as if I was
indoors."

"Oh, don't mention it. Yesterday I saw that your mind was
occupied. You couldn't have thought of such practical things. Why
don't you come in; there's still a lot of time before the train leaves."

"Thank you so much, sir. I'm sorry to turn down your hospitality,
but I really must be going. It's hard to find transport this early in

the morning. And besides, the coffee was still hot this morning. I had some and so I don't need anything else."

"Farewell then," he said in response. "Until we meet again."

"Till we meet again," Hanafi rejoined. "And please take care of my wife's grave. I'm much indebted to you."

"You can trust me, Mr. Han. By the way, did you happen to speak with the lady from the orphanage about the perimeter walls?"

"Yes, I did. Thank you, once again, a thousand thanks for your kindness. If Corrie and I had met kind people like you… I'm sure we'd still be living together happily."

The old man only half-understood Hanafi's last comment. Nevertheless, he smiled and looked at him kindly. "We are here on this earth only for a short time," he said. "So instead of making enemies, why not make friends? Whoever does good deeds will receive goodness in return. That's what my wife always said."

"Sir, I'm leaving Java. We will probably never meet again. So I want you to know that I will always feel indebted to you, immeasurably."

"Let's not owe and be owed, Mr. Han. A debt must be paid, and a payment must be accepted. I'm only acting as a human being obeying the commandment of Allah."

"God bless you, sir. I'm afraid I will miss my train. Once again, thank you."

The two men shook hands and Hanafi walked away.

23

Back to Earth

After returning to Batavia, Hanafi sold his books and the few things he had in his room. He sold most everything, except for some clothes. He was going on a long journey, and he reasoned it was better to convert everything to cash. And what would he do after that? His only plan was to get as far away from Batavia as he could.

A few days later he was standing on the deck of a ship at Tanjung Priok harbor.

Piet, his former landlord, came on board to see him off. "Just so you know, Han," he said as he shook Hanafi's hand, "I have never agreed with those who ostracized you. As far as I'm concerned, people can do what they wish so long as they don't disturb me."

"Thank you, Piet. If more people thought like you, I wouldn't have been ostracized just for being different."

"But that's human nature, Han. You've got to remember that. If someone has different values, or does things differently, other people immediately meddle in his affairs, even if he has done nothing to provoke them. If you want to live in peace, it's better to follow the crowd. Low with the cows and bleat with the goats, isn't that what your people say? Those are words to live by, Han."

"I see your point now. Maybe I will live by those words, if I can."

"You have to, if you want to live in peace. Here, in your country, we live in a small world. This is not Europe. There, people have more freedom. You don't have to worry too much about what other people think. But even there, there are still rules of propriety you have to follow. Supposing I were to smoke a palm-leaf cigarette in public, my picture would be in the next day's paper, I'm sure.

"Of course," said Hanafi, dropping his gaze. "But I sometimes wonder what's the good of living if a man can't do as he pleases with his own life, without being harassed by his fellow men?"

"Because I want to enjoy my life, I don't mind putting on a mask at times," Piet told him with a smile.

The ship's whistle blew for the third time, and Piet hurried to disembark. "Goodbye, Han," he waved his last goodbye from the edge of the pier. "And remember my words," he shouted, "if you want to live in peace."

"Farewell, Piet. And thank you."

The ship steamed out of the harbor, and Hanafi went to sit alone on the deck. For a long while, he simply stared at the vast blue sea, his heart sinking with the weight of his sorrow. And then he overheard some Dutchmen complaining among themselves. One of them was showing the others an article in the newspaper. It was a Batavia Dutch-language paper, notorious for its hatred towards natives. The article was about an Indonesian student in Holland who married a Dutchwoman, a classmate at the university he attended. The writer attacked not only the one student but all Indonesian students and intellectuals as well as their demand for ethical policies. He even attacked some of their prominent Dutch sympathizers. But for Hanafi, what was worse than the article, were the insulting comments the men made as they read the newspaper.

"As Europeans, our freedom is being curbed," one of them shouted as he pounded the table. And then he got up and started pacing back and forth. "We're pushed back everywhere we go. And we always have to give in. It's the same thing with taxes. Who is it who pays the largest share? We do, that's who, and it's all because of this ethical policy business!"

Though Hanafi covered his ears with his hands, he could still see the men gesturing as they ranted about the injustice done towards them. Finally, he got up and hurried into his cabin. If that's the way it was with the press, and with those influenced by the press, how sweet in comparison, he thought, was his landlady in Batavia. At least she was civil.

And he thought to himself, that although he would always be faithful to his love for Corrie, he would not advise a mixed marriage for anyone. The world was simply not ready for it. Of all the Europeans he knew, there were perhaps only two or three who could sincerely accept a mixed marriage. The rest condemned it outright.

The natives, too, disapproved of it, though not with so much hatred. "It's a big mistake," they would say, and "never the twain shall meet." He recalled again his mother's words—words he had considered to be a sign of ignorance—when she warned him not to pursue his interest in Corrie. Now, one by one, her words had been proven true.

And he thought of what Piet had said, that most Westerners would respect a native who had a Western education and yet had not abandoned his native ways. But it was too late for him. He had been misguided from the beginning, and he was convinced more than ever that a happy life was now impossible. Hanafi dropped his head and hid his face in his hands. At best, he could hope that his son Syafei would not follow in his footsteps. He might obtain a Western education, so he could replace the bad qualities of the native people with the good qualities of the Europeans. But, as a native, his character must be nurtured in the native way.

When Hanafi arrived in Padang, he went to the smallest inn he could find, not to save money, but to avoid running into anyone. But later that night, when he went out to eat, a flyer about a night fair caught his eye. And he thought that perhaps the diversion might help relieve the burden in his heart.

After dinner, he went, and soon found himself standing in the quietest corner on the fair ground. He stood for a long time, blankly staring this way and that. It was as though he was in a dream. His eyes and ears could see and hear the festivities around him, but his mind could not fully comprehend the scene. Indeed, he was barely aware that he was in Padang.

And then a child caught his attention. It was a little boy, being carried on a man's shoulders, and he was pummeling the man's head and face with his little fists. "Those balloons over there, I want those balloons," he cried.

"But they cost ten cents, Pei," said the man, "and your mother gave us only five."

"I want the balloons," the boy cried louder as he continued to hit his mount. "Let's just give the man five cents and take them."

"That's the same as stealing."

"Don't you have any money?" the child whined.

"I don't have a single cent, Pei."

"Go find Mother. Ask her for more."

Seeing his old houseboy with his son startled him out of his daze. "Buyung, Buyung!" Hanafi called out.

"Sir, is that you?" When did you come?"

"This evening," he answered, and turned toward Syafei. The little boy hid his face as though he was afraid of him. Hanafi led them to the balloon stall and asked the boy, "Now, tell me, which one do you want?"

Syafei, wide-eyed, looked over all the balloons, which were tied to a branch of palm. "The red one!" he shouted, forgetting all his apprehension.

But when the vendor untied the red balloon and was about to hand it to him, Syafei suddenly directed his attention to the other balloons. "Maybe I like the blue one better. But the purple one is nice, too. Maybe the purple one."

"How much for all the balloons?" Hanafi asked the vendor.

The vendor counted ten balloons. "One rupiah, sir."

"We'll take them all."

Syafei clapped his hands, cheering for joy. He slid off Buyung's arms and walked over to take his present from Hanafi.

"Who are you, sir?" asked the boy confidently, as he clutched the palm branch with all the balloons.

"A stranger," replied Hanafi.

"Why are you being good to me?"

"Because I'm a good person."

"Like my father, he's a good person."

"Where is your father?"

"Mother said he's in Batavia, going to school."

Hanafi fell silent for a moment. What would this little boy say, if he told him that his father was standing right here in front of him? "Your father is a good person?" Hanafi asked.

"Yes, very good. Mother said no one is as good a person as my father and that when he comes back from Batavia, he will give me all the balloons I want, just like you did."

"Does your mother often talk to you about your father?"

"Everyday, but only when Grandma is not around," the boy confided. "Only when it's just the two of us at home."

"When will your father come back?"

"When he finishes going to school. I don't know, maybe still a long time."

The little boy's statement struck him. What Rapiah told their son was right. He was getting an education. Yes, indeed, and had now graduated. But at what price had he learned his lessons?

The crowd was moving all around them, pushing Syafei closer and closer to Hanafi, causing him to look up at Buyung for help.

"I could carry you so that people won't run into you," Hanafi suggested.

Syafei paused before he answered. "Since you're a good person, like my father, and you gave me all those balloons, I guess that's all right."

Hanafi scooped Syafei into his arms.

"When your father comes back from Batavia, would you like him to carry you?" he asked the boy.

"For sure."

"Do you want to meet your father?"

"Of course, but Batavia is far away and you have to cross the ocean on a big ship to get there. Mother said that when I am big, I can go there to visit my father."

"What about your mother, does she want to see your father?"

"She wants to see him very much, but she's afraid of Grandma."

A young woman suddenly rushed toward them and snatched Syafei out of Hanafi's arms. "If you get tired of carrying him, just put him down," she snapped at Buyung. Before Hanafi could stop her, she had disappeared into the crowd.

"Rapiah!" Hanafi shouted.

"Hanafi!" He heard an old woman's voice, and then saw his mother's face appear in the crowd.

"Mother!" he called.

"When did you arrive? Where are you staying?"

"I just arrived. I'm staying nearby, at Belantung Inn."

"Who are you with?"

"I'm alone, Mother."

Hanafi's mother paused for a moment, her lips quivering as she thought of asking about Corrie. But she held herself back. "There's much I want to talk to you about, but not here. Tomorrow morning I will come to the inn," she said, and then mumbled under her breath, "I'll put up with going to a place like that if it's to see my son. Tonight, I must go with the group to where we are staying."

"Who is Rapiah with?"

"Her parents," she said. "They saw you too but no one dared to come near you."

"But they're my own aunt and uncle, Mother."

"They're simple village folks, Hanafi. You know, ignorant people."

Hanafi made no reply.

"Tomorrow morning at seven," his mother said, "I'll meet you at the inn."

"Where are you staying? I could meet you there. Wouldn't that be better?"

"I'm staying with Rapiah's family, in Tuanku Demang's house. I don't think you should go there before you settle things with Rapiah. If you do, it might put me in a difficult position. We'll have to find out first if Tuanku Demang's door is open or closed."

She then turned around and walked away. Buyung followed behind her, leaving Hanafi alone with his thoughts. He recalled how his country relatives used to insist that he visit them whenever he was in the area, and how much he used to dread those visits. Now they were barring him from their door.

He was puzzled by what he had heard from Syafei. He was certain Syafei was not lying when he told him that Rapiah talked about him all the time, and described him as a good person. Children do not lie about such things. Did that mean Rapiah still loved him? Why then, did she snatch Syafei from his arms with such determination? She even said she would rather have Syafei walk than be carried by him.

It suddenly occurred to him that she must have overheard him asking Syafei if his mother would like to see his father. And that she must have also heard Syafei's answer: "She wants to see him very much, but she's afraid of Grandma." When Syafei said that, she was probably standing behind him. It would have embarrassed her. That, he supposed, was why she acted the way she did.

In fact, Hanafi barely recognized Rapiah. Her movements were strong, her figure slender and lithe and when she snapped at Buyung, it showed a woman who knew what she wanted.

How small he felt compared to her, this simple country girl, who as his wife had received nothing from him but abuse yet had nothing but praise for him. At the same time, he was also sure that even in her "victory" over him, she would have no intention of revenge. Was that not the sign of a noble character? Hanafi had no wish for her forgiveness, he simply wanted to be acknowledged.

Corrie too had a noble soul. He was the despicable one, a scoundrel! Twice he had found a wife who could make him happy. And twice he had let the woman slip through his fingers. Now he had only his misery.

In his bookshelf there had been books with titles such as *Secrets of a Happy Marriage, Customs and Etiquette,* and *Keeping Love Alive.* But what good was all that knowledge, if he could not put it into practice?

Where did he go wrong, he asked himself. Perhaps his upbringing was partly to blame. For at a young age, after losing his father and being so tenderly sheltered by his mother, he had been sent away to live with a Dutch family, cut off from his mother's guiding hand and all Eastern values. Could it be that it was this loss of connection that led him astray later in life?

Rapiah and Corrie, he realized, were equally noble, each with her own beauty. One was a flower from the East, the other from the West. At first, he thought he was at one with the West, and would find happiness with Corrie. But he now realized that there was a part of him that was so Eastern, that it could not be erased by any education. So deeply was it planted in his soul, and so thoroughly absorbed into his blood, that it was as though he had drunk this essence of Easternness in his mother's milk.

He now admitted that it had been difficult to bring this part of himself in line with his Western values. For the two worlds were indeed far apart. When it came to family life, for example, an Easterner loves to be in the company of his family and relatives even after he has a family of his own, but a Westerner prefers to live apart as soon as he marries.

As he looked back, he saw that there was indeed much misunderstanding between him and Corrie, even when they were together. And this misunderstanding had its roots in their difference of sensibilities. In a friendship, one can still keep one's distance, and this difference can be discussed without locking horns. But between a husband and wife, the relationship is so intimate that such a discussion easily can erupt into a quarrel, especially if both parties think of themselves as the more educated one.

And what of his education? It turned out to be no more than a thin veneer, inadequate to satisfy a Western woman in marriage. And as for Rapiah, she simply could not receive the proper guidance from him, a half-baked Westerner. If only she had had a proper husband, he was sure she would have bloomed into a beautiful flower. But now her life hung in limbo because she had fallen into the wrong hands.

Both his wives lacked neither heart nor soul, nor love for him. But he mistreated them all the same. And it was all because he was a half-baked man, neither Eastern nor Western. He was brought up wrong, and they had fallen victim to his faulty upbringing.

Hanafi had now completed his education; he had returned from his long sojourn.

For a long time, he stood in a daze amidst the goings-on of the fair. When he finally regained his senses, he was in his room at the inn. It was one o'clock in the morning. And with a wavering heart he lay on his bed waiting for daylight.

24

The Journey Home

At seven o'clock the next morning Hanafi's mother was already at the inn, looking for him.

"The rest of the group—your mother- and father-in-law, Rapiah and Syafei—left for Bonjol on the six o'clock train this morning," she told him.

"What? Didn't they want me to see my son?" Hanafi asked, surprised.

"No, your uncle was adamant about that."

"But he's my son, not theirs."

"But you know, Hanafi, according to Minangkabau custom, Rapiah and her maternal uncles have a greater claim on Syafei than you do, even though you are his father." She turned to another subject. "Let me ask about your life. Where is your wife?"

"She passed away, Mother," he replied, and wiped his eyes.

"Truly, we are Allah's and to Him we shall return," she recited the Islamic eulogy. "What happened? Was she ill?" she asked with true concern.

"It was cholera, Mother." Hanafi paused. "It's my fate," he said.

Hanafi's mother's could feel her son's sorrow in his voice. "How long has it been since she passed away?" she asked softly.

"Less than half a month."

She fell silent as her eyes fell on her son who was staring blankly out the window, as if to fend off further questions. His face looked so different. "I sense that you were disturbed to hear that Rapiah had gone back to Bonjol," she said after a pause. "Why? Did you want her to stay?"

"No, Mother, it makes no difference to me. Last night, she snatched Syafei from my arms, which I suppose was her way of saying that she wanted to sever all ties with me. And that's fine by me. I don't think you should harbor any hope of bringing her and I back together. I believe a man has only one true love in his lifetime."

"Then why were you concerned when I said she and the others had gone back to Bonjol?"

"It's the elders. They have no idea why I'm here. I could be visiting just for a couple of days, or maybe I'm here to see my son for the last time. Shouldn't they first find out, before they took him away to Bonjol, my own flesh and blood?"

"You have a point, Hanafi. And don't think that I didn't argue with them and tried to get them to stay, but Rapiah's parents were obstinate. When seeing you, they first hoped that you would take Rapiah back; her being without a husband for so long has brought shame to their house. But then, when they remembered how you had treated her in the past, they weren't so sure. So now they want to find out about you first, whether you're still married or not. If you're not, whether you are planning to find work here in West Sumatra. And, finally, if you would go to Bonjol to ask for their forgiveness. Then, maybe, they will give Rapiah back to you. You have to understand, Hanafi, a parent does not willing give away her child to someone who doesn't t appreciate her worth."

Although his heart was heavy, Hanafi laughed, not a happy, confident laugh, but an agitated one. "So now they're afraid I might run away with Rapiah, is that it? Please tell them, Mother, that it is I who worry about being forced to take her back."

"After all this time, Hanafi, it seems you still can't tell the difference between gold and dross."

"I don't deny it, Mother, Rapiah is pure gold. But as I just said, true love happens only once. And since Corrie has taken that love with her to the grave, there can be no replacement. You can tell Rapiah's parents that they need not hide their daughter."

Hanafi looked away, his eyes distant as though lost in a dream.

"So what are your plans now?" she asked him.

"I don't know."

"Have you taken a leave of absence?"

"Yes, but I intend to resign."

For a long while his mother looked at his face. She could see the burden in his mind, and sense his reticence.

"What if we go back to the village, Hanafi? We can think of our future there."

"Fine, Mother."

"Is it all right with you if we leave today?"

"That's fine."

"At nine o'clock?"

"Fine."

"But we'll have to get ready and leave soon."

"Fine," he repeated, yet did not move a muscle. His eyes remained fixed on a point faraway. His mother called a bellboy, and told him to quickly pack up Hanafi's luggage, for they had to catch the nine o'clock train to Solok.

"There's not much time left, we have to hurry," said the bellboy as he ran up to Hanafi's room. Hanafi eventually followed him, and helped pack his suitcases. Another bellboy brought the bill to Hanafi's mother. Outside, a buggy was already waiting for them.

Seeing Hanafi's state of mind, his mother decided not to stop at Tuanku Demang's house although her belongings were still there. Hanafi was simply in no condition for a visit. And besides, they were late. They went straight to Padang station, and the train pulled out just as they boarded the first-class carriage.

Throughout the journey, Hanafi hardly uttered a word. Everything he saw and heard passed by him unnoticed, as though he was asleep with his eyes open. Whenever his mother tried to initiate small talk, he answered her only with, "Yes, Mother," "No, Mother," or "I don't know."

When they arrived in Solok his spirit seemed to improve. His eyes began to sparkle, and his bearing brightened as well.

"Before continuing on to Koto Anau, let's take a look around in Solok," he said as they got off the train. "I want to see our old house."

"All right, Hanafi. But we can't go inside, because the house is now rented to someone else."

But it was not the house that interested him; it was the tennis court. For it was there that he had been happy, when he was courting Corrie. As they passed by it, Hanafi told the buggy driver to stop, and got off.

"I'll wait here in the buggy," said his mother. "It's cooler here."

Hanafi got off, and went into the court. No one was there, although one could tell that it was still in use from its meticulous condition. He sat on the bench, the same bench he had shared with Corrie. They hadn't replaced it. The heart that he had carved into the wood, with the letters C and H in its center, was still there, so faint that one could hardly see it. He had carved it with his pocketknife in the days when he fell secretly in love with the lovely Corrie du Bussée. And all this time, he had never once told her about it.

How many times had he sat on that bench chatting with Corrie? He smiled at the memory then turned to look at the tall almond tree in the yard of his old house nearby. How easily he could still picture the small table and chairs, where he had waited on countless, agonizing afternoons for Corrie to come for tea before tennis.

While he sat with his thoughts, the afternoon had turned to evening, and evening began to fade into darkness. Finally, his mother gave in to her restlessness and sent the driver to deliver a message to him.

It was he who startled Hanafi from his daydream, "Madam says that it's too late to go to Koto Anau, now, that you are to wait here until she makes arrangements for a place to stay for the night. We'll come back to pick you up later."

"Fine," Hanafi answered without turning his head.

If she had been by herself, Hanafi's mother would not have needed to make any arrangements. She could arrive unannounced at her relatives' door in the middle of the night, and they would be glad to see her. But because she was with Hanafi, she felt she had to warn them of his condition, so they would not be offended when he arrived.

When finally she did return to the tennis court, accompanied by their host, it was already half past eight. Hanafi was still sitting on the bench, daydreaming.

"It's late now, Hanafi," she said gently as she approached him. "Tomorrow morning we will start for Koto Anau. Tonight, we can stay with your uncle, here."

"All right, Mother." Hanafi rose and walked past his uncle, without even a gesture of acknowledgement. But thanks to his mother's warning, the elder took no offense. When they arrived at his uncle's house, Hanafi said he would like to go to bed right away. And it was only after a great deal of persuading and cajoling from his mother that he agreed to take some food in his room.

His mother nevertheless drew a sigh of relief. His eyes did not seem so blank, though he still would not look at anyone in the eye, except for her. And the expression on his face was less muddled. There was sadness and resignation in it, but she was convinced that that too would change with time.

25

Paying His Debt

Hanafi's condition remained the same the next day and even after he and his mother arrived in Koto Anau. In the days that followed, many family friends and relatives came to visit him in the family's long house. For a whole week the family had to entertain villagers who flocked to their house to see the one they called "The Pride of the Village Who Never Set Foot in the Village after He Became a Man." But the one they came to see did not receive even a single one of his guests. While they ate and drank in the common room, he buried himself in his room, refusing to see anyone. Luckily, no one took offense, for his mother had already informed everyone of his condition. Besides, even if he was that way, he was still a source of pride for them and they felt honored just to set foot in his family's house.

His mother alone would see him in his room. Noticing that he had regained his old, proud and quiet bearing, she felt somewhat encouraged. When he spoke, his words were no longer incoherent, and some calm had returned to his face.

After the visitors stopped coming Hanafi began to venture out of the house. He would go to the rice paddies behind his house, where he sat and gazed dreamily at the mountains and the serene countryside. At midday he would return, have his lunch, and then nap. Later, after his shower and tea, again he would go out to seek quiet, out-of-the-way places. If anyone greeted him, he answered shortly, and then moved on. And if he ran into someone on the footpath, he would turn around and hurry away.

The village children gave him many titles: "The Mute One," "The Daydream King," and other such names. Sometimes they reached his ears, but he paid no heed.

All that his mother could do was wait, knowing she must not initiate any conversation about his past, especially regarding his two wives. She must simply be patient, until he brought up the topic himself.

For his part, Hanafi seemed to have come to terms with his loss. With resignation and forbearance, he accepted Corrie's death. And although he had no religion, he bore the conviction that he would someday be reunited with his beloved wife.

While he knew of no place he could go to find happiness, he also knew he could not stay in Koto Anau forever. His presence there had brought only misery to his mother. When he was away, living in Batavia, she had many relatives and friends coming to visit her everyday. She also had Rapiah and Syafei and he could picture how happy they were together. Now, because he was back, they had to live separately. The long house was virtually empty, and his mother sat idly alone all day. Hanafi came to realize how much he cared for her and, for the first time, began thinking of his mother's future.

He knew that above all she wanted all four of them to be reunited. But that was impossible. His heart was with Corrie, and he had to stay faithful to her until the day they met again in the after world. What was he to do?

One afternoon, upon returning from his walk, he approached his mother. "I was wondering, Mother," he said, "before I came back, did you live alone in this house?"

The old woman was so happy to see her son speaking to her. "No, Hanafi," she said, "besides your elders, whom I have asked to move to the upper house, Rapiah and Syafei also lived here with me. After you left for Batavia, the three of us were inseparable."

"So, after I left, the two of them came here with you."

"That's right."

"But on the evening that I arrived, they moved back to Bonjol."

"That's right, Hanafi."

"And while I was in Batavia, did Rapiah's father ever ask her to move home?"

"He asked her once, but she wouldn't go. She wanted to live with me, and I with her. Even now, I think she would rather live with me than with her parents."

"You never felt burdened taking care of her and Syafei?"

"No, Hanafi. When you were away, they were your replacement. If they hadn't been here, I don't know..." She shook her head as her voice faltered, "I don't think I could have survived without them."

He was silent for a moment.

What was he worth to Rapiah, Syafei, and to his mother, he asked himself. As it stood now, his life was consumed entirely by his hope for a future meeting with Corrie. He had to die faithful to her, and nothing else meant anything to him. He had no other dreams and no plans. Nothing aroused his interest. Not only was he useless to others, he assumed, but wherever he went, his presence could only mar the happiness of those around him. And most importantly, he had become a burden to his aging mother. It would be so much better if she could have Rapiah and Syafei there with her instead of him. They would make her happy, and she, in turn, could help bring up Syafei, who was yet to become a man, instead of waiting on him, a mere remnant of one.

For a long time Hanafi sat quietly, contemplating the path that had become clear to him. His mother thought he was considering bringing Rapiah and Syafei back to Koto Anau. "Yes, Hanafi," she said, "now that you're home, I would be really happy if my grandson were here too."

"Syafei should never be apart from you, Mother."

"I meant if he could come here with Rapiah," she said.

Hanafi's face hardened. "Don't even think about it, Mother. Corrie is my only wife," he said curtly.

His mother bowed her head. From that day on, Hanafi never mentioned another word about the matter. His condition also worsened. He ate little and rarely slept. His face grew pale and gaunt. He no longer went for his walk among the rice paddies, but instead spent his days buried in his room.

And then one night, near dawn, the air was shattered by a sharp cry from Hanafi's room. His mother jumped from her bed, and rushed to his room. Luckily his door was unlocked and there she saw him, his head hanging over the edge of his bed, his sheet and the mat on the floor soaked in blood.

"Hanafi!" she cried. "Tell me what's wrong."

"It's just a stomach ache. I feel better now."

"But you have been throwing up blood," she said as she lifted his head back onto the bed. "Oh, who could be so evil as to poison you like this?"

"I was like this once before, when I was in Batavia."

Without saying another word, his mother ran to their relatives' house for help. They all rushed over. And roused by the commotion, other villagers also rose, and were soon swarming towards Hanafi's house. The yard was now full of people. Everybody wanted to know what was going on.

One of Hanafi's uncles, a traditional healer, asked for betel leaves and cold water in a saucer. He put the leaves in the water, and recited a prayer over it as he shook his head from side to side. He discerned that the evil spell must have come from far away, perhaps from his enemies across the ocean.

He told Hanafi the water he had blessed could repel the evil attack. Hanafi drank it in one gulp, just to please his mother. But she was not satisfied. As much as she believed in the man's ability to heal, she also wanted to bring a doctor. So, without telling anyone, she sent a messenger to Solok to fetch a doctor, no matter what the cost.

The sun rose high in the sky. It was late in the morning, and Hanafi's condition had worsened. He spoke only in broken syllables, and kept vomiting more blood.

Hanafi's relatives agreed that the evil spell had come from afar and all the healers that there were among them tried their best to neutralize it. One stabbed a chicken with a dagger, while others fervently recited prayers in the adjacent room, directly on the other side of the wall from where they thought Hanafi's head lay. One brought a bundle of seven roots and seven leaves, which he ordered boiled in the kitchen, and another dipped the hilt of his dagger in a glass of water to be given to Hanafi.

Before Hanafi had a chance to drink the magic water, the doctor arrived. He was a young man and though he had never met Hanafi, Hanafi's story was well known to him. Thus, when the messenger told him that Hanafi was vomiting blood, he knew exactly what medicines to bring.

Before the doctor began his treatment, he ordered everyone, except for Hanafi's mother, to leave the room. The relatives, even the healers among them complied, although not without grumbling.

After they had gone, the doctor immediately set to work. From his bag, he took out a small pump along with some vials of medicine.

Hanafi was exhausted but still conscious. "Do you know what I'm suffering from, doctor?" he said in Dutch, smiling faintly.

"I do, Mr. Han."

"But the poison, doctor, I didn't take it by mistake."

"Even so, it's my duty to help."

"It's too late, doctor, I drank a lot. You have no right to help me. I took it because I wanted to go."

"Forgive me for being blunt, Mr. Han, but this is the act of a coward. Think of your mother, your wife and your son."

"So be it, doctor, I'm a coward. But my life is empty, no dreams, and no future. It's better if I go."

"One does not live for one's dreams alone, but also for one's duties, especially toward one's family."

"Do you know my life story?"

"Even the children in the village know your life story."

"So you know that I have long abandoned those duties."

"All the more reason for you to make amends now. I have prepared the medicine, now I must pump your stomach. And if you don't let me, I will have to use force. Let's get on with it. Look at your mother and how you have made her worry."

"All right, doctor, go ahead. But my poor mother, please don't tell her that I did this to myself."

"If you wish."

"Doctor," Hanafi said as the doctor was about to begin, "do you know love?"

The doctor paused for a moment. He knew there was very little he could do to help a patient who had chosen to die. If he saved him this time—which he doubted if he could—what would prevent him from trying to kill himself again? And yet as a doctor it was his duty to try his best.

Drawing close to Hanafi, he whispered, "Your condition is critical. You must not talk. Listen to me: I am speaking as a doctor and as a human being. I may be young but don't think that I don't know what love is. In my opinion, a lover is proven true only if he can endure his trials patiently and knows how to keep his head up in a storm. Yes, love asks for sacrifice, but this is not sacrifice. You're only running away from difficulty. And that's not love.

"You're wrong to think that your life is empty and without purpose. You may have lost your wife but you still have your mother and your son. You are the only roof over their heads, the only pillar they can lean on. They have a right to your love. And as for your love for your dearly departed wife, you must sanctify that love by accepting the duties that come with it.

"Now, about my duty as a doctor and a human being. I came here at the request of your mother. So let's try our best, if only to satisfy your mother. How things will turn out, only God knows."

"As you wish, doctor."

The doctor then began to pump Hanafi's stomach, even though he did not believe it would save him. After he had finished, he told Hanafi's mother that Hanafi had a rare stomach disease, one that could rarely be cured. Then he left, leaving behind the healer and elders who were still busy deliberating what to do.

When he regained consciousness, Hanafi gestured to his mother. "Mother," he said, "please forgive my sins. And please take good care of Syafei. Don't let him follow in my footsteps."

"Oh, my son, I forgave you long ago. And don't worry about your son. Now recite the creed, Hanafi. Say the name of God and his prophet, so your path may be straight."

Hanafi rested his sad eyes on his mother, and murmured *"Lailaha illallah. Muhammad dar Rasulullah."*

As he took his mother's hand, his soul departed.

26

Epilogue

Of all the young men studying in Batavia who went sightseeing to Lake Singkarak or Sawahlunto, not one failed to stop by the small yet meticulously kept house in Solok. Hanafi's mother had bought the house and lived there with Rapiah who remained steadfast in her decision not to remarry. The two of them made a pact never to part.

Whenever a student came to visit, Hanafi's mother would have a chicken slaughtered for a special meal. The young men doted on her; they thought of her as a wise old woman. Often, they would gather around her to receive guidance. They discussed the way of life for Easterners, who must never become half-baked Westerners.

Syafei always sat beside his grandmother. He promised that after his study in Holland, he would return to look after his mother's rice fields.

Hanafi's body had been brought back to Solok for burial but even in death his status remained unclear. While some family members argued that Hanafi, having taken on European status, must be buried in the Dutch cemetery, others continued to claim him as a native son whose body must be buried in accordance with local traditions. It was only after a long deliberation among the elders and in consultation with the Assistant District Commissioner, that a consensus was reached: Hanafi would return to the land from which he was born. Shortly before nightfall of the day after he died, he was buried in the Malay cemetery. It was there that every Friday, his mother and Rapiah brought flowers and water for his grave.

Translator's Note

I first encountered *Salah Asuhan* as an eighth grade student in Jakarta as mandatory reading in my Indonesian literature class. As I recall, the story made little impression on either myself or my classmates. In light of modern pedagogy, it would be easy to blame the educational system; as students we were expected to do no more than memorize what our teachers said in order to be able to regurgitate it, word for word, in our exams. But I don't think this is necessarily the case. I suspect that the real reason *Salah Asuhan* left no indelible impression on me at that time was that I was simply too young. To be moved by a work of art, one needs life experience, so the problem of human existence that is evoked in the work can resonate in one's own heart. I believe this is true of literature more than of any other art form. As for my classmates and I, at fourteen, perhaps to learn our teacher's interpretation by rote was all that *should* be expected from us, with the hope that it will one day prove useful in our lives, long after we have passed our exams.

Many years later, I encountered *Salah Asuhan* for the second time under very different circumstances. I had been living in Canada for quite some time, long enough to call it my second home and to feel that I had a stake in the country's main cultural discourse: gender politics, racism and multiculturalism. At the same time, a feeling of nostalgia for Indonesia that ran much deeper than mere homesickness, had also crept in. The time was ripe to reread *Salah Asuhan*, which by some lucky chance did come across my path. How excited I was to find that the very issues that beset my time and my world were all there in *Salah Asuhan*, penned by my fellow countryman in 1928! As if by reflex, I suddenly remembered the imposed interpretation from grade eight, which did turn out to be quite useful in helping me form my own ideas.

For the benefit of those who never took grade eight Indonesian literature, here is a very brief summary: Hanafi, the protagonist of this novel, is madly in love with the beautiful Corrie du Bussée, though he has long been betrothed, according to West Sumatran tradition, to his cousin, Rapiah.

We were taught that the struggle Hanafi faces as his life is torn between the two women serves as an allegory for pre-independent Indonesia as it struggled toward national identity. Corrie, the feisty, liberated Western woman, represents progress and modernity, while the simple-hearted Rapiah represents traditional values. Which woman should Hanafi marry? Which course should the emerging nation take? Staying on the old path means being stuck precisely in that dark world of superstitions and ignorance that had rendered the nation powerless for so long against Dutch colonialism. But treading the new, unknown path of progress may lead one to become a confused, half-baked man, who is neither Eastern nor Western.

Although I was impressed by how contemporary, or maybe timeless, this theme is, I have to admit that the "hidden" symbolism came to life only after I was moved by the love story in the foreground. Moeis' characters do serve as mouthpieces for conflicting ideologies. But they are also real human beings who must suffer the conflict of their time, the burden of duty, and the pain and passion that is love.

I had never translated Indonesian literature before. But the idea of rendering *Salah Asuhan* into English came naturally to my mind soon after that second reading. There was an impulse in me to share this story with the Western world which, after all, is represented in it as one side of the cultural dialogue. But above all, I simply wanted to share this novel with men and women of heart who love a good story.

Translating this work into English would not have been possible without the constant help and support of my wife Bev Komori. I would also like to thank John McGlynn at Lontar for his patience and commitment throughout the long process and Jamie James for his editing skills.

Robin Susanto

About the Author

Born in 1890, Abdoel Moeis was actively involved in the early years of institution building that marked the beginnings of Indonesia's nationalist period. After an apprenticeship as a civil servant he left government service for journalism, quickly becoming involved in nationalist publications like *Kaoem Moeda*, a paper he co-founded in 1912. In essays

published in the Dutch language newspaper, *De Express*, he strongly criticized Dutch attitudes towards Indonesians. Around this same time, he joined the Syarikat Islam (Islamic Union), rising quickly through the ranks to become its representative to the Netherlands in negotiations aimed at obtaining direct representation for Indonesia in the Dutch parliamentary system.

Within several years he became an important member of the central leadership of the Islamic Union. In 1919 he was arrested when a Dutch Controleur in North Sulawesi was murdered just after Moeis had completed a speaking tour there. However, he remained undeterred in his union activities until 1922 when he was arrested again and exiled to Garut, West Java, for a period of three years. (Previously, he had married to a Sundanese woman from that area.)

Correspondence that Moeis initiated with Balai Pustaka publishing house in late 1927 shows a major change in the man's life focus with him now concentrating more on creative-writing than political thought. In addition to *Salah Asuhan (Never the*

Twain), he published three other major novels and four novels in Indonesian translation.

He exercised a strong influence on Dutch figures who established what is now the Bandung Institute of Technology and, after independence, he founded Persatuan Perjuangan Priangan, whose focus was the development of West Java and the Sundanese people.

Moeis died in 1959. For his years of dedication to the nationalist cause he was that same year named a national hero by President Sukarno.

CPSIA information can be obtained at www.ICGtesting.com
Printed in the USA
LVOW12s2202230913

353804LV00001B/49/P